Eliza Jane

Eliza Jane

Lila Osborn Mechling

Donkeys Ears
Publishing Co.

ELIZA JANE
Donkeys Ears Publishing Company, Portland, OR
© 2018 by Lila L. Mechling

All rights reserved. Published by Donkeys Ears Publishing Company. No part of this publication may be reproduced or distributed in any form or by any means, or stored in a database or retrieval system, without the prior written permission of the publisher.

Editing and design by Indigo: Editing, Design, and More

ISBN: 978-1-7328167-0-1
LCCN: 2018914159

*This book is dedicated to my grandmother Eliza Mary Ludlow Engel,
Georgie's oldest daughter, and to Laura Wood, Eliza Jane's daughter, who
completed the Ludlow-Herrington family tree. Thank you for sending me
dreams about the "old house" until I had to go find out for myself.*

Acknowledgments

I would like to thank my wonderful husband, Mike Mechling, for his patience over the past several years accompanying me on trips to Michigan, wandering through the countryside of Huron County, the old farm and graveyards, Port Hope, and Huron City, and searching through the stacks at the county clerk's office in Bad Axe.

Chapter 1

Summer, 1879, Western New York

As I sprinkled flour across the wood of the sideboard with one hand, I brushed stray strings of my straight brown hair off my sticky forehead. I could feel drops of sweat trickle down my spine under my long-sleeved blouse. I longed to be outside with the younger children playing school under the shade of the old oak tree behind the house. Would that we had a summer kitchen like Grandma had in her day, but I could only daydream.

"How're those biscuits coming?" Grandma asked as she removed the lid from the kettle of stew bubbling merrily on the cast-iron stove. It filled the room with savory smell and even more heat.

"Almost ready," I lied. I kneaded the biscuit dough and counted—under my breath so as not to overwork it.

My younger brother Dick came tromping in from the yard. At fifteen years old, his stomach always led him home at mealtimes. With his dark hair overlong and hanging in his eyes, he slouched over to me. I slapped his hand as he snatched a piece of dough and popped it in his mouth. I glared at him.

"What?" His boy-man voice cracked over the word, and he feigned innocence as he yanked my braid.

"Go away," I ordered him, trying to act the big sister though he stood several inches taller than me.

"Stop bossin' me around, Eliza. I'm almost as old as you are," he said.

"You are not. I've got two years on you," I said. "Now go away."

He sidled over to the kitchen table where my next younger sister Roseanne sat snapping off the ends of green beans. He snatched up little bits of stems and flicked them at her face. The bits got caught in her dark, wavy hair, and she screamed and flinched.

"Richard," Mumma said to him, using his full name like she always did when she was cross, "for heaven's sake, will you please find something useful to do?"

"Here, help me open this," Grandma said. She handed him a jar of last year's tomatoes, which he opened. When he handed it back, she told him, "Go find Grandpa and help finish whatever he's up to before supper." She poured the tomatoes into the stew.

"All right," he grumbled then stomped over to the screen door and slammed it behind him.

"That boy has too much time on his hands," Grandma tutted, shaking her head.

Hunched in the corner chair over her mending, Mumma said, "We'll be in Michigan soon, and then he'll have plenty to keep him busy."

Michigan. I swallowed, my stomach suddenly tightening. I'd lived in New York for as long as I could remember. I wished with all my heart that everything could just remain the same. I floured the end of a glass and pressed it into the dough to make neat circles.

"Maybe we won't be going to Michigan after all," I ventured.

"What do you mean?" Roseanne asked. "What makes you think we aren't going?"

I shrugged my shoulders. "I don't know. I just don't feel like we should move. I just feel like maybe we should stay here." I hesitated, glancing at Mumma over my shoulder. "Every time I think about moving, I get a stomach ache."

"Oooh," Roseanne crooned spookily as she pretended to rub goose-flesh on her arms. "It might be a premonition." She giggled and scooped the pile of green beans into a pan.

Mumma let out her breath in a huff. "She isn't having a premonition. She just doesn't want to go." We'd talked about this, she and I. I knew she was disappointed in me, but I couldn't help the way I felt. I didn't want to go.

"My mum had the sight. It often runs in families," Grandma said knowingly.

"She doesn't have the sight," Mumma said, clearly impatient now.

"We haven't even had word from Papa yet, and it's already July," I said. "Maybe something happened to him?"

"Eliza Jane, stop," Mumma said so sternly I felt as if I'd been slapped.

I should've known better than to say anything when she was cranky. I stuck my fingers into the jar of grease and smeared it onto two metal baking sheets.

Roseanne walked over to me and whispered, "Mumma got a letter today."

Placing the biscuits in neat rows on the pans, I glanced at her. She pointed to her apron pocket.

"You worry too much, dearie," Grandma said, patting me kindly on the arm.

"Worrywart," Roseanne mocked. I stuck my tongue out at her and finished cutting the last bit of dough.

We'd been living at Grandma and Grandpa Ludlow's house for months, since my seventeenth birthday in March, while we waited for word from my pa. He and my three older brothers had left for Michigan as soon as the boats were able to break through the ice on the Erie Canal, leaving Mumma, me, and my younger brothers and sisters behind.

After the biscuits were baked and the beans were boiled, I called everyone in to eat. Suppertime in our family was always chaotic, with everyone trying to wash up at once and fitting the ten of us around the table. It was a tight squeeze. I lifted little Ben into the old high chair. There was much noisy scraping of chair legs against the wood floor as we scooted into place, elbow to elbow. Grandpa led the blessing, and the food dishes began to make their way around.

When everyone was settled and had begun to eat, Mumma announced, "I received a letter from Papa today." She reached into her apron pocket and pulled out an envelope.

I glowered at her. "You could have told me," I said.

She winked at me, pulled the letter from the envelope, and unfolded it.

With a clinking of forks landing on plates, everyone stopped eating and watched her. She skimmed the contents and began to read. "On Monday of this week, I made a deal to purchase forty acres. It is a fine piece of land on the tip of the thumb, on the shore road, between Huron City and Port Hope."

"What does 'tip of the thumb' mean?" eight-year-old Georgie said.

Impatient to hear Papa's letter, I held up my hand like I was wearing a mitten and quickly said, "This is Michigan." I pointed to the tip of my thumb and said, "This is where Papa is."

Mumma continued, "There is a cabin with a loft. We'll be a bit crowded but, if the older girls work out, it will do us for a time."

What? I looked quickly at my sister. She looked back at me with wide eyes.

"Both the house and the land need work. It was owned by a small logging company, so we'll have a lot of clearing to do before it can be tilled. People hereabouts are friendly. Some of them have mentioned having a barn raising, so we might have it up by the end of summer. I haven't had a chance to ride over to Bad Axe to register the deed but will take care of that by the end of the week."

She glanced up from her reading. It was a rare moment—all was quiet. Then, as a fire when it takes, everyone burst into chatter at once.

"What does he mean, 'if the older girls work out'? What about Dick? Why doesn't he have to get a job?" Roseanne demanded.

"I will have a job," Dick said importantly. "I'm the farmhand."

Roseanne crossed her arms on her chest and narrowed her eyes, staring at him. He ignored her and went back to eating.

"Is there a school?" Emma asked. As a twelve-year-old, she loved going to school. "How long will it take to get there?"

"How will we get all of our stuff there?" Dick asked.

"We'll be going on the train, of course," Roseanne said. "Won't we, Mumma?"

"What about the dog?" Georgie nearly shouted.

Mumma looked to Grandpa, who said calmly, "You'll be traveling by water, the same way your pa did. The furniture will be shipped, now that we know where to send it, and everything else will go with you. The dog," he nodded pointedly at Georgie, "is going to stay right here with Grandma and me."

Roseanne and Georgie wilted like old flowers, and Emma repeated her question, "But will there be a school?"

I could hardly breathe. I swallowed hard around the lump in my throat and blinked threatening tears quickly away before Mumma noticed. Suddenly it was happening. I stirred my fork through the food on my plate, not willing to take another bite while my stomach churned. I looked at Grandma, and she met my eyes. Sadness fell like a veil across her face, and she seemed to slouch just a little. She stood to pick up Ben, who was struggling to get free from the high chair. When she looked back at me she was smiling, but her eyes still looked sad.

After she'd recovered from her momentary disappointment, Roseanne chattered with Emma and Dick about the two new towns. Grandpa told Georgie he would probably be able to get another dog once we got settled in Michigan.

Nellie, being forgotten in the midst of the ruckus, began to cry. She was almost five and so small, her little face was barely visible above the edge of the big oak table. I pushed my chair back, and she climbed up into my lap. I smoothed her snarled, honey-colored hair away from her face.

"I want Papa," she said.

"I do too," I replied and hugged her.

That night, when I lay down on top of the covers in the bed I shared with Roseanne, sleep wouldn't come. Tossing and turning, I was unable to stop the thoughts racing through my head.

"What's the matter?" Roseanne whispered so as not to disturb Emma and Nellie in the other bed.

I didn't want to answer. I couldn't admit to her—again—all of my fears just to get teased.

"I can't sleep either. I'm so excited," she went on. "New towns, new people. I certainly don't want to get stuck out on a farm, miles from anything and anyone."

"I don't think you need to worry about that," I said gloomily, "since you'll probably be working as a maid in one of the towns."

"I know," she said, sighing wistfully. "I wish I was like you, old enough to be courted and fall in love. I'd rather get married than empty chamber pots for some rich family."

I groaned aloud and rolled over away from her.

"How long are you going to wait, Eliza?" She pressed on, "You don't want to end up an old maid, do you?"

Courting, marrying, getting a job, I thought to myself. *Moving, leaving Grandma.* I felt like I was drowning. I rolled onto my stomach and buried my face in my pillow. Why couldn't I just stay in New York?

* * *

The following day, I awoke with a heavy heart. Papa's words, *If the older girls work out,* followed me throughout the morning like a dark-gray cloud over my head. When I tried to talk it over with Mumma, I realized she and Papa were depending on the money Roseanne and I would be able to earn to help make ends meet.

"Just until we get on our feet," Mumma explained.

"But you're going to need a lot of help on the farm and with the little ones, won't you?" I suggested.

"We'll need the money more," she said.

"Maybe I could wait just a little while, until after things get settled," I said hopefully.

"Eliza, you are seventeen. It's time to grow up." Her voice was soft but with an edge. "You aren't going to be with us forever. Someday soon you'll leave us to make your own home."

My teeth and fists were clenched. I wanted to scream at her. Instead, I turned and ran upstairs to the bedroom, which was deserted now in the middle of the day. I picked up the hand mirror from the dresser and sat down on the bed to look intently at my reflection. Pale-blue eyes stared back at me. Straight, straggly hair the color of mud was pulled back from an unremarkable face. *A plain Jane, that's who I am,* I thought, tossing the mirror aside. And to make matters worse, I was short and puny. No hope at seventeen of ever becoming taller.

How could any young man be attracted to a me? I thought. *I look like a twelve-year-old.* I flopped facedown across the bed and groaned aloud.

Just then the door opened, and Grandma poked her head in. "My word, child, don't you have anything better to do than sit and sulk? What's the problem, dearie?"

I sat up, sighed, and shrugged my shoulders.

She sat down next to me and took my hands in her worn and wrinkled ones. "You worry too much," she said, not for the first time. "Tell me what's bothering you. Maybe I can help."

"I don't want to go," I said in anguish. "Couldn't I stay here with you and Grandpa? I don't want to have to find a job and live with strangers."

"You've always been a shy one," she allowed, "but that's nothing to cry about."

"I'm not crying," I insisted, sniffing. "Roseanne says I'm going to be an old maid, and Mumma told me I should be thinking about getting married and having babies. Look at me," I wailed. "Who's going to want to marry me?"

"What do you mean? You're a very pretty and very sweet young lady," she said.

I shook my head mournfully. "I look like a little girl."

"You're just a late bloomer is all," Grandma said. "I was much the same. Too busy to put on any weight. Many of the women in our family are of short stature. There's nothing wrong with that except not being able to reach things up high."

"That's true." I smiled at her and sniffed again. "But Roseanne's younger than me and looks all grown up. And she's beautiful."

"Mark my words, when you're my age, you'll be glad to look so young. And beauty is in the eye of the beholder."

Morose, I said nothing but just looked down at my lap.

"You can't stop life, Eliza Jane," she said gently. "Time moves on for us all. Try to look on the bright side. When you get to Michigan, you may learn to love it there."

I shrugged my shoulders again. "Maybe," I conceded.

"Enough of this self-pity, now." She patted my hand and stood up. "Let's go see what we can get done this afternoon, shall we?"

Staying busy was just the thing I needed to get past my ill mood. I worked in the garden pulling weeds, took the children on a walk while Ben took a nap, and helped Grandma with supper.

That evening, after the dishes were done, I joined Mumma on the back porch. I sat down on the lower step. Our old, black mutt timidly crept up to me to have his ears scratched. I looked at the paper Mumma had been writing on.

"Making lists?" I asked.

"I don't want to forget anything," she said and leaned her head against the weathered wood of the door frame. Her brown hair, which was exactly the same color as mine, had just begun to sprout a few wiry, gray strands. I looked at her face, pale in the fading light, and noticed how the crow's feet around her eyes had sagged into lines of fatigue. I felt guilty about how I'd been acting.

I took the paper and pencil, wrote one entry at the bottom, then handed it back to her.

"Georgie's shoes and socks," she read aloud and chuckled, a smile replacing her frown. My little brother had a bad habit of never keeping shoes on his feet. "Are you over your sulks then?" she asked.

I nodded, then voiced the dreaded question, "When are we going?"

"Early next week."

So soon, I thought. *Too soon.*

I sat there for a long moment, taking another look at her list. Most of the furniture, including the old grandfather clock from Mumma's side of the family and the cast-iron stove, would be shipped separately, like Grandpa had said. The rest would travel with us: Papa's tools that he'd left behind, dishes, pots, pans, and kitchen utensils from the old house, as well as our clothing and bedding. It was daunting. No wonder Mumma looked so worn.

The crickets began chirping as the evening sun set beneath the horizon and brought on twilight. I handed the paper back to her, and she went into the house.

I sat outside mulling things over until the fireflies could be seen twinkling across the field. I still got a lump in my throat thinking about leaving Grandma. How I would miss her and the stories she told while we were cooking, sewing, or gardening about her life in Ireland and my pa when he was a boy. I wondered if I would ever be able to return to New York. What if I were never to see her again? I gulped. Grandma was right; I did have a lot of worries.

Chapter 2

Morning dawned bright and clear the day we left New York. It was already warm at daybreak. I quickly dressed in my brown skirt and white blouse over a camisole and layers of petticoats. I combed out my hair and pulled it back into a tail. Then I wrapped it round and round and pinned it securely into place at the back of my head. I scooped up the scanty stash of coins I'd been saving for a rainy day, tied them into a handkerchief, and pinned it to the inside of my waistband.

Myself taken care of, I helped the younger children get cleaned up and dressed, making sure to tell Georgie to keep his socks and shoes on. Grandma had made a breakfast of hotcakes and bacon to send us on our way with full stomachs. I didn't have much of an appetite, but the boys ate second helpings, which put a smile on Grandma's face.

There seemed to be endless last-minute tasks, thanks to the lists Mumma had made. Emma and I washed and dried the dishes. Mumma took the biscuits she'd made the night before, split each of them, and added butter and cheese and the leftover bacon. Then she placed them into a couple of tins for the first part of the voyage.

"Is this all we're having to eat for the trip?" Roseanne asked as she took the tins from her and put them in a well-worn carpetbag.

"Of course not. It's just to tide us over," Mumma called over her shoulder. "There'll be places to eat along the canal."

Grandpa and Dick had loaded trunks and crates containing our belongings onto the wagon the day before and delivered them to

Brockport, where they waited on the dock, stamped and labeled with our shipping information. This morning Grandpa and Dick moved the remaining two trunks, in which the bedding and quilts had been folded and stuffed, onto the wagon. Into the carpetbag and Mumma's satchel, we packed a small toy for each of the little ones, a deck of playing cards, a comb and brush, hair pins, and a couple of washrags. Mumma added a shipping company brochure, and each of us girls had chosen a small sewing project to keep us busy while traveling.

I grabbed my most prized possession, a book by Louisa May Alcott called *Little Women*. The only book I owned, it was a gift from my best school friend. Books were difficult to come by, unless you knew someone who was rich enough to have a collection or you were able to borrow from the library. I placed it into the pocket of my skirt.

Dick stepped into the house and called, "Grandpa says if we're going to get to the boat on time, we should leave now."

"Girls, don't forget your bonnets," Mumma said.

My sisters and I grabbed the two bags, the smallest children, and our sunbonnets and dashed outside. I stooped to pick up Nellie's cloth doll, which had been removed from the satchel and forgotten on the floor. I stuffed it into the other skirt pocket.

Grandma stood in the middle of the yard and pulled her tattered old shawl around her shoulders in spite of the warm morning. Each of the children took a turn kissing her good-bye before they climbed up into the wagon.

My turn. The moment was finally upon me. "I love you, Grandma," I said with tears streaming down my cheeks. "I'm going to miss you and all your stories." I hugged her one last time, not wishing to let go.

She said into my ear, "It's time to start your own stories, Eliza Jane." Then she laid her soft, warm, comforting hand on my cheek and said, "Don't forget to write."

"I won't," I promised, wiping my tears with my sleeve. I gave her a quavering smile, turned my back on her, and climbed into the wagon.

Mumma handed Ben up to me, did a quick double check of the house and yard, and kissed Grandma good-bye. "Let's go," she called out with finality and climbed up alongside Grandpa.

Out of habit, I started counting noses: Roseanne, Richard, Emma, Nellie, Ben… "Wait!" I called out. "Georgie's not here."

The wagon, which had barely inched forward, jolted to a stop. Everyone groaned loudly.

"Where did that scamp run off to now?" Grandma said, turning in a circle and holding a hand up to her brow to shade her eyes.

Dick, who was ready to get going, let out a loud sigh and murmured something rude under his breath. Roseanne giggled and elbowed him in the ribs.

I had a feeling I knew where he would be. I climbed back out of the wagon and hurried across the yard and behind the house. There I found him sitting between the back steps and the wall of the house, his formerly clean shirt and pants now a rumpled, dusty mess, with his face buried in the matted black fur of our old dog.

When I spotted him I called, "Georgie, it's time to go." He didn't move. I went to him and pulled on his shirt. "Come on," I said, trying hard to keep impatience from my voice. "We've got to go. Now."

"I don't want to leave him," he said, sniffing loudly. The dog sat up, whined, and licked his face.

"I know you don't," I sighed, aware of the minutes ticking by, "but Grandpa would miss him terribly if we took him away. He's gotten so attached to him. You don't want Grandpa to be any lonelier than he's already going to be after we're gone, do you?"

He sniffed and wiped his nose on his shirt sleeve. He let out a weary sigh and gave the dog one more embrace. I pulled him up by the hand. We jogged back to where the wagon waited with the dog hobbling after us on stiff, arthritic legs, awkwardly wagging his tail and whining.

Grandma placed her hands on her hips and said, "Another two minutes and you'd have been left behind for sure, George Ludlow."

She spat on her hankie and gave his face a quick wipe along with a hug and a kiss. We climbed into the wagon.

I settled Ben on my lap and Nellie in the crook of my arm.

"All set," Dick called out, and the wagon slowly creaked forward.

We had gone no more than ten feet down the drive when Nellie, struggling to stand, began to yell, "Stop! Stop! I forgot Hattie," and she began to cry in earnest.

"It's okay, I've got her," I said. I pulled the doll from my pocket and handed it to her.

"Have we forgotten anyone or anything else?" Mumma asked. "Put that doll into my satchel, Eliza, so it doesn't get lost."

Roseanne grabbed the doll from Nellie and put it away. Once again, the wagon began to roll forward. We were on our way. I looked at Grandma standing alone in the yard with the grubby old dog beside her. She pushed back some white hairs that had come loose from her bun then raised a hand in farewell. I closed my eyes and pressed that picture of her into my memory. The wagon turned onto the roadway, and soon she was out of sight.

* * *

We took the old Indian trail road to Brockport. As the wagon creaked along through ruts and holes, I was jostled about while trying to keep Ben balanced on my lap. We left the farms and countryside behind and approached the dwellings on the outskirts of the village where the road was much smoother and better maintained. Soon I was admiring the beautiful, grandiose houses, and I craned my neck to look up at the tower of the First National Bank.

There was so much to see: majestic stone churches with their tall spires reaching for the heavens, stories-high brick buildings, and people in townie clothes walking along the boardwalk or crossing the street as our wagon went past.

Crossing over the bridge at the end of the street, we sat up taller as we caught sight of the Erie Canal. The smaller children had never seen it. Even Georgie perked up. It was a busy place, this manmade waterway. There were barges and boats coming and going and long-shoremen on both sides of the canal moving freight to and from the boats that were tied off in slips.

"Look at that one!" Georgie exclaimed, pointing.

Dick yelled, "That's a steamboat! I'd like to work on a boat like that."

"It really stinks here," Roseanne said, her nose scrunched up and her mouth turned down.

She was right. The summer sky was hazy. The dank smell of the canal, acrid smoke from the outlying factories, and animal excrement all blended together into one strong stench. Roseanne and I pinched our noses. Emma, Nellie, and Ben copied us, giggling.

Grandpa turned east down Canal Street. There were several boats of various kinds tied off along this side of the waterway. A way down, near the end of the line, was an older one, shabby and worn, its tow rope slack. A boy, equally as ragged, stood idly with two mules, their tails swishing idly at flies, on the path that ran parallel to the canal. It was near this boat that Grandpa stopped the wagon. He gave Mumma a hand to help her down. We all clambered from the wagon and stood watching.

"Oh my," said Roseanne, her eyes wide as she motioned to the same boat I'd spotted. "Is that ours?"

It looked like a flat-topped house built inside of a long, narrow boat. *Marguerite* was written in merry red letters across its stern. The bright sun having taken its toll, the red, white, and blue paint was cracked and peeling. The house, which was almost as long as the boat itself, had windows, big double doors, and a ladder going up on top where an odd collection of passengers were lounging.

"Other than needing a new coat of paint," I said, "it looks like it will remain afloat."

"We could've taken the train to Michigan if we weren't so poor," Roseanne lamented in a whiny voice. "It certainly would've been quicker."

"The train would've taken a long time, too, with all the stops it makes along the way," Dick said. "And if you think it stinks here, what do you think a train would smell like?"

She glared at him stubbornly.

"You've seen the pictures, Roseanne, all that smoke," he went on.

"We'll have a lot of stops on the canal, you just wait," she snapped.

Georgie pulled on my sleeve and quietly asked, "Are we poor?"

Glaring at Roseanne, I said to him, "Have you ever been hungry and not had any food to eat?"

"No," he said, wide-eyed.

"Have you had a roof over your head and clothes to wear?"

"Yes," he nodded.

"Then you aren't poor," I said.

"Donkeys!" Emma exclaimed, pointing. "What happened to horses?"

"I don't know, and I don't really care," Roseanne said with a sniff while looping the crocheted strap of her little drawstring purse around the wrist of her white-gloved hand. "I just know they stink," she remarked.

"Those are mules," I said. Remembering what I'd been taught in school, I added, "They pull the boat down the canal."

"All the way?" Emma asked.

"I hope so," I said, "otherwise how will we get to Buffalo?"

"Seems like they would get tired," Georgie said.

Mules are the least of my worries, I thought, but I smiled down at him and said, "They are very hardworking animals."

"I'm glad I'm not a mule!" he declared.

As we stood watching, the scruffy-looking boy walked behind the animals while holding one by its tail, right across a wooden plank bridge and onto the forward end of the boat. We watched in fascination as they disappeared from our sight below the deck.

"And they ride on the boat?" Roseanne said. "This trip just keeps getting better and better."

Picking up our two bags, Dick led the way to where Grandpa and Mumma beckoned.

Mumma hugged Grandpa and crossed over another little wooden bridge onto the back of the boat, where the captain was greeting his passengers. We took turns saying our farewells. I was last with Ben and Nellie.

Grandpa kissed each of the little ones and then me. "God bless you, Eliza Jane," he said. I looked up into his eyes; wells of tears had gathered there.

"I'll miss you," I said, hugging him. "Tell Grandma I'll write as soon as I can."

I picked Ben up to carry him on my hip and held Nellie's hand. As I approached the crossing, I hesitated for fear of tripping on the hem of my skirt and falling, kids and all, into the water. Ben was squirmy, and Nellie was tugging on my arm.

"Nellie, take his other hand," I said, setting Ben down. She led the way across.

"Follow me, and I'll give you a quick tour," a stout older woman said to Mumma. She was wearing a faded blue dress topped with a yellowed linen apron and tatty shawl. She introduced herself as Mrs. Fields, the captain's wife.

We stepped after her through a narrow doorway, down a few steps, and into a room that stretched the width of the boat. There were small windows with open shutters on each side.

"During the day, this is a place where you can sit and read or play games out of the sun," Mrs. Fields said, indicating the benches that lined the walls. "You may store your satchels under the seats. At night, we hang bunks in here for sleeping." She indicated the ceiling, which was lined with large hooks.

Behind me, Dick dropped our bags in a corner. He pulled on Georgie's sleeve and dragged him back out the door.

"How many people sleep in here?" I asked.

"Oh, as many as fifty or more, though most of the time the men sleep up on top, if they sleep at all," she replied.

We all stared at the hooks.

"The bunks hang on ropes, like hammocks, one below the other," Mrs. Fields added.

"We'd better put the little ones on the top," Roseanne said, under her breath, "to keep them from being crushed."

"They are very sturdy," Mrs. Fields added, looking directly at Roseanne. "If needs be, some can even sleep on the floor under the bunks. But you needn't worry about that now," she added. "We're only half full this trip."

Hard to imagine twice as many people, I thought as I grabbed Ben, who was trying to make a getaway.

She led us past the storage area by way of a passageway along the narrow deck outside. "The cargo bay is, of course, the largest area," Mrs. Fields said. We looked through double doors and out the other side, where dockworkers were still loading. She pointed up where beams arched across the ceiling. "It's strong enough to support passengers and more cargo above. There's also room below deck for animals, although I won't be showing it to you now. Best we remain topside."

That answers the question about where the mules went, I thought.

We moved on to the third and last room, the living quarters. There was a long plank table and benches, a sideboard, and a rocking chair in the corner.

"This is the galley where the crew eats their meals and sleeps when they're off duty. There's a privy over in the corner," she pointed to a small area hidden by a curtain, "but most people go ashore when necessary."

"We can go ashore?" Emma said hopefully.

"There'll be lots of opportunities to do so. Little towns all along the canal," Mrs. Fields answered. She turned abruptly at the sound of someone calling to her and bustled off.

With the tour finished, we retraced our steps back to the sleeping quarters. Roseanne and Emma went up on top to find the boys. Mumma picked up our bags where Dick had dropped them and found an open space on one of the benches. She took out a biscuit tin then stashed the bags into cubbies under the bench. She broke a biscuit in half and handed a piece to each of the little ones. She offered me the tin, but I shook my head, so she placed it on the floor near her feet.

I leaned back against the wall and looked around at our fellow passengers, mostly women and children, who were sitting near us in the stuffy, crowded room. Some were dressed for travel in their Sunday best, with the ladies wearing gloves and bonnets or hats. I hid my hands in the folds of my skirt lest someone thought I wasn't appropriately attired. Others wore what was possibly the best they owned—patched, dirty, and bedraggled. They searched for cubbies large enough to stow their odds and ends.

There was one large family who looked to be immigrants. They had probably already traveled a long way and were still in transit. I didn't recognize the language as they murmured their conversations. The women had plain dresses and aprons. The bearded men wore long frock coats, high boots, and round hats. One of the older girls looked across the room at me with serious blue eyes, her blond hair pulled tight and covered with a small white cap. I gave her a tentative smile, but she looked away.

The cargo doors slammed shut, jarring the whole boat. *It won't be long now,* I thought. I should have been excited about this trip, this experience of a lifetime, but instead I felt like someone had pulled a rug out from under me. I stood up to get a better look through the window.

Lurching suddenly, the *Marguerite* began to move forward. Out on the towpath, the long rope was pulled taut as the mule boy lashed the animals with his short crop and they began their arduous job of pulling the boat along the canal.

CHAPTER 3

"Take these and offer them to the children," Mumma said, handing the biscuit tin to me.

I was grateful for the excuse to leave her and go out where I could see the sights. I found the ladder at the end of the cabin and climbed up to the top just as the boat was going under the Brockport Bridge. Startled, I ducked my head for fear of being decapitated. I looked up and laughed aloud at myself. Feeling foolish, I took the final step up. There was plenty of room for the boat, extra trunks, and furniture, as well the passengers—not all of whom were seated—to pass under the seemingly low-lying bridge.

"Low bridge, ev'rybody down! Low bridge, for now we're goin' through a town."

A man in travel-worn clothing sat leaning against a small tower of precariously piled packages and bundles that had been tied atop the roof. He wore an old leather cap that was tipped back on his head to reveal dark, merry eyes that crinkled at the corners. Tufts of grizzled gray hair stuck out over each of his ears, and his crooked yellow teeth were mostly hidden by an overlong mustache. With deft fingers he played a banjo to accompany his singing. My brothers and sisters were laughing and clapping as they sat at his knee

"I've got an old mule an' her name is Sal, fifteen miles on the Erie Canal. She's a good ol' worker and a good ol' pal…"

The rooftop was crowded with folks at their leisure watching as we were pulled along on our way out of town. It felt so pleasant, with the sunshine and the gentle breeze created by the movement of the line boat.

I handed the biscuits to Roseanne. "Mumma says to have something to eat if you're hungry." I took one myself and found a spot to sit nearby. Gazing at the lovely, fluffy biscuit stuffed with rich cheese, butter, and bacon made my mouth water. I was suddenly ravenous. It had been hours since my meager breakfast. I chewed each bite slowly so as not to miss one moment of its deliciousness.

A man standing with a large pole near the edge of the roof was dressed in a faded linen shirt, the sleeves of which were as wide as the legs of a pair of bloomers and ended in long cuffs. It was tucked into his black trousers, which in turn were tucked into a pair of leather boots, crusty and cracked with age and use. A blue kerchief stained dark from perspiration encircled his neck, and a brown, brimmed cap perched low over his eyes to shade the sun. I couldn't tell if he was old or young, his whiskery face having that weatherworn look of someone who spends all their days outdoors. He nodded to me as he moved toward the tail end of the boat. I smiled sheepishly, embarrassed to be caught staring.

I turned my attention to the outskirts of town, where the businesses and factories stood. It was strange to think that the rest of the world was going about their daily business while we were sitting on a floating house headed to someplace new. The peculiar feeling of not having any chores to do made me restless. I picked up the tin, replaced the lid, and went below to put it away.

I found Mumma where I'd left her, with her head tipped back against the wall and eyes closed. Exhausted from so much excitement, the little ones were both asleep. They lay to either side of her on the bench with their heads in her lap. Not wanting to disturb them, I gently set the tin on the floor. Mumma opened an eye and smiled at me. I went back up on top, where Roseanne and Emma were playing cat's cradle with the loop of yarn Emma kept wound around her wrist. Dick and Georgie were lying on their stomachs with heads hanging over the side. Georgie had removed his shoes and socks, and his bare feet, ankles, and skinny calves were sticking out of the ends of his trousers.

"Be careful," I warned, picturing him toppling over the edge and down into the water.

Dick glanced at me. "Stop fretting, Liza. This boat's as gentle as they come."

I picked up the discarded shoes and socks and put them in my lap as I sat down again in my former spot where I had a good view up and down the canal.

This section of the Erie Canal was long and straight. I could see another line boat that looked a lot like ours a little way ahead of us, and a barge was being towed the other direction. The boats blew their whistles as they passed each other, the pole man and other friendly people waved, and the captains called to each other by name.

I watched for a while, taking in the sights and sounds, then I reached into my pocket and pulled out *Little Women*. At home, I'd just gotten to the part where Jo, hoping to help Marmee get to Washington, DC, to their injured father, earns twenty-five dollars by selling her hair, much to her sisters' horror. That was when Papa's letter had arrived, and I hadn't had a chance to read since. In no time at all, I was lost in the world of the March sisters.

My peaceful diversion came to an end when the boys got bored and the little ones awoke from their nap. The crew had stopped the boat at Albion to change the mule team, and I could hear my sisters begging Mumma to let them go ashore to walk for a while.

"See if Eliza will go with you," Mumma said.

I stood up, slipped my book into my pocket, collected Georgie's discarded shoes, and went down the ladder.

"Here I am," I announced. "I'll go along."

The girls clasped their hands and smiled. Dick and Georgie wanted to come too, and Georgie quickly put his shoes back on without untying them. Nellie was pulling on my skirt, not wishing to be left behind.

"Make sure to keep up with the boat," Mumma said.

Dick looked back at her and laughed. "Maybe the boat will have to keep up with us!"

We made our way single file back across the same little bridge the mules had just used, climbed up to the path, crossed the Main Street Bridge, and walked onto the boardwalk of the town. The children were laughing and chattering gleefully.

Smaller than Brockport, Albion was one of many stopping places for boats. There was a general store, an inn, and a livery stable on the canal road. We headed straight into the general store. After my eyes adjusted to the dimness, I looked around at all sorts of goods the store had to offer travelers, from shirts and boots to dried soups and meats.

Emma spotted the candy at the front counter and turned to me, begging with hands folded. "Could we have some? Please?"

The rest gathered round and chorused, "Please, Eliza?"

I felt for the knotted hanky of coins tucked into the waist of my skirt. I asked the shopkeeper for two of our favorites, molasses toffees and peppermints, which he wrapped in brown paper cones for me.

Back out on the walk, I passed out candy to everyone and put the rest into my pocket. The boys popped whole toffees into their mouths and began to chew. Roseanne and Emma chose peppermints, and Nellie and I nibbled our molasses candy trying to make it last longer. *Oh, the delicious sweetness,* I thought, as each tiny bite melted in my mouth.

"Worth every penny," I said, smiling with pleasure.

"Mmmmm," Nellie said.

"Thank you, Liza," Emma said with a sigh of pleasure, and the rest echoed her.

Walking back over the bridge to the tow path, we found the *Marguerite* was already underway. The boys ran, the girls skipped behind them, and last Nellie and I held hands and walked. I was not concerned about catching up, as I knew there would be many more slow spots for the line boat along the way. Every time we approached another boat being towed, our boat would have to wait while the other lowered its tow rope to allow us to pass. We would easily keep up.

Wildflowers grew amongst the tall summer grass beside the pathway: Queen Anne's lace with its delicate white flowers, purple iris, and black-eyed Susans. Nellie started skipping from one patch to the next, her long golden hair bouncing against her back as she picked blossoms and handed them to me.

"What are you planning to do with these?" I asked her.

"I'm picking them for Mumma," she said in her sweet singsong voice.

"I'm sure she'll appreciate that. If you pick long enough stems, Emma might weave them into a crown for you." Emma had a wonderful knack for making pretty things.

I tucked the sides of my skirt into my waist to form a deep pocket. Nellie continued gathering her precious flower blossoms. Eventually, she grew tired in the heat of the day, and her bonnet fell back onto her shoulders. Her excited skipping from flower to flower slowed to a walk while she twirled a blue aster between her fingers. I turned to her and took her little face in my hands. Her clear blue eyes squinted up at me in the bright sunshine. I saw her cheeks were red, and she was perspiring.

"Come on," I said, stooping down. "It's time for a piggyback ride."

Up ahead Dick and Georgie were laughing boisterously, and I hurried to catch up. Georgie was pointing at the mules, and the girls were holding their noses again. I grinned. Their laughter was infectious. I didn't see the humor in animal droppings, but they thought it was hilarious. I was careful to step around the piles.

When I finally caught up with the group, the boy driving the mules raised a hand to his cap.

"This is Peter," Dick said by way of introduction. "He's a hoggee."

"A hoggee?" I said. I stooped and put Nellie down to give my back a rest.

"That's his job," Georgie supplied.

"She can ride on one of the mules, if you'd like, Miss," Peter said.

Nellie, eyes alight with fear, shook her head no and buried her face in my skirt.

"I'll ride with you, Nellie," said Georgie, his face bright and hopeful.

I looked back at the hoggee, and he nodded approval.

Without pausing to stop the animals, Dick boosted Georgie onto the back of one of the mules. Once he was astride and settled, Dick lifted Nellie and set her down behind him. She put her small arms around his waist and lay her head against his back.

"What's his name?" Georgie asked.

Peter said, "She's called Petunia. The other is her daughter, Daisy."

"Good girl, Petunia," Georgie said, patting the animal's neck.

I smiled to myself. Daisy and Petunia. Their names were the only sweet-smelling thing about them.

Dick kept an eye on Nellie, and I dropped back to walk with the girls. Emma checked the flowers in my makeshift pocket. She reached in and pulled a couple out then knotted the stems skillfully together. By the time we rejoined the *Marguerite*, Emma had woven a ring of flowers, which she set onto Nellie's fair head.

Mumma and Ben met us as we came across the bridge and back onto the boat. Nellie handed a bunch of the now-wilted flowers to Mumma.

"Look, Mumma," she chirped excitedly, "Emma made me a flower crown. Do you want her to make one for you too?"

Mumma smiled.

"And we got to ride Petunia," Georgie added.

The boys went up to the roof again to play some cards, Roseanne went inside to get out of the sun, and Emma found a corner to sit where she and Nellie could sort through the rest of her floral treasure.

I handed Mumma the wadded brown bags of leftover candy then knelt down in front of a pouting Ben. He wasn't happy about having been left behind. I held my closed hands out in front of him. "Which hand?" I asked. He tapped one, and I opened it to show him a piece of candy. A bright smile lit up his face and replaced his tears.

Our next stop was Gasport, where we had supper at a tavern. The meal was an appetizing pot pie loaded with meat, potatoes, and vegetables in a savory gravy, fresh-baked bread and butter, and milk for the children. It was a refreshing break from the slow-moving boat and a long day under the hot sun.

By evening we were back aboard and underway. So far, the scenery had changed very little: fields and farms on the outskirts of small villages; trees in full leaf, a few just beginning to curl in the heat of midsummer; low-lying shrubbery and wildflowers; birds and bees. The kind of scenery I'd grown up with near home. But now the terrain was becoming rugged. The sun's slow descent made it difficult to see, but there were definitely hills ahead.

The captain was sitting at the bow holding his pipe in one knotty hand and visiting with some of our fellow travelers. My brothers and sisters crowded in to listen, and I inhaled the delicious smell of his tobacco, a poignant reminder of how much I missed Papa. Mumma was managing a squirming and cranky Ben, so I took Nellie and found a spot on a wooden storage box near the fresh water barrel.

Captain Fields was a seasoned old man, his sun-browned face a map of lines framed by the frizzled white whiskers of his long sideburns. His cap was as weathered as his face, and he wore an old blue jacket over his white linen shirt.

"I've been a canaller for over forty years," he was saying, his voice deep and resonant. "I've seen thousands of settlers on the canal heading west. I was just a youngster when Clinton's Ditch was a cockamamie idea in someone's head. There was a lot of arguing among the politicians back then 'bout money, and some thought it an impossible dream. But after all was said and done, we had a waterway that cut across the whole of New York State from the Atlantic to the Great Lakes."

"Built mostly by the work of Irishmen, my pa says," Dick put in.

"True," the captain agreed, nodding, "and a lot of other folks as well."

"How are we going to get over those hills?" Dick asked, pointing westward.

"Now there's a good question, lad," he replied. "One of the best parts of the Erie Canal. This," he said with a wide gesture of his arm, "is the beginning of the great Niagara Escarpment, the highest elevation we have to climb on our way to Buffalo. A man by the name of Nathan Roberts, 'bout fifty years ago or so, engineered the locks that would make it possible for boats to climb those mountains."

My brother whistled between his teeth, eyes alight. "Amazing!" he said.

"Yes, it is," the old man agreed. He took his pipe from the corner of his mouth to refill and relight it, something I'd always loved watching Papa do. When he was finished with this ritual, he looked up at Dick and nodded. "An 'amazing feat of engineering' they called it. And I can tell you, after all these years of going through the Lockport Locks, I'm still in awe."

The twittering birds and buzzing bees of the afternoon gave way to the pesky mosquitoes of early evening. Every so often you would see someone swat one and scratch, but too late to prevent a bite. Georgie was already itching at spots on his neck and cheek. The captain noticed, crossed one leg over the other, and puffed out aromatic smoke that drifted lazily off into the air as we moved slowly along.

"Back when the canal was first carved out of the earth," the old storyteller continued, "they had to dig up along the Montezuma Swamp this side of Syracuse." He pointed with his pipe eastward. "The Indians told 'em not to go into the swamp but, o'course, they didn't listen, and they were almost massacred by hordes of mosquitoes. Story's been talked about ever since. Men came out o' the swamp with hands and faces so swollen they weren't recognizable. Thousands or more came down with a sickness called malaria they caught from the bugs, and a lot of 'em died. Wasn't until cold weather they were able to finish the diggin' in that part of the country."

Just hearing the story made my skin crawl and itch more than it already did. I could imagine the poor, pathetic figures crawling out of the swamp with eyes so swollen they were unable to see and skin covered in bugs and bloody pustules. I gave myself a quick shake. Thoughts like that were what nightmares were made of.

Georgie's eyes were wide with alarm. "Are we going to get eaten alive?"

The captain chuckled. "No, son. Have no fear, the boat'll keep movin', and we'll pass through this area of the blood-suckin' insects soon enough."

Roseanne leaned back and said in a stage whisper, "Or when they've had their fill of our sweet blood."

Before the climb to Lockport, we stopped to change the mule team, and then we were off again. The sun finally set, making a silhouette of the approaching hills. Most of the passengers were milling about enjoying the cooler evening air, as they didn't want to miss this greatest of sights on our journey. The boat was abuzz with more than just mosquitoes. People chattered away with anticipation as the hills along the ridge were now upon us. I was glad to have a seat with a good view to the west.

Closer and closer we got to those hills until we were floating right along between canyon-like walls of earth. I looked up to see the first stars just beginning to appear. The Captain's wife had gone around lighting the lamps at both ends of the boat. As we approached Lockport, the five double locks rising up like a great huge staircase were aglow with many gaslights, which were reflected by the ripples in the water that sparkled and gleamed. The captain called up to the pole man, and the boat slowed to a halt. There were only a couple of vessels ahead of us and, for a time, we just sat watching as each took its turn to enter the locks.

"Captain Fields, how do the locks work?" Dick asked.

"When the gates open, the boat enters the lock," the captain said, pitching his voice so others could hear. "Then, once the boat is in, the lock gates close and the sluice gates open to fill the lock with water. The boat is lifted to the level of the next lock. And while we're busy goin' up, often there're boats on the other side comin' down." He pointed with the stem of his pipe. I noticed workers above and below managing the gates.

Slowly, our boat crept forward, and soon we were next in the queue. The boat whistle blew three times as we approached the first lock. Just as we had watched the ones before us do, we slipped through the big wooden gates. They slammed shut, and the sound of water rushing in surrounded us.

I glanced over the side of the boat, and an exclamation of surprise escaped my mouth as the boat began to rise with the water level. As we rose one level after another, Peter, the hoggee, had the strenuous task of climbing the elevation on the towpath, giving the mules a swipe with his crop to keep them moving at a pace. When we completed the fifth and final lock, we were over sixty feet above where we had started, a dizzying height to be sure.

I was captivated by Lockport and wished I had some time to explore. Although it was evening, the town was still humming with activity. The lamplighter had completed his nightly task, and the streets were lined with bright lights atop their poles. People strolled along the boardwalk in the cooler nighttime air. Our line boat continued under two bridges and then stopped and tied off to change teams.

Mumma and I and the rest of the children joined the small crowd of passengers and disembarked to take a stroll to view the canal from the topside. We walked halfway across the bridge nearest the locks and leaned against the railing. Such a pretty sight, as the water twinkled with reflected light from the lamps. Then we stopped at the local hotel for tea before heading back to the boat.

We found Mrs. Fields and her crew had been hard at work hanging bunks in compact rows in the long cabin, which was now turned into sleeping quarters. Richard and Georgie remained outdoors hoping for more of the captain's stories. They would sleep in the open air up on top. I went with Mumma and the girls to help get the little ones tucked in. Roseanne and Emma also got into bunks as it had been quite a long day.

"Eliza, aren't you going to sleep?" Mumma asked when, a short time later, I clumsily climbed back out of my canvas bed.

"I don't feel the least bit tired," I said. "I'll just sit outside for a while."

One would think that growing up in a large family I would've been able to sleep in a room full of strangers, but I felt restless and couldn't settle myself down. I found my spot near the bow of the boat. I had butterflies in the pit of my stomach, kind of like the feeling you get when you jump from a high place—a little bit scared and a little bit excited.

I sat down and listened to the captain's soft voice telling his canal stories to a small audience of men and boys up on the rooftop. The banjo player was strumming a tune quietly in the background. The now-familiar sounds of life on the Erie Canal were hushed in the oncoming night. The waxing moon was a crescent turned over on its back, giving off little light and allowing a good view of the stars. It was pleasant and relaxing to stargaze in the cooler air. My many fears, which had bothered me for weeks, no longer seemed important now that we were well on our way west. Fatigue from the day slowly overtook me as the gentle motion of the boat lulled me like a baby. My eyes began to feel heavy. I tiptoed into the sleeping quarters and crawled back into my hanging bed.

For the next several hours, I slept as the *Marguerite* continued its lolling journey westward down the canal toward Buffalo. I woke up to three whistle blasts in the wee hours—the signal that we had reached the final lock at Black Rock. The sun had not yet risen.

We tumbled out of our hammocks, rumpled and wrinkled. After a drink from the fresh water barrel and wiping hands and faces, Mumma took out the remainder of the biscuits, which were somewhat stale by now, broke them in half to make enough, and passed them around. We each gratefully took one and ate, along with a few more sips of water.

Daylight heralded sunrise as the line boat floated into Buffalo Harbor. Buffalo was no small town; it was larger by far than anyplace we had yet reached on our journey. I could see the outline of tall buildings that made up the city's skyline in the glow of the oncoming morning.

Our boat continued right into the heart of the waterfront under one bridge after another then moved into one of the slips, where we stopped and tied off. The sky was streaked in shades of pinks and reds.

"Red sky at night, sailors delight. Red sky at morning, sailors take warning." I absentmindedly recited the old proverb under my breath as I took charge of Nellie and Ben. We followed the others off the boat, across the perilous little plank bridge, and onto the solid ground of the westernmost city of New York.

CHAPTER 4

I STOOD GAWKING IN THE LIGHT OF DAWN AT BUILDINGS, WAREHOUSES, train tracks, and ships—big ships. They were larger than I had ever seen up close, some with tall masts and bare rigging, others modern steamships with towering smoke stacks, all resting in place along the water's edge. I wasn't the only one gaping. My brothers and sisters, and the many passengers who had disembarked in Buffalo with us, were all talking at once in excitement. Ben grabbed hold of my skirt, not wanting to get lost in the shuffle.

A cacophony of shipping activity surrounded us: stevedores moving crates, boxes, and baggage to and from boats; a train screeching and hissing as it pulled up alongside a loading dock across the way; the foreman shouting orders to his crew; and in the near distance the loud, deep moaning of ships' whistles out in the harbor. All of these blended together in a disharmony of scents and sounds that inundated the senses and gave us our first taste of the big city of Buffalo. People were expressing their wonderment and pondering where to go from here, their loud voices raised above the din.

Many began to move purposefully along the dock toward the street. Mumma unfolded the steamship company brochure and glanced around her. She had never been to Buffalo, and I wondered how we were going to find our way. She turned the paper over, and there was a crude map sketched on the back. Looking around her, she decided upon a route and followed the crowd.

There were ships that did the Lake Erie route to Detroit, Michigan, daily. Grandpa and Mumma had booked our passage with an agent in Brockport. We were supposed to take a steamer owned by the East & West Transit Company called the *Wissahickon* to Detroit and then another ship called the *Flora* from Detroit to Port Hope.

We went to the berth that was printed on our ticket, but the *Wissahickon* was not to be found. A different ship was there. The wrong ship. Not a steamer, but a smaller fishing vessel. We continued to hike the whole stretch of Front Street that bordered the canal but were still unable to locate ours, so we went all the way back to find a ticket office. It was easy to spot because there was a long waiting line of travelers. We weren't the only ones missing a ship.

I remained outside with the children while Dick went with Mumma to wait in line for an agent. I glanced at the sky again. The red of the sunrise had faded, and the sun was well up. Yesterday's clear sky was now dotted with mares' tails, but there didn't seem to be much of a breeze moving the air. Gulls flew overhead, squawking raucously and alighting on ropes that ran diagonally tying the ships to the dock. One was perched high over my head where the topmost sail was rolled up. I wondered vaguely what the world must look like from up there.

"What are you looking at, Eliza?" Roseanne asked me.

"Watching the gulls," I answered, "and remembering what Grandma used to say about the weather."

Roseanne looked at the sky doubtfully. "Do you think it will rain?"

"If there's enough blue sky," I began to recite, mimicking Grandma's voice.

"To make a pair of Dutchman's pants," Emma joined in.

"It's not going to rain," we finished together laughing, and we simultaneously looked back at the sky.

Emma shook her head thoughtfully. "I don't think there's enough blue."

"I don't care," Roseanne said, her chin jutting stubbornly, "as long as we are on the ship before it starts."

Quite a long while later, Mumma and a grinning Dick came back out of the office with the news that the *Wissahickon* had had to go into dry dock for repairs.

"What are we going to do now?" Emma wailed.

"Don't worry. Our passage was transferred to the *Buffalo*, with a cabin at no additional cost, to make up for all our trouble," she said.

The *Buffalo*, a steamboat, was owned by a ferry company and did the lake route between Buffalo and Detroit, with stops at Cleveland and Toledo. It would take longer to reach Detroit with the extra stops, but it would save us from needing lodging until our second ship was due to sail.

We walked back along the wharf to where the *Buffalo* was moored. I gazed at the enormous ship as we made our way to where we would board. I felt dwarfed staring upward at its metal bulkhead. To the people watching from above, we must have looked like a line of tiny little mice. The ship had three decks and was as long as a couple of buildings. A smoke stack towered above. Never in my life had I imagined I would ever travel on a ship so large.

"I wish we'd thought to ask about our baggage," Dick said to Mumma.

"For now, let's just concentrate on getting ourselves where we're going. All of our belongings have the ships' names and our destination printed on them, so even if they don't arrive in time, they will eventually get to Port Hope." We followed her up the gangway to the second deck, where a steward was greeting passengers.

I wanted to find our cabin, but my sisters dashed off. They were excited to get to the railing on the open deck to look down from above and join the crowd of other passengers waving to people below. Dick dropped the carpetbag and satchel at my feet and ran off after them with Georgie in tow. Mumma went in search of a water closet for Nellie.

"Well, Ben," I said, "I guess it's just you and me. Shall we go find the cabin?"

Chewing on his finger, he nodded to me. I put one bag over my shoulder, picked him up, settled him on my hip, and grabbed the other bag. I felt like a pack mule trudging along the narrow corridors searching for our room. When I finally found it, I opened the door and peered in. Being belowdecks, there was no porthole to let in light. I left the door open to allow the lamplight from the passageway to illuminate the room. Two bunks were built against one wall and two on the adjacent wall, with barely enough room between them to turn around. I dropped the bags onto one of the lower bunks, and went back out the door.

We found the others, who had pushed their way through the noisy crowd to the railing on the open deck. Standing in back of everybody, I held Ben in my arms and stood on my tiptoes but we didn't get to see much, being as short as I am. Nellie had a good view, though, from where she perched on Dick's shoulder.

The weather was definitely changing. It seemed warmer and muggier than yesterday. *The calm before the storm*, I thought. In the back of my mind, a fear was creeping. I did not want to be on the water in a storm.

Three loud blasts of the ship's horn, and the *Buffalo* began to move. A thrill of excitement surged inside of me. This truly was the trip of a lifetime. Even though we had no one to wish us *bon voyage*, we all yelled and waved excitedly as the ship proceeded slowly from its berth. It made its way along the quay to open water. Once we cleared the city's harbor, the ship picked up speed into the vast sea of blue that was Lake Erie.

After we were underway, we walked along the deck and back down the stairs to the inside passage to locate the dining room. The mealtimes and menu were posted, and I started to look forward to the noon meal. My previous sense of excitement was wearing off. Roseanne and Emma escaped Mumma's watchful eye to roam the ship with Dick and Georgie, leaving me behind again to entertain the younger children.

"I'm sorry, Eliza," Mumma said. "Do you mind very much taking care of them for a bit? I would love a nap."

After the stress of locating our ship, her face was flushed, and I could see by her eyes she was very tired. I walked with her back to our cabin and lit the lamp so she could see. She curled up on one of the bunks and smiled at me. I pulled Nellie's pocket doll and Ben's cloth ball from the satchel, and we left her alone in the stuffy little room. Taking each child by the hand, I led them upstairs in search of a place to play out of everyone's way.

The toys kept the little ones entertained for a time, and when they became bored, I took them outside for a walk on the deck. Later, we sat down and watched the waves, but the wind had picked up so much that it wasn't very pleasant. Finally, I resorted to storytelling. As the family teller of tales, I had a collection of stories the children loved to hear over and over again. I was relieved when Mumma arrived a couple of hours later.

"There you are," she said. "I've been looking high and low for you."

"I'm so glad you're here," I said. "I was beginning to run out of ideas."

"She told us a story about a funny rabbit," Nellie said, giggling.

Relieved to be off-duty for a while, I gathered up the toys and followed Mumma to the dining hall. We were being spoiled with all the good food on this trip. Ham and boiled potatoes with gravy was served for lunch with warm bread and butter, milk, and tea. We were unused to being treated so extravagantly. Roseanne was especially happy to have a place to practice her airs. She carefully removed her white gloves, gently pulling one finger at a time, then placing them into her little purse. I hid my bare hands in the folds of my skirt in my lap.

The boys quickly tired of having to watch their manners. They wolfed down their food and Mumma had to remind them repeatedly to not talk with their mouths full. When they finally asked to be excused, Mumma insisted that Dick and Georgie take a turn supervising Ben.

Emma fetched the satchel with our sewing projects, and we found a place to sit indoors facing large windows. Emma pulled out a small crochet hook and some fine yarn, and Roseanne had her squares of fabric she was piecing for a quilt block. Nellie wanted to learn to crochet like Emma, so Mumma was showing her how to make a chain. I was meant to be embroidering a pillowcase with delicate flowers, but I was distracted by the darkening sky. Unfortunately, those mares' tails I had spotted that morning had foretold of weather change, for storm clouds had gathered, the wind had picked up, and the waves were capped in white.

"Oh, that's so pretty," Roseanne was saying.

I turned my attention to Emma's project. She was deftly forming the loops of an intricate crochet stitch.

"It looks like lace," I said.

"I saw a woman with this pattern on the collar of her dress," she said. "I wanted to make one for my brown dress to fancy it up."

"When I get married," Roseanne began, and I couldn't help but roll my eyes, "I'm going to have a brand-new dress with lace at the collar, cuffs, and hem."

"The hem too?" Emma said.

"Of course," Roseanne said. "It will be like a real wedding gown." I snorted. She turned to me. "Oh, I know what you're thinking. You think it's all I ever talk about."

"You do talk about it a lot," I said. "One would think there was nothing else to do in life except get married."

"You could become a teacher," Emma said. "That's what I'm going to do when I finish school."

Roseanne laughed unkindly. "That's a good idea, Liza. You'd make a wonderful spinster teacher."

"Roseanne, you needn't be so mean-spirited," Mumma said, pulling Nellie's first chain out and winding the yarn onto the ball.

Roseanne was petulant. "Do I have to wait for Eliza to marry before I can?"

"It's customary for the eldest to marry first," Mumma said, "but why don't we get to Michigan before we start making wedding plans?"

"You're too young to get married anyway," Emma said.

"I'm not too young to start looking for a husband. I'm already sixteen. If I wait too long, all the good ones will be gone."

"Oh, my," I said, wide-eyed. "Emma, maybe you should get started on that collar for Roseanne's wedding dress. If you wait too long, you might not have enough time to get it done."

"At least you could try to be interested in courting," Roseanne spat back. "You're going to end up an old maid, and where will that leave me?"

"No one is going to be an old maid, young lady," Mumma said, putting an end to the subject. An uncomfortable silence fell. My cheeks felt hot.

After a long moment, Nellie piped up. "Well, I'm not ready to get married," she said decisively. "I'm going to go to school."

"I'll go with you," Emma agreed, holding up her project and regarding it with a critical eye.

Nellie went off to join Georgie when he came by with Ben on their walk around the deck. The rest of us continued to work, alone with our thoughts. My head bent over my sewing, I started removing my last few uneven stitches as worrisome thoughts about my future flew through my head. *An old maid? A spinster at seventeen? This is ridiculous. Roseanne is being so unfair.* That awful feeling of inadequacy once again invaded my mind as I recalled my conversation with Grandma. I knew someday I'd have to get married and have babies. Everyone did.

Mumma put her head back and closed her eyes. The motion of the ship was becoming rockier. We seemed to be wind bound as the choppy waves became higher and the ship began to pitch and roll. Summer storms could be violent, sometimes even bringing a tornado. There was a streak of white-hot lighting against the dark, angry clouds, followed closely by a clap of thunder. It was too hard to keep my stitches neat and my stomach settled at the same time. I gave up. I wove my needle into the fabric to keep from losing it, folded the pillowcase, and put it back into Mumma's satchel. My sisters followed suit. Rain started blowing by the window, and just as I was ready to go out and collect the little ones, Georgie came running through the door, cheeks red and breathing hard, his hair wet and windblown every which way.

Trying to catch his breath, he said, "I can't find them," and burst into tears.

Chapter 5

"Where are the little ones?" I asked, jumping up from my seat.

"I can't find them," he yelled back at me, stamping a foot.

Mumma woke with a start.

Georgie swallowed hard, trying to stop crying. He shrugged his shoulders helplessly. "I was watching Dick and some other boys playing cards. I turned around and," he hesitated, "I thought they were right there with me, but when I looked, they were gone!" He wailed.

"Calm down, George," Mumma said. "Now tell me again slowly."

"I just stopped to watch Dick's card game. I turned around and they were gone."

"What if they fell overboard?" Roseanne, her voice shrill, spoke the worst.

Was it possible for two small children to go overboard unnoticed? I wondered. I recalled the railing where we had stood when the ship left port. It was built so nobody could climb it or slip through. I whispered a quick prayer: *Please, Lord, keep them safe.*

Mumma said, "Don't panic. Let's just think for a moment."

"Let's split up and search the ship," I suggested.

"Good idea," she agreed. "Roseanne, you and Emma search the deck above. Eliza, keep Georgie with you and search down here. I will go find one of the crew. And all of you, be careful."

A difficult and frenzied hunt ensued. I tried to imagine where two small children might hide and knew I'd have to check every nook and cranny. I struggled to keep my balance as the ship rolled over the waves.

Outdoors, we walked headlong into the wind and rain against the onslaught of passengers seeking shelter indoors. Georgie and I left the girls at the stairway and started along the now-deserted deck. Going back inside, we checked the parlor where I had entertained them, the library, and even the toilets. I inquired of each group of passengers that went by if they had seen a little girl and boy wandering about the ship, to no avail. We cut through to the other side of the ship and started over, with no luck.

"Where is Dick?" I asked Georgie.

"He was playing cards."

No sooner had I asked the question when I spotted him at a table with a group of men and boys. I felt like scolding Dick. He should have been watching the children, not Georgie. As we approached, he glanced up and then looked away, trying to ignore us.

I pulled on his shirtsleeve and said urgently, "We need your help."

He pulled away from me irritably. "I'm in the middle of a game here, Liza, can't this wait?"

"No, it can't," I said emphatically, desperation making my voice overloud. "Nellie and Ben are missing. Georgie was keeping track of them, and they got away from him somehow."

Dick threw his cards into the middle of the table, apologized to the others, and scooped up his winnings.

"Are you gambling?" I said, incredulous.

"Just some penny ante. No harm in it," he said, stuffing the money into his pocket.

"Poker. Well, I'm not going to bother Mumma with that now, but seriously, you should know better. Mumma entrusted you with the children, not Georgie."

He looked down at me defiantly. "Georgie was just here a while ago. I didn't see the children with him."

"Did it occur to you to ask? He doesn't know where they went," I said, panic rising, my voice tight with emotion.

We went back to the parlor, where we met the others with similar reports. Roseanne's brow was wrinkled with worry, and Emma had tears rolling down her cheeks. I was beginning to feel light-headed. Mumma was giving a description of Nellie and Ben to the third mate. He wrote notes on a small pad and assured Mumma that they would be found.

Suddenly a young woman came through the door with the little ones in tow. "Are you missing some precious cargo?" She smiled.

The tall young woman dressed in a beautiful, dark-green traveling ensemble walked toward us. She held Ben and Nellie each by the hand. Both children's faces, pink from the wind and wet from the rain, lit up when they saw us. Ben began to cry and went into Mumma's welcoming arms. I stooped and wrapped my arms around Nellie, giving her a fierce hug, so relieved was I to have them back safe and sound.

"Oh, thank heavens," Mumma exclaimed. "Wherever did you find them?"

"They were on the top deck, outside the pilot house in the pouring rain," the woman replied. "I was there visiting the captain, a family friend. There they were, sitting next to the railing watching the waves. I assumed they had become separated from their family."

Crisis averted, the third mate excused himself.

Mumma passed Ben to me and took the young lady's gloved hand into her own. "I am so grateful, Miss."

"Miss Stafford," she said and shook Mumma's hand.

"Thank you so very much, Miss Stafford," Mumma said. "I'm Mrs. Thomas Ludlow, and these are my children." She motioned to all of us gathered around her.

Miss Stafford was quite handsome and exquisite. I noticed Roseanne taking in every detail of her expensive outfit, from the pert little hat perched atop her light-brown curly hair to the beautifully fitted white gloves, handbag, and small, matching umbrella that hung from her wrist. At least Roseanne had the good sense to be properly dressed with her own white gloves. I looked down at my rumpled, travel-weary dress and work-worn hands. My sister was always telling me I should take more care with my appearance. Under normal circumstances I wouldn't have given it another thought, but I suddenly felt shorter than usual and wished I was better dressed—or was in another place and time.

Nellie was clinging to my skirt, so I squatted down and put Ben on my knee. I pulled a hankie from my pocket to wipe their tears and dripping noses.

Mumma went around the circle and introduced each of us. "We are destined for Port Hope, Michigan."

"An amazing coincidence," Miss Stafford exclaimed. "Port Hope is my home. Will you be taking the *Flora* from Detroit?"

"Yes," Mumma confirmed. "I understand it makes regular stops in the town."

Miss Stafford nodded. "I'm a frequent passenger whenever I travel. The *Flora* picks me up at Detroit and drops me off at my father's dock in Port Hope."

"My husband has just purchased land north of the village with intentions of farming," Mumma explained. "He and our older sons are there now."

I had just opened my mouth to inquire about the possibility of employment in the town when Ben threw up all down the front of me and burst into tears again. Immediately, Nellie leaned in toward my lap and did the same. Miss Stafford put a delicate hand over her mouth. She and the others took a quick step back, away from me. I broke into a sudden sweat, my smile drooping to dismay, and stood up with my hands out to my sides. I was dripping with vomit. I looked around stupidly as everyone continue to stare at me.

Face hot and eyes brimming with tears, I took the crying children each by a hand, mumbled, "Please excuse me," and dashed off.

Humiliated, I dragged the little ones along and rushed toward our cabin, ignoring the looks of others as I made my way down the stairs and through the passageway. As soon as we got into the room, I stripped off the children's outer clothing. I poured water from the pitcher into the basin on the small stand between the bunks, then used a wash cloth to clean their faces. I tucked them into one of the bottom bunks, where I hoped the motion of the ship would encourage sleep rather seasickness.

"Can you fix Hattie?" Nellie asked, pointing to the doll who was lying on the floor.

I frowned, anxious to get myself cleaned up, but picked it up anyway. I looked at the toy impatiently, not wishing to bother with it. I pushed it into the water basin, furiously rubbed it with the soap bar, and dunked it a couple more times to rinse it. I must have looked quite fierce while I did this, for Nellie was watching me wide-eyed from the bed.

I let out my breath and smiled at her. "By tomorrow, she'll be ready for you to play with again." I wrung the doll out and hung her up on the end of the bed to drip dry. Satisfied, Nellie rolled over on her side and closed her eyes.

I washed off the few bits and pieces of partially digested food that were stuck to the children's clothes and hung them on the wall pegs. My skirt and blouse were a different story. I sighed, looking hopelessly down at my soiled clothing. I wished I could go find our luggage and get something clean to put on. I settled for another pitcher of clean water, the bar of soap, and a washrag and towel. Stripped to my camisole and petticoats, I cleaned my skirt and blouse the best I could. By the time I was finished, they were wet all the way through and still smelled like sick. Even my undergarments were damp and smelly. I tried to blot them dry with the towel. There was nothing more I could do with them until I arrived at my new home.

Alone in the room with Nellie and Ben napping, the situation unexpectedly struck me as funny. I was choking down laughter when Mumma walked in to check on me, but as soon as I saw her, I burst into tears. Mumma hugged me cautiously.

"I'm so sorry, Eliza Jane," she said.

"Where are the girls?" I asked, sniffing.

"When I left them, they were still visiting with Miss Stafford. She's just a couple of years older than you and attends Michigan Normal School," Mumma said.

"What? Two years older than me?" I said sarcastically. "And not yet married? Roseanne must be so disappointed."

Mumma ignored my outburst. "Roseanne and Emma had questions for her about Port Hope. They can tell you the details later."

I was feeling quite resentful. I would have loved to have been a part of that conversation. She was, after all, our first contact with someone from our new home and could be a promising prospect in my search for a job. "Hopefully, Roseanne will think to ask appropriate questions rather than how many eligible bachelors reside in the town," I spat.

"Put your clothes on and go for a walk," Mumma sighed.

I gave her a withering look. "They're soaked through. And they stink."

"They'll dry faster in the open air," she said. Then she added, "Leave the door open when you go."

Reluctantly, I got back into my putrid apparel and left the room. I was so angry I wished I could slam the door, but I was robbed of even that small satisfaction.

My sisters found me standing at the rail. The rain had stopped, and passengers were once again free to roam the ship.

"Oh, Eliza, of all the things to happen," Roseanne said, giggling. "Weren't you embarrassed?"

"Are you all right?" Emma asked.

"With the exception of my pride," I said. "Where is Miss Stafford?"

"She returned to her traveling companions," Roseanne said airily. "And, Eliza," her voice brimmed with excitement, "she invited me to call on her after we get settled."

"But did you ask about the possibility of getting a job?" I asked impatiently.

"Well, no. I was more concerned with making her acquaintance. Her father owns the whole town. He's the mayor or something," she said.

"And she told me all about the schools and the teachers," Emma said.

"I'm so happy for you," I said hotly.

"Don't get mad at us just because you were indisposed. It wasn't our fault, Eliza," Roseanne said.

"Don't mind me," I said, deflated. "I'm not in a very good mood, having to spend the remainder of our trip smelling like this." I motioned toward my still-wet clothing.

"You really do smell sour," Roseanne grimaced. "Come on, Emma."

They left me and walked back along the deck arm in arm. I looked out toward the water. The spray from the waves dampened my face and mingled with the bitter tears leaking out of my eyes. *An opportunity missed*, I sighed. *Surely it won't be the only opportunity.*

As the ship pulled into port at Cleveland, I remained where I was. I watched the dock workers move cargo and livestock off and onto the ship. Families disembarked and walked down the ramp toward awaiting loved ones. Most looked travel worn and bedraggled. It had been a rough voyage. I hadn't been the only one who had to deal with seasickness. Some of them, I knew, had come from other countries, their trip being much further and longer than my own. There was much rushing about as men, women, and children were reunited with spouses and parents, some driving off in fancy carriages and some in farm wagons. Others walked toward the nearby station to continue onward by train.

It had been a very long and trying day. I let out a sigh of fatigue. I wished to be off the ship as well. Would that I could already be in Michigan, on the farm. I was sure all would set itself aright, and this day would just be an unpleasant memory. The late afternoon sun peeked through the clouds. Until the ship was underway again, the air would remain humid and uncomfortable.

By the end of the day, my soiled skirt dried, but my sisters didn't want to stand or sit near me. They were at a table a little ways away entertaining Nellie and Georgie by playing Go Fish.

"How much farther do we have to go?" Georgie called out to me.

I figured we were about a third of the way to our final destination. The next port of call would be Toledo and then on to Detroit, where we would change ships and eventually arrive at Port Hope.

"We're getting close to halfway there," I said encouragingly. He put his cards down on the table and came to join me. I put my arm around his shoulders. Never one to be sensitive to odors or dirt, he leaned against my side.

Exhaling loudly, he moaned, "I'm tired."

"Maybe you need a nap."

"Not that kind of tired," he said impatiently. "I'm tired of being on a boat."

"You need some food." Food was always the answer with Georgie. "It's almost time for dinner."

Arriving with a squirming Ben, Mumma led the way to the dining room. We were waited on by servers, and we enjoyed another delicious and satisfying meal that none of us had had to prepare. It was such a treat and did much to restore my mood. I savored every luscious bite of the sour cherry pie I had for dessert.

Finished with dinner, we all went back outside for a walk. I wasn't surprised to see how the sky had darkened. Storm clouds in shades of indigo and gray had gathered again. A ship's mate walked by wearing a rain slicker and carrying a lamp.

"It's going to be a rough one, ma'am," he said to Mumma, remembering her from their encounter over the lost children. "Best you keep your young'uns inside." He tipped his hat and went on his way.

We remained where we were for a few more moments. Abruptly, snake lightning streaked across the sky followed by an earsplitting crack of thunder. There was no rain yet, but the thunder and lightning were putting on quite a show. Ben watched from Mumma's arms, and Nellie hid her face in my skirt. Both were a little scared, but not Georgie; he was excited.

"One thousand one, one thousand two, one thousand three...," Emma counted after the next lighting strike, "...one thousand six." The thunder rumbled again.

"I don't like it," Nellie said, hands over her ears.

The wind had picked up and heavy rain began to splatter across the deck. Not wanting to get caught in the deluge, we hurried inside.

We turned in early, sleeping two to a bed that night on the narrow and not very comfortable bunks. We didn't mind. We were used to sharing. In spite of the fact that there was no ventilation in the small cabin and the ship continued to pitch over the rough water, nobody had any complaints. Luckily for me, nobody got sick again. Eager for this day to be over, I fell immediately asleep.

CHAPTER 6

I SLEPT THROUGH THE NIGHT, MISSING OUR STOP AT TOLEDO COMPLETELY, and woke with a start when the ship's whistle sounded several loud blasts. I sat up in the pitch dark of the tiny cabin, felt around until I found my wilted skirt and blouse at the end of the bed, and slipped them on, fumbling with the buttons. I grabbed my shoes and tiptoed out the door. I paused for a moment to make sure I had everything fastened, tuck the blouse into my skirt, and slip my shoes on, quickly tightening and tying the laces. I headed down the passageway to the staircase then went up to the middle deck and toward the bow. It was a lot cooler this morning, but I didn't mind. The air, fresh from the storm the night before, felt wonderful. The sky was just beginning to lighten on the horizon, and I could see stars peeking through the scattered clouds above.

"Excuse me," I said to a ship's mate as he passed on his rounds, "can you please tell me where we are?"

"Just entering the mouth of the Detroit River, miss," he said and continued on his way.

"Thank you," I said.

I looked at the sky to orient myself, so I could tell we were traveling north as we left Lake Erie. Recalling my maps from school, I knew that Ontario, Canada, would be to my right and Michigan to my left. I'm not sure what I expected of the Detroit River, but this section at least was really wide, forming a channel between the two countries. Awestruck at its power, I could feel the energy of the water as it poured into the lake.

As the sky continued to lighten, Dick and some other early risers joined me at the rail.

"Looks like we're almost to Detroit," he said. "How long have you been up here?"

"A little while. I awoke when the ship's whistle blared."

"Me too," he said. "The water's really rough."

"Yes, it is," I said. "Do you think that's from the weather last night or because of the river flowing into the lake?"

He shrugged his shoulders. "Probably from the river emptying into the lake. We're traveling against the current."

Regardless of how rough it seemed, the ship made its way upriver with ease. The sun rose above the horizon—a lovely sight after the angry clouds of yesterday. It was going to be a beautiful day. We stood there for quite a while watching the river narrow the further north we traveled.

"Canada seems so close. On a map it looks like you could almost touch it," Dick remarked.

"How long do you think it will be before we arrive at Detroit?" I asked him.

"It won't be long now. We just passed the lighthouse on that point over there."

"Maybe we should go make sure everyone is up. It's impossible to tell day from night in that dark cabin."

We went below and found chaos and confusion, with Mumma and the children all getting up and dressed in the small space. Dick took Georgie out to get him cleaned up, I combed and braided the girls' hair, and Mumma dealt with Ben. We stuffed leftover odds and ends back into the two bags we had been dragging along with us throughout the trip.

Detroit replaced Buffalo as the largest city I had ever seen. Factory warehouses, storehouses, and trains along the railroad tracks lined the waterfront for miles outside the city proper. Tall city buildings formed the skyline in the distance.

After disembarking, we found ourselves standing with our few belongings and looking toward the crowded metropolis of towering buildings, businesses, and church steeples that seemed to scrape the sky.

"We have some time to spare. Shall we go for a little walk?" Mumma asked.

"Yes," Roseanne and Emma replied enthusiastically.

We headed up Woodward Avenue, the wide main street going up from the wharf. The horses pulling their wagons, fancy carriages, and street cars clip-clopped along the street paved with cedar blocks. Looping arms with Emma, Mumma led the way. I brought up the rear carrying Ben, making sure nobody strayed off and got lost again, and trying not to gawk.

At a large intersection, Mumma pointed and said, "Let's go across to that hotel and have something to eat and a nice cup of tea."

An hour later, after a breakfast of ham and eggs, fresh warm bread and butter, and a delicious cup of tea, we were impatient to begin the last leg of our journey. As my family trooped back out the door, I paused to clean Ben's messy face and hands and tie Nellie's shoes. I looked up to see that the others had gone on without us. I grabbed the children by the hands, and we stepped outside. I looked up and down the busy street. They were nowhere in sight. We crossed over to the plaza in the middle of the intersection.

I was afraid to venture too far in a strange city, so I said, "Let's just wait here for a moment."

"Where's Mumma?" Nellie asked.

"I don't know," I replied with as much calmness as I could muster.

Unperturbed, she said, "What's that?" and pointed up to a bronze statue of an Indian queen wearing a winged helmet and wielding a sword and shield.

"It's a monument," I told her.

We walked over to take a closer look. The base of the structure was an octagon with four eagles with wings spread standing on four blocks. Above them stood the figures of four men, one each for the navy, infantry, cavalry, and artillery.

I squinted my eyes and looked up to the plaque. I read aloud, "Erected by the people of Michigan in honor of the martyrs who fell and the heroes who fought in defense of liberty and union."

"What's a martyr?" Nellie asked.

"People who die for something they believe in," I told her.

"What did they believe in?" she asked.

"Freedom," I answered. "When I was Ben's age, the Civil War happened. Papa fought in that war in the New York State Militia as part of the Irish Brigade."

"Oh," she replied. Then she put her arms out to her sides and started walking along the shadow of the telephone wires and trying not to fall off. Ben followed.

I sat down of one of the benches and looked around again for the family. The Detroit business day was in full swing, with people bustling this way and that. They all seemed to be in a hurry. A horse-drawn wagon loaded with fresh vegetables and fruits clopped past us on its way up the street. I wondered if I should just start down to the waterfront on my own. Surely that's where they would have gone. To my relief, Dick came jogging toward us.

"Where have you been?" he asked, slightly out of breath.

"What do you mean, where have I been?" I said, piqued. "I turned around, and you'd all left."

"Well, where did you think we'd go?" he retorted and shook his head. "You're such a goose sometimes, Eliza,"

Too relieved to argue with him, I picked up Ben and placed him securely in Dick's arms and then took Nellie by the hand. He led the way to where the others waited. They had made a detour down Jefferson Avenue to admire the majestic homes that were there facing the river. A cart, like the one I'd noticed earlier, was parked on the corner and people were examining the produce.

Mumma looked at me, her mouth a stern line. "Come along," she said, "and try to keep up, would you?"

* * *

It was almost noon when we finally departed on our next leg of the journey. The trip up the Detroit River, across Lake St. Clair, up the St. Clair River, and into Lake Huron was painfully slow. The *Flora* had a sidewheel propeller and it was as slow as the *Marguerite*, minus the mule changes. A passenger and freight ship, it also delivered mail to all the little towns. It stopped at nearly every village along the way. At each port of call, there was the moving of stowage off and onto the ship as well as the going and coming of passengers. When there wasn't a dock, passengers and cargo were rowed ashore, which took even longer.

"Where is the illustrious Miss Stafford?" I asked Roseanne while we waited through one such stop. I had secretly hoped for another chance encounter. "I thought the *Flora* always delivered her right to her father's dock," I said, not able to keep the envy from my voice.

"Oh, yes, that's right," Roseanne said, ignoring my tone, "but she's visiting friends in the city before she returns home."

"Ah, probably in one of those mansions you were drooling over?" I scoffed.

"How would I know, Eliza? She was really very nice, which you'd have discovered for yourself if you hadn't been indisposed."

True but unfair, I thought. "I didn't ask to get thrown up on, you know."

"Stop taking it out on me, then," she said. "She invited me to call on her. You may come along if you wish," she added with her nose in the air.

"Roseanne," I said impatiently, "she—or rather, her family—is a potential employer, not a budding friendship."

"It could turn out to be both," she insisted. "You never know."

The children were beginning to get antsy. Even I was tiring of the same stories, songs, and games. That afternoon, after arguments broke out over even the simplest game of Go Fish, I resorted to Mother May I, reserving an area of deck that wasn't being used by anyone. Soon they even tired of that game. I finally gave up and let them do as they pleased and watched from the deck chair in which I slouched.

Nellie held onto her doll's foot and ran along the deck with the poor little thing flying behind her. I wondered what would happen to the doll if she should let go—she'd probably fly over the railing and into the waves below, with no hope of retrieving her. I sat up and called to Nellie.

"You'd better bring Hattie to me for safekeeping." I stuffed her headfirst into my pocket, where she'd already spent a good portion of our journey.

It was a long, sluggish day. We were so close to our destination and yet still so far away. We docked at Port Huron and remained there through the night. Sleeping in another tiny, stuffy, windowless cabin, we shared the bunks that hung along the walls. The ship itself did not sleep, however. The noise of unloading and loading cargo and the yelling back and forth of the crew did not lend itself to a restful night. I gave up on sleep just before dawn, when the *Flora* left port.

I had to admit that, although the all-night commotion on the ship didn't help, it was my excitement that kept me restless and vigilant. My heart leapt at the thought of seeing Papa again.

Breakfast was tumultuous. The boys were running rampant, and no matter how much we tried to clean up, we all looked rumpled and untidy. Even Roseanne had given up on her prissy white gloves, the palms of which would never be white again, and stuffed them into her little crocheted handbag. Mumma, clearly at her wits' end, removed Georgie from the table and hauled him out for a talking to. Somewhat unrepentant, he did attempt to stifle his giggles and keep his hands to himself, though it was difficult when Dick kept making jokes. I kicked Dick's leg under the table and glared at him. But it was Roseanne who finally said what he needed to hear.

"Grow up, Dick," she said in a scathing tone. He stared at her across the table but shut his mouth.

I took the smallest children out for a walk while the rest finished eating. I gave Hattie back to Nellie as I didn't want to walk around again today with the doll's legs hanging from the side of my skirt. Roseanne and Emma caught up with us.

"We've been traveling for days, and it still feels like we are never going to get there with all these stops," Roseanne complained.

"I know," I agreed. "I've been counting the hours."

"And the minutes and seconds," Emma said.

"It's kind of like one of those dreams where you want to hurry but your feet are stuck," Roseanne said.

"I've had a dream like that before!" Emma exclaimed.

We sat outside and tried to occupy the time with cards or reading or sewing. My hands were too nervous to sew, and I was so preoccupied with anticipation that I couldn't even enjoy reading my book. The smaller children were underfoot. They, too, were ship-weary and full of nervous energy.

Later that morning Dick found a discarded map of the Michigan coastline along Lake Huron. We spread it out on a table and traced our trip from Detroit through Lake St. Clair to Port Huron, locating each of the stops we'd made. Then we looked to see how far we were from Port Hope. Had it only been a couple more miles, it would still have been too far, so impatient were we to reach our journey's end. Finally, by midafternoon we were at White Rock and a while after that, Sand Beach. Our excitement began to mount.

Mumma joined us with a sleepy-eyed Ben. "That was the last stop before Port Hope," she announced. "We'll be there before you know it. Eliza, gather everyone up and make sure nothing is left behind." She set Ben down and dropped our bags at my feet.

"You mean nobody is left behind," Roseanne laughed.

I rushed around gathering the discarded toys and cards and stuffed them into one of the bags then checked to see if Georgie had his shoes on. He did, but without socks. In the back of my mind, I wondered where he'd left them, but there was no time to look now. I handed the satchel and carpetbag to Dick and Emma and herded the children into a line behind Mumma. I stood at the end of our group holding onto Ben.

At long last we landed at Port Hope. It was late afternoon. Wrinkled and bedraggled, I leaned against the railing as the ship slowed and approached the dock. I shaded my eyes with my free hand and scanned the area for Papa.

"There he is!" Dick called out and started waving his arm.

My sisters did the same, and Nellie had tears rolling down her cheeks. I don't think I have ever been so happy to see anyone in my whole life. I had such a feeling of relief, it almost made me dizzy. Until that moment I hadn't realized I'd been so worried about finding Papa in this new place.

CHAPTER 7

Papa was pacing back and forth along the dock, slapping his old hat against the leg of his work-worn overalls. Then he caught sight of us waving and calling from the ship's rail, and his sun-browned, furrowed face beamed with joy and he smiled from ear to ear.

"Look, Ben, there's Papa," I said, pointing to where he stood on the dock waving back to us. It took him a moment, but when he spotted him, his whole face lit up. He began yelling, "Papa, Papa!"

We followed Mumma down the ramp. Papa hurried toward her, taking long strides to close the gap between them, until they were in each other's arms. Roseanne and Emma giggled, and Dick cleared his voice, embarrassed at their show of affection. Papa hugged me and my sisters in turn and shook hands with Georgie and Dick. Then he stooped down and gathered the little ones up in his strong arms. Nellie wrapped her arms in a stranglehold around his head.

With his hair and beard scraggly and overlong, Papa looked as if he'd been living rough. His clothing hung on his tall, lean frame, but other than that, he looked well. We all walked toward where the horse and wagon stood waiting. I looked around for my older brothers but they were nowhere to be found.

"Where are the boys?" I asked Papa.

"John and Will are working their farm and Tom has a job in Grindstone City," he replied, and setting the little ones down added, "Come and take care of these two, would you?" He turned to Mumma, "Dick and George can come with me to get the baggage loaded while you and the other children go up to the village to pick up some groceries. We'll meet you up there."

He and the boys started to walk away, but then Papa turned back and said to Mumma. "Go to McDonald's. He's got better prices."

Roseanne and Emma went on ahead, skipping together arm in arm. I walked with Mumma and the little ones up the road from the lake to the town. We crossed Main Street, where McDonald's Mercantile was located on the corner of State Street.

Roseanne and I looked at each other. A town with more than one store! We were impressed. Port Hope was bigger than we had imagined. We followed Mumma into the shop and looked around. She went straight to the counter while I took Ben by the hand and wandered around looking at the stacks of clothing, shoes, and bolts of cloth. I gave Emma the remaining coins tied in my hanky, and she and Nellie made a beeline for the candy shelf.

"Save us a piece," I said as they dashed away.

Mumma handed her list of staples to the woman behind the counter. She looked over the list and began stacking bags, cans, and packages, including soap bars, lard, flour, cornmeal, coffee, tea, molasses, sugar, dried beans and peas, potatoes, salt, and baking soda.

"You folks just arriving?" the woman said while wrapping salt pork and bacon in paper.

"Yes," said Mumma, "we came in on the *Flora*."

"From where?"

"Brockport, New York," Mumma said.

"Well, welcome to Port Hope," she said jovially. "Where are you staying?"

"My husband purchased land to farm just north of here. He and our older boys have been here for a few months now."

"Hard work, farming is," said the shopkeeper, a man with a handlebar mustache and wearing an apron. "I'm Angus McDonald," he said, shaking Mumma's hand politely.

"I'm Mrs. Thomas Ludlow," Mumma smiled.

"Do you need help loading these supplies?" Mr. McDonald asked.

"Thank you, my husband and sons will be along momentarily."

Papa and the boys arrived with our heavily laden wagon. I was relieved to see that our belongings had found their way to Port Hope after all. We had to reorganize a bit to make room for the purchases Mr. McDonald had stacked neatly on the bench outside his store. Papa helped Mumma up onto the seat next to Dick and put Ben between them. He lifted Nellie onto the back of the wagon next to the food, and she held on tightly to the side. The rest of us walked along behind, except for Georgie, who ran ahead, frolicking like a young colt on a spring day.

It was a few miles from the village to our farm, but we were so pleased to be off the boat and on dry land again, although I still had that floating feeling you get after being on the water. The road north was on the bluff above the lake and followed the shoreline. With the exception of deep and uneven ruts making the walking a little tricky and the pesky flies that hung out near animal droppings, the walk wasn't too unpleasant. Already grimy from days of travel, we didn't give a care for how dirty our skirt hems and shoes got. There were puddles here and there from the storm of a couple of days earlier, which the horses sloshed into and everyone else, except Georgie, stepped around. On either side of the roadway, the dried golden-yellow grass was waist-high and peppered with prickly thistles that grabbed at my skirts if I wasn't careful.

Inland, when the presence of trees didn't obscure my view, I could see farms, some with well-constructed barns and good clapboard houses. Sadly there were just as many meager-looking ones with log cabins.

"Those houses probably have dirt floors," Roseanne whispered.

"Do you think so?" I said.

She nodded with a look of dread upon her face. "And with our luck, that's what our house is going to look like."

I hoped not. It was hard enough to keep things clean and tidy without having a dirt floor.

"There was a fire here almost a decade ago," Papa told us. "Many of the logging companies went out of business. There are still several in the area, but more and more farmers are buying up the land."

As we hiked alongside the wagon, my sisters chattered to Papa. They told him the tale of the missing children, how I became indisposed, and meeting the illustrious Miss Stafford.

"Her father is a very important person here," Roseanne said.

"Yes, he is," Papa nodded.

"She asked me to call on her at Stafford House," Roseanne went on. "Do you think I'll be able to do that someday soon?"

"We'll see," Papa said to her. Then he gave my shoulders a squeeze. "Sounds like you had a rough trip, daughter."

I smiled back ruefully. "Yes, it was quite an adventure. Where do you suppose we should look for work?" I asked him.

"Maybe with the Staffords," he winked at me. "Or in Huron City."

"Papa, how's the farm coming?" Dick called down from the wagon.

"You'll soon be able to see for yourself," he replied.

"What about the school?" Emma said.

"Can I just do the farm?" Georgie interrupted. "I don't want to go to school."

"Even farmers have to know how to read and write and figure numbers," Papa said.

Georgie's shoulders slumped briefly, but then he dashed off again.

"Don't go too far ahead," Papa called, "we're almost there. This is all our land along here," he said, waving his arm.

It was an area that looked as if it had been logged off and was now overgrown with thin trees, shrubs, and sticker bushes. As we walked around a curve in the road, a house came into view. Roseanne had been right; my heart sank. It was a log cabin. But it was quite a bit bigger than those we'd seen along the way.

"Here we are," Papa announced. We followed the wagon into the drive.

Papa had been busy. He'd cultivated a large garden near the house with chicken wire fencing around it to keep out small animals, and he'd built a chicken coop that housed several laying hens. There was even a newly constructed outhouse.

Mumma climbed down from the wagon and looked around, her face inscrutable. Papa led her up two steps onto a wooden porch where there was a stand with a water basin, a small framed mirror, and a long bench with two washtubs lying upside down.

"I want to add onto the porch, put a roof over it, and screen it in so we have a pleasant place to sit, free of mosquitoes and rain," Papa said.

Then he opened the door to the house and Mumma went in first. As soon as my eyes adjusted to the dimness, I looked at the floor. I stomped my foot a couple of times to reassure myself it was made of wooden planks, and then smiled at my sister, who mimed wiping her brow in relief.

Dingy windows let in a little light. A stone fireplace and hearth were on the wall of the main room, two bedrooms were at the back, and above those was a loft. There were no stairs, just a simple ladder attached to the wall that Dick, Emma, and Georgie scrambled up.

After a quick inspection of the house, Mumma set to work stooping over the hearth to lay a fire. We would have to do the cooking over the fire until Mumma's stove arrived from New York.

"There," she said, standing up again with her hands on her hips. "Now it's starting to feel a bit more like home."

She was right. There was nothing like the glow of a fire to make things feel homey, although it was quite warm in the house already from the heat of the day.

"Come on, boys," Papa called. "There's work to be done before we lose the light."

They clambered down the ladder and out the door. Trunks, crates, and Mumma's rocking chair were brought in and placed against the back wall, except for the rocker, which was placed near the window. Not much in the way of furniture had arrived with us, but there were clothing, bedding, towels, and dishes to be unpacked. Papa's tools were stored on the porch next to the washtubs for the time being.

The kitchen was part of the main room, built into the corner along the wall adjacent to the fireplace. I inspected the larder, which was a tall cupboard built against the wall, at the far end of the room opposite the fireplace. I pulled the tight-fitting doors apart and peeked inside. Nothing much was in there. *No wonder Papa looks so gaunt,* I thought. A smooth wooden work surface ran along the wall under a window, upon which sat a tin water pail. There were open shelves built above and below and a sink that drained to the outside of the house. But sadly, no indoor pump. A long table with benches and two high-backed chairs on either side of the fireplace completed the room's furnishings.

Grabbing the bucket, I went outside to fill it with fresh water at the pump. I lugged it back in using both hands, set it in its place of honor on the sideboard, and hung a dipper from the lip. There was a cast-iron skillet, a kettle, a three-legged Dutch oven, and a big stewpot on the hearth. I filled the kettle and handed it to Mumma, which she hung over the fire to heat. We lit the kerosene lamps to light the dim room. Roseanne unpacked the dishes, each of which had been carefully wrapped, and we were relieved that none had shattered during the passage over canal, lakes, rivers, and roads. She handed them to Emma, who set the table.

Mumma and I unpacked the food supplies, placing perishable items in the larder. Our first meal in our new home would be a simple one: pork and boiled potatoes, and a very satisfying cup of tea.

A couple of hours later, sitting down for supper, Papa said grace, thanking God for a safe journey and food to fill our bellies that had been prepared in our new home. Ben and Nellie were nodding off before they finished eating. I felt like doing the same, but before I could go to bed there was still much that needed doing to prepare for the next day.

It was a quiet evening, as we were all spent from the excitement of the day. Each of us silently went about our final tasks knowing that rest, sweet rest, awaited us. I fed the sourdough starter, which had arrived intact, with flour and water to make bread dough, and placed a few cups of beans in a bowl to soak overnight. Combined with the leftover pork, we would have soup for tomorrow. Roseanne and Emma washed up the dishes. Mumma and Papa sorted out all the blankets and quilts, placing bedding on the floor of the loft and extra bedroom. Dick took a lantern and led the younger children to the outhouse.

When most everyone had turned in, I gathered dirty laundry and carried it out onto the front porch, separating the darks and lights by the glow of the lantern. I put the most soiled items, including my skirt, blouse, and Nellie's doll, into a tub full of soapy water in hopes that overnight most of the stains and stench would be removed.

It was very late when I finally settled down. I shared the extra bedroom with Ben and Nellie in case they woke up during the night. There wasn't a peep heard from Roseanne, Dick, Emma, and Georgie up in the loft. We'd opened all of the windows, including the ones in the main room, so the cool night air would circulate. There were screens attached to them, a luxury I hadn't expected, so there wouldn't be as much of a problem with the annoying flies, moths, and mosquitoes. A chamber pot was placed just outside the door on the porch, in case anyone had to go during the night.

I lay down on my makeshift bed, sleeping one more night in my chemise. Sleep did not immediately come. I thought of Grandma, who was probably missing me as much as I was already missing her. I wondered if this place would ever feel like home to me. I concentrated on the quiet, even breathing of the little ones next to me. Sounds of insects, and croaking frogs, and the gentle rustling of leaves floated in through the window with the breeze off the lake. I sighed, and I closed my eyes.

Chapter 8

"And on the seventh day He rested." I recited the verse from Genesis under my breath as I trudged along through the clumps of dirt and sod. I was removing knotted roots of grass and other debris as we worked to clear the field for plowing. God may have rested but not Papa. He worked from sunup to sundown seven days a week. And if Papa was working, everyone was working. We had been on the farm for a little over a month and had not stopped our toils for anything except meals and a night's sleep.

"Oh, my goodness," I groaned, standing up straight and rubbing the small of my back.

It was midmorning of a late summer day. That morning was only slightly cooler than the many before it. I pushed the strands of hair that had escaped from my braid off my forehead with a loud sigh and wiped the sweat from my brow with a corner of my dingy muslin apron. Quickly surveying the area, I checked to see if Georgie and Nellie were still at their task of stacking kindling in a neat pile near the door to the house. To the south of where I was standing, Dick and Papa had put the harness and chain on the horse, and they were well into another day of stump pulling. Roseanne, Emma, and I were working behind them, cleaning up the slag, clearing out brush, and salvaging all wood of a decent size.

The largest of the stumps were left over from when the land had been logged off years ago. But there were also trees of all sorts—weed trees, Papa called them, which had sprung up in the last few years. They also needed to be felled, chopped up, and cleared away before the land could be tilled. The only trees left around the property, when we were finished, would be the apple, plum, and pear trees that someone had had the good sense to plant, and a few sugar maples. Papa hoped to work as long as the weather allowed so he'd be ready to plant in the new year.

I walked over to the edge of the path that led to the house where a pail of cool, fresh water sat. I took off my bonnet, filled the dipper, and drank. It had the slightly bitter tang of iron, but how refreshing it was! Emma and Roseanne followed me. They dropped to the ground and pushed their bonnets back off their heads. I refilled the dipper and passed it them.

"Thanks," Emma breathed.

"My hands are a mess," Roseanne said, her brows knit with dismay as she looked down at her nails.

I looked at my own hands. The blisters that had bothered me during the first week had dried up and turned to calluses. That was a relief. My fingernails were cracked and broken, and the only thing that would make them clean would be doing the week's washing for Mumma.

"Put some lard on them tonight and sleep with your mittens on," I suggested.

She considered my advice, sighed, and stood up. "There's no hope for it," she said. "Come on. If I sit here any longer, I won't want to get back up."

We went back to work until the sun was high and Mumma called us in for the noon meal. We took turns washing at the basin on the back porch. It felt so good to eat a delicious, filling meal, then it was back out into the hot sun until suppertime. That was the pattern to our days: eat, work, eat, work, eat, and sleep, with the regular chores sprinkled in between. I didn't mind the work in the mornings so much, but afternoons were hardest when the sun was at its hottest, and I was already tired from the earlier half of the day.

Roseanne, soprano voice pitched high, began to sing, "Oh-oh, where have you been, Billy Boy, Billy Boy? Oh-oh, where have you been, charming Billy…" We joined in with her verse after verse. Singing was a great distraction to the mindless, back-breaking work that made up our existence that summer. We took turns shouting out the next titles: "Hush Little Baby," "Johnny Comes Marching Home," "Mary Had a Little Lamb," and other ditties we'd learned in school. About the time we thought the day would never end, we sang "The Battle Hymn of the Republic." A patriotic song, it was most invigorating, and we raised our voices and practically shouted, "Glory, glory hallelujah! Glory, glory hallelujah! Glory, glory hallelujah! His truth is marching on!"

I hadn't had trouble falling asleep since the first night in the cabin. Every night since we'd started clearing, I'd dropped onto my makeshift bed and slept soundly until the rooster crowed at sunrise. The saving grace from this grueling toil was the fact that we were finally able to see progress being made. An entire field was almost cleared and ready to be cultivated.

The dog days of summer stretched into September without a cloud in sight. The last rain we'd seen had been on the trip from New York. Papa said other farmers were talking drought, but I later learned that farmers always talked drought, as it was the worst of their fears. The dryness made the ground hard as Dick and Papa took pick and shovel to help us remove tree roots or the tangled webs of grass roots. The lack of rain, however, was one kind of blessing. We lost no time due to summer storms.

We had so much to do before the weather turned—not the least of which was to erect a barn to shelter the animals. Besides the horse, we had acquired two milk cows, a sow and a hog, and more chickens.

My older brothers, John, Tommy, and Will, took time from their own work to help Papa mark the dimensions of the barn with stakes and string, then Tommy led the building of the foundation out of stone and mortar. Word spread fast throughout the farming community of our need for a barn. Papa ordered lumber and supplies from Huron City and went on horseback to visit a few of our neighbors.

At dawn one Saturday in late September, farmers, along with their older sons and farmhands, arrived with tools and ladders ready to work. A barn-raising, I can attest, is a sight to behold. These farmers, who had barely made Papa's acquaintance, were willing to give up a day of their own labors to see that our family got this barn—the most important of all buildings on a farm—constructed. Greeting one another in friendly fashion, all the men seemed to know each other by name.

"Oh, my goodness," Roseanne whispered to me, smiling like a cat stalking a tasty mouse. "We needn't have worried about whether or not there were eligible men in the area."

I shook my head but grinned at her. "Roseanne, you are absolutely shameless. You are not here to flirt."

"I'm just going to peruse the possibilities," she said and winked at me.

"As long as it's peruse and not pursue," I warned her.

"Seriously, Eliza, you're not getting any younger."

"What? I'm seventeen and a half. I'm not an old maid yet," I said, annoyed. "Are you going to help me get the table set up?"

We went into the house and lifted the long plank table then carried it clumsily through the doorway. Noticing our struggle, Mumma and Emma helped us lift, and soon the table was placed in the yard. We did the same with the long benches, and then Mumma brought a long linen tablecloth to cover it. Emma pumped water into a couple of pails with dippers for the men to drink. I helped her carry the water over near the building site so it would be convenient for the workers.

What could have been a massive job that would take weeks, if not months, turned out to be a daylong neighborhood party. *Many hands make light work*, Grandma used to say. It was never as true as when watching a village at a barn-raising. The men were skilled with tools and knowhow, and one older man in a wide-brimmed brown hat, with a pipe stuck in the corner of his mouth, seemed to be the resident expert and took on the role of foreman. He strode about barking orders at the others and making sure the job was done correctly. Measuring, sawing, and hammering produced one framed wall followed by another. Working in unison, they raised one and attached it to the foundation. Pegging the walls was the least liked job of all, and there was a lot of "Let the youngsters do it!" being shouted about.

Since he was old enough and strong enough to be part of the crew, Dick pitched in with hammer and nails. Georgie, anxious to be a part of the fun, made himself useful by dragging one piece of wood after another to the men. He would probably end up with hands full of splinters by the end of the day.

Just before noon the farmers' wives, daughters, and smaller children arrived with kettles of soup, stew, smoked fish, fresh bread, butter, and cheese to share. It was our first social event on the farm.

Mumma was excited to meet other farmwives in the district. Emma and Nellie made instant friends with several children with whom they would go to school. Roseanne and I finished putting out dishes, utensils, and napkins, and Mumma brought out two large dishes of apple betty and some blackberry buckle she had baked for the occasion.

Mr. Bruce, whose farm was closest to ours toward Huron City, was there with his older boys John, Bill, and George. His wife, Bridget and daughter, Annie, were part of the party of women who joined us at lunchtime, and they brought the younger Bruces along. Annie was close to me in age and the oldest daughter. She and I took over tending the little ones, including Robert Bruce and our Ben, to keep them out from under foot.

"I have to laugh at Andrew," Annie said of her brother who was the same age as Georgie. "At home he isn't usually this excited to help."

"Georgie is the opposite. He always wants to help. He would rather stay home to work with Papa and Dick than go to school," I said.

"Andrew doesn't like school either," she said. "He has a lot of trouble paying attention. He's very fidgety."

"Sounds just like Georgie. He's become quite the fisherman too. He goes with Dick to the lake in the evenings. We've been eating a lot of bass lately."

"I surely miss going to school," Annie said. "I read in my spare time now, but I do miss school."

"I haven't had any spare time since we moved here," I laughed, "and Roseanne and I need to find jobs."

"I'm the only girl in my family," she laughed. "I think my mum would starve before she'd part with the extra set of hands."

I gave her a knowing look. "Emma is twelve and able to do the work I usually do, and Mumma and Papa will need the money we can bring in, at least for a while."

"I met your brother John last week," she said. "He was over to our house with my brother John. They not only have the same name, they're the same age."

"That is a coincidence," I said. "John has a farm right up the road from here with Tommy and Will. Will helps with the farm, but Tommy has a job at Grindstone City."

She nodded and grinned. "Yes, that's what he was saying. His farm is pretty much just across the road from us. He stayed for dinner, so I got all sorts of information about you and your sisters from him."

"Oh, my, I hope it was all good," I said.

"Yes, it was. He said you are the best with the children, and Roseanne sings really well."

"And Emma has the longest hair and Nellie is the sweetest," I said smiling, "but he should have described Roseanne as the biggest flirt. She's impatient with me because she wants me to court and marry. It doesn't seem to matter who the man is or whether or not I'm interested."

"It's the opposite at my house. My mother doesn't want me to go anywhere."

We laughed together. I found out that she loved to cook more than any other task and that she'd been born in Ireland, which I could tell by her gentle accent. Papa and her father were already friends. Her dad had helped mine to find our farm and had also sold us our cows and pigs. Annie, just a year older than me, had brown hair, blue eyes, and freckles, just like me. We could have been sisters, except she was so pretty. I hoped we would be close friends.

John came over to say hello to us and get a drink of water.

"Speak of the devil," I laughed and winked at Annie. She beamed at him. Tall and strong, and twenty-one years of age, my brother was a good-looking young man. Since coming to Michigan, he'd grown a beard, which he kept trimmed. I wondered if he and Annie might become sweethearts someday.

One of the women had given Mumma a steel triangle as a house-warming gift. At lunchtime, she held it by the loop at the top and rolled the metal wand around the middle, creating a ringing loud enough for all to hear. Almost in unison, the men, boys, and young children dropped what they were doing and came to the yard for dinner.

Each filled a plate then took their food and sat on the ground, picnic style, but without a blanket or tablecloth. Nobody seemed to mind. I spotted Roseanne, who had targeted one of the Bruce boys and was sitting with him. He looked a little shy as she turned on the charm. Emma and Nellie sat with the same group of girls they'd been playing with. Georgie and Andrew Bruce were nowhere to be found, which was concerning.

"I'll go look for them," I said, as Annie tried to get Ben and Robert to sit down and eat.

I walked all the way around the building site to make sure they weren't getting into any mischief and then to the other side of the house. I found them sitting in the long grass with the Bruces' Irish setter between them.

"She's a really nice dog. I like her shiny fur," Georgie was saying. "I really miss my dog."

I stood silently in the shadow of the house and listened, smiling to myself.

"Did he die or something?" Andrew asked.

"No, but he was pretty old. We left him in New York. Liza said he had to stay and take care of Grandma and Grandpa."

"You going to get a new dog?"

"I want to, but Pa's been too busy to ask him about it," Georgie said, glumly picking at the grass.

"I'm hungry," Andrew said.

"Let's go eat," Georgie agreed, springing to his feet. "There's lots of dessert."

I stepped out from my hiding place. "There you are! I've been looking all over for you."

"We're coming," they said together and sprinted past me followed by the big red dog.

After the meal was finished, the women and children waved good-bye and set off for home, and the men went back to work.

"Eliza, be sure to take a walk one day soon to visit me," Annie called from the back of their wagon, "and bring your sisters."

"I will," I shouted, smiling and waving good-bye. I was so happy to have made my first friend in Michigan.

Progress on the barn continued nonstop through the long afternoon as joists were constructed for the roof and the older boys hammered the floor of the loft into place. Then, using a rope and pulley, they hoisted the joists up and secured them. Leaving framed openings for windows, boards were hammered into place to complete the walls. Big double doors were constructed and hung at both ends and another at the hayloft. It was a sight to behold.

In the evening the men headed out, receiving thankful handshakes from Papa. My brothers, who were still up on the roof putting on the shingles, whooped when Mumma called them for supper. She served the meal on the table outside, and we enjoyed a delicious dinner of leftovers from the potluck. I looked around the table thinking how long it had been since we'd been all together at one table.

After the meal, Papa and the boys finished the last of the shingles, and Tommy attached lightning rods. Roseanne, Emma, and I watched as he completed this task. I nervously eyed the sky, even though it was a perfectly clear day.

"What would happen if lightning struck right now?" Georgie asked, reading my mind.

"Don't even think it," I said.

"Why don't we have those on the house?" Emma asked.

"Because the barn is taller. Lightning always strikes whatever's tallest," I said.

"Is that true?" Georgie asked.

I shrugged my shoulders. "That's what they say."

Tommy's task was finished as the wire was dropped down and buried in the ground. There was still work to be done on the inside of the building, with stalls and such, but rather than spend money on windows, Papa would put up shutters. For tonight, though, the job was finished.

Mumma and I were cleaning up well into the evening. Papa sat in his chair and lit his pipe, doubtless savoring the good feeling of what had been accomplished that day. The children fell into bed without a peep and were quickly asleep, as they had been playing since sunrise.

It was the most productive day I had ever witnessed, and as I fell asleep that night, I thanked God that I had a new friend and that we were a part of such a welcoming and generous community.

Chapter 9

The week after the barn was built, Mumma's long-awaited cast-iron stove, the beds, dressers, and the heirloom grandfather clock arrived from New York. And along with them came the laundry boiler. We were so excited you'd think the clouds were raining pennies.

Thrilled to have an excuse not to work in the field, Roseanne and I took over the next wash day, and Mumma became reacquainted with her stove by pickling some of the late summer vegetables from the garden. At daybreak I had started the boiler to heat over the fire out in the yard. The most soiled work clothes had been soaking since the night before. I gathered the rest of the laundry and sorted it. Roseanne poured boiling water through stains on dresses, shirts, and aprons. I put the first batch of whites, mostly undergarments, into water and added some soap shavings. Then I began to scrub. When I finished the first batch, I moved it to the boiler, put the lid back on, and started with the next batch.

Papa's and Dick's work clothes were the most soiled and toughest to get clean. I pulled them out of the soaking tub and put them into the warm wash water. Emma emptied the soaking tub and cleaned it up for rinsing. I worked over each pair of pants and each shirt with the soap bar and scrubbed them furiously against the washboard. Meanwhile, Roseanne moved the whites from the boiler into the rinse tub and added more water to the boiler. It was quite a laborious process, but still it was a welcome break from our usual work.

I fed the clean clothes through the wringer while turning the crank and watched with satisfaction as the pieces came out compressed and flat and dropped into a basket. Then we shook them out and pinned them to the wire line with wooden clothespins to dry in the breeze. By the end of the day, all of it was clean, dry, and folded, and a new batch of mending was placed in Mumma's pile for darning, patching, or just stitching up loose seams.

* * *

The days were shorter and the evenings cooler, although there still hadn't been any rain. When the children started the winter term at the school in Huron City, Mumma and Papa told us it was time to begin our search for employment.

"We should go to Huron City," I said. "It's so much closer and there's a big house there and a store."

"Only one house and one store," Roseanne argued.

"I know what you're thinking," I said. "You want to meet Miss Stafford again."

"Eliza, you're a genius!" Roseanne exclaimed. "Of course we should go to Port Hope. If we accidentally ran into her I'd be so embarrassed that I hadn't even attempted to call on her after she so kindly invited me. I'll write her a note now."

Baffled, I looked at my sister. She had a one-track mind. If I dared to stand in her way she would plow right through me.

In two days' time, Roseanne received a reply from Miss Stafford in the mail. We set off for the village. It was a two-hour walk, and we had to keep our eyes down lest we step into one of the frequent holes in the uneven, rutted roadway. It was either that or trudge through the long, dry, dusty grass on the roadside, which was no fun at all in a long skirt.

"Do you think we'll have to board there?" I said, voicing my anxiety.

"It would be easier than making this hike every day," she said.

"I tried to tell you we should have gone to Huron City," I said.

"It would have been easier," she conceded. "But I still think we have a better chance at Stafford House. Only problem is how can I keep Billy interested in me if I never get to see him?"

My sister had set her cap for Billy Bruce. They were very close in age, which meant he was probably only my age and worked on his pa's farm, not exactly in a position to court a girl.

"Are you sure he wants to court you?"

"Of course," she said. "I know he likes me."

"Do you, now?" I said doubtfully. "And what makes you think he likes you?"

"A girl just knows," she said with a smug smile.

She probably did know. I envied her self-confidence. What boy wouldn't be interested in her, with her lustrous hair and lively personality? If a young man were interested in me, I'd probably be the last to find out.

"Really, Eliza, if you'd just wake up and look around, you might be surprised to find there are lots of young men to fancy."

"I'll take your word for it," I said, not wanting her to start nagging me. "Right now, I'm more concerned with getting a job than finding a beau."

She shrugged her shoulders. "There's no reason you can't do both. You didn't even notice the ones who were at our barn-raising, did you?"

"I noticed three very handsome ones," I said, grinning.

She looked at me with raised brows.

"Unfortunately," I continued, "they're all related to us."

She laughed. "Yes, and did you see John and Annie Bruce? I think he likes her."

I let out my breath, exasperated. "Seriously, Roseanne, you aren't going to be satisfied until everyone is matched up." I secretly agreed with her, but I wasn't going to tell her that. It would only encourage her obsession.

We finally arrived at Stafford House. I'd had my first glimpse of it as we passed by the day we arrived on the *Flora*. This time I took a moment to really appreciate it. The house had three stories with a gabled roofline. There was a covered porch that wrapped all the way around it and a grand walkway and stairs leading up to the front door. There were tall windows on every side, and a sleek black carriage was parked on the drive. The house was not the only large one in town, but it was the most striking, as it was situated on the main road facing the lake.

Awestruck, I followed my sister, who marched right up to the front door to call on Miss Stafford as if she were one of her best friends.

"This is very presumptuous. Shouldn't we go around to the service entrance at the back?"

She ignored me and rang the bell. Nothing happened. We stood there for some time. I felt awkward and wondered if we should ring again or walk away, but the door opened. An elderly woman in a plain black dress stood there.

"I am here to call on Miss Stafford," Roseanne announced importantly.

"May I ask who is calling, miss?" the woman asked.

"Miss Roseanne Ludlow and my sister, Miss Eliza Jane Ludlow," she answered with more self-assuredness than I could've ever conjured.

The servant showed us to the sitting room. We didn't have to wait long.

Miss Stafford came into the room smiling. "Miss Ludlow," she said taking my sister's hand, "I was delighted to receive your note." Roseanne had worn her delicate gloves to hide her work-worn hands. She had had to soap and scrub them then soak them in bluing to make them look white again.

"And Miss Ludlow," she said, turning to me and shaking my hand. "Lovely to see you both. To what do I owe the pleasure?"

"We came to town in search of employment," my sister said, using her well-bred young lady voice.

"Ah yes, I do recall our conversation. How are your mother and the younger children?" she said with a slight pull at the corners of her lips.

I grimaced, sure she was remembering my shipboard mishap with the seasick children. A memorable meeting it had been.

"Everyone is fine and happy to be home at last. Thank you for asking," Roseanne said. "The children have started school and the summer work is winding down, so we decided to begin inquiring."

"I'm very happy you came today. You've just caught me because tomorrow I am leaving for school as well. Let me call for tea, and we'll sit down and have a chat with my stepmother."

Mrs. Stafford was a pleasant woman who did not seem at all put out that she was having tea with two complete strangers. "Mary Ellen tells me she met you on the ship coming from New York and that you are seeking employment."

"Yes ma'am," Roseanne answered. I nodded my head and smiled, still not having said a word.

"My best friend growing up was named Roseanne," she said and added, "a lovely name."

Mumma had raised us to know how to behave in different situations, but I was almost paralyzed with shyness. A better time it was for my sister, who was truly practiced in using appropriate manners. She was quite comfortable being invited to tea by such influential people. Miss Stafford and her stepmother were clearly enchanted with her, and Mrs. Stafford interviewed her throughout the tea. I felt like an ugly duckling. I sat there stiff as a board and smiled until my face felt as if it would crack. Neither of the women paid me any mind.

"We are already well-fixed with a cook and two maids," the matron said, "but are you able to sew, and do you have good penmanship?"

"Oh yes," I finally spoke up. Mrs. Stafford turned her attention briefly in my direction.

"Our mother has taught all of her daughters to sew," Roseanne said, drawing the attention back to herself. "I will demonstrate my penmanship if you'd like."

Mrs. Stafford continued the interview, asking details about family and background. I was impressed at the poise and control Roseanne exhibited. Soon the tea was finished, and we were escorted back to the foyer.

"We have a seamstress who makes our clothing seasonally, but I could use someone to handle the day-to-day mending and to help me with my letter writing," she explained. "I would very much like to offer you the position, Miss Ludlow, if you are interested." Then she turned to me and shook my hand. "I'm sorry, but I have no other positions at this time, Miss Ludlow. Thank you so much for calling."

And just like that I found myself dismissed. I had to return home alone and unsuccessful. Roseanne remained behind to discuss the details of her new job, to have a tour of the house, and to meet the staff.

Mortified, embarrassed, frustrated, and jealous, I marched myself down the drive to the road. *I can sew. Better than Roseanne. Shame on you, Eliza Jane,* I said to myself. *You know perfectly well why Roseanne got the job and you didn't. Because when you met the lovely Miss Stafford, you had the great misfortune of being vomited on, not once, but twice.* But the other side of my mind argued: *It's because you didn't speak up. You never speak up for yourself, Eliza Jane.* I hated to admit it, but that was the truth. My eyes stung with unshed tears. I picked up my pace, wanting to be home.

CHAPTER 10

The whole awful scenario at Stafford House played out in my mind over and over again. I was so angry with myself. Tears threatened and obscured my view but I didn't slow down. In my rush I didn't see the pothole in my path. Stepping into it, I rolled my ankle and sprawled headlong onto the wagon-rutted road. My hands barely broke my fall, and the wind was knocked out of me.

In shock I sat up, my heart pounding out of my chest and my foot throbbing. The tears I had tried hard not to shed coursed down my cheeks in pain and self-pity. I looked at my hands, which were scraped and stinging. Impatiently I rubbed them against my skirt, loosened the laces of my dusty shoe, and pulled it carefully away from my ankle and off my foot. Then I gingerly peeled my stocking down to examine the damage.

"What in the world is wrong with you, Eliza Jane?" I scolded myself.

Cheeks hot and wet, I wiped my tears with the palms of my scuffed hands. *Of all the ridiculous situations,* I thought. I wriggled my toes and moved my foot back and forth and side to side. There was a bruise already forming on the outside of my ankle, and it was beginning to swell. I pulled my stocking back on and laced my shoe tightly to give it some support. There wasn't anything nearby to hold onto while I pulled myself up, so I clumsily crawled onto my knees and stood up onto my left foot. Slowly, I put weight onto my right. Pain shot through my ankle. I tried limping, just stepping on my toes. It was no good. There was no way I could walk the remaining miles home.

I sat back down rather than chance stumbling and having another fall and scooted myself off the road a little way to the shade of a nearby bush. I had only been there a few minutes, hardly even enough time to consider my predicament, when I heard the sound of a shod horse clip-clopping on the hard-packed roadway. Looking up, I was relieved to see a wagon coming my way. I waved and called out. Fortunately, the driver, a young man, saw me sitting there, a dusty lump of waving arms.

He set the brake and jumped down beside me, removing his hat as he did.

"Hello," he said. "Are you in need of some help?"

I looked up at him and smiled in relief. He looked to be about the same age as one of my older brothers, with a long narrow face, curly brown hair cut short, and the finest pair of blue eyes I'd ever seen. It wasn't so much the color of his eyes that was so compelling. Most of the people in my family had blue eyes. But his were so clear and bright, and when he looked at me I caught my breath for an instant at their intensity.

"I'm Ethan Kilpatrick," he said, bending down and offering a hand. He wasn't a large man; he was slender and of average height. He had a tight sinewy strength about him, like most men who were used to hard work.

I put my hand in his, and he helped me to stand. For a second I felt light-headed and thought I might plummet back to the ground.

"Whoa, there," he said, and took hold of my elbow to steady me.

Grimacing with the renewed pain in my ankle, I said, "I'm sorry, Mr. Kilpatrick. I've had a fall. I stepped into a hole, and I think I've sprained my ankle."

"Do you live close by, miss?"

"Ludlow," I finally had sense enough to tell him my name. "Eliza Jane Ludlow," I said, shaking his hand this time. "I do live fairly close. Up the road between here and Huron City."

"Would you like me to drive you home, Miss Ludlow?"

"I would be very appreciative, if it isn't too far out of your way."

"Not at all," he told me. "Right on my way home."

He helped me up onto the wagon seat. I almost lost my balance again as my one good foot missed the step. He grabbed hold of me and gave me a boost up.

"Are you usually accident prone?" he asked.

My face, already warm from embarrassment, became hotter still. Giving up all pretenses, I laughed out loud. "No. I don't know what the matter is with me today."

He walked around to the other side, put his hat back on, and climbed up onto the bench beside me. He was looking right at me. I was still giggling, which further humiliated me. I didn't want him to think I was a giddy schoolgirl without a brain in her head. I wasn't inclined to hysterics but, for a moment, I simply couldn't stop laughing.

Smiling at me crookedly, he removed the brake and gave the reins a shake. The wagon lurched forward. Not wanting to tumble off the wagon seat and confirm that I must be a halfwit, I held on tightly to the edge.

"Ludlow," he pondered the name. "Is it your family just arrived a while back? I think I know your brothers."

"I do have three older brothers: John, Tom, and Will," I said.

He was nodding his head. "Yes, that's them. We've played cards together a couple of times. Your brother Tom works at Grindstone City?"

"Yes, he does, and all three like to play cards," I said, recalling my brothers' penchant for poker.

"So where have you been this fine day?"

My smile fell. "My sister and I went to Stafford House in Port Hope to inquire about work," I told him ruefully. "We made the acquaintance of Miss Stafford aboard our ship coming from Buffalo. Well, I should say, my sister made her acquaintance. I was otherwise occupied at the time."

"Where is your sister now?"

"She was hired by the lady of the house," I said.

"But not you?"

"No. I'm afraid I didn't make a very good impression."

"Ah, there's a story there, I think," he teased, his voice revealing a hint of an Irish lilt.

"Yes, there is, but one I'd rather not remember."

"Now you really have me curious," he said.

"It's just too humiliating." My eyes started to tear up, and I turned my face away.

We sat there quietly, side by side, for a time. Anxious to take his attention off of me, I asked, "Have you lived in Michigan long?"

"Going on four years," he said. "I came out with my folks, same as you. I'm the eldest and, until a couple of years ago, was the only son. I have four younger sisters and a baby brother. I work for my dad on the farm."

"Where is your farm?" I asked.

"A bit south and west of Huron City. We have family in the area, some of my dad's cousins, who farm nearby."

"Not too far from us then?" I asked.

"Not too far. Do you ever get to Huron City?" he asked.

"No reason to, except maybe to keep looking for work. Papa goes to the general store there for supplies sometimes."

"There's a church there. My family attends, when we aren't too busy with planting and harvesting," he said.

"This is the back of our land," I pointed, as we passed Stoddard Road. "The drive is up there around the curve."

"This used to be Mr. Huffman's old place. He was mostly in logging. You are really close to Pointe aux Barques," he said.

"The lighthouse? Yes, we took a walk over there a couple of weeks ago."

"Have you been swimming in the lake?" he asked.

"I've gotten my feet wet, but I'm not much of a swimmer," I said. In truth, I wasn't a swimmer at all. "Everyone has been so busy working to get the farm up and running there hasn't been time for much else."

He nodded his head in understanding. "I know what that's like. We're still working on expanding our fields and pasture. Farming is a never-ending enterprise—and exhausting. But there's no better feeling than coaxing life out of the dirt."

"I wouldn't know about that yet. We've barely gotten the first field cleared," I said and smiled at him.

He looked at me then and grinned back. "You have a really nice smile," he said.

I felt very self-conscious all of a sudden, but his gaze held mine, and I did not look away.

He turned into the drive and pulled up alongside the house. Mumma came out the door wiping her hands on her apron.

"Hello," she said, shielding her eyes in the bright sun.

Mr. Kilpatrick quickly jumped down from the wagon and removed his hat. "Hello, Mrs. Ludlow, I'm Ethan Kilpatrick. I'm here to deliver your daughter home. She's had a bit of an accident." He shook Mumma's hand and continued around to my side of the wagon where I was trying to lift my weight on one foot to climb down.

Mumma's face changed from friendly smile into brow-furrowed concern as the young man put his hands around my waist and lifted me to the ground.

"I stepped into a hole and twisted my ankle," I told her.

With one arm around my waist and my arm on his shoulder, he supported me as I limped painfully into the house and to one of the high-backed chairs.

"Thank you very much, Mr. Kilpatrick," I said.

He flashed me a charming smile and said, "You're very welcome, Miss Ludlow."

"Would you like some tea?" Mumma asked.

"No thank you, ma'am," he said. "I've got to be getting home with the supplies."

"Thank you so much for assisting my daughter," Mumma said.

"My pleasure, ma'am," he replied. Turning, he nodded to me and went out the door.

I smiled to myself. *Every cloud has a silver lining,* Grandma used to say.

Chapter 11

"What in the world happened?" Mumma asked after Mr. Kilpatrick departed. "And where is Roseanne?"

"Oh Mumma, it was dreadful. I was an absolute dunce," I said and tried to relate my entire misadventure. By the time I got through the whole appalling experience at Stafford House, my frustrated tears had started anew. But I changed quickly to giggling when I told her how Mr. Kilpatrick had looked at me like I was crazy when I couldn't stop laughing. She alternately commiserated and chuckled through my story. When I was finished, I felt suddenly exhausted.

Mumma carefully unlaced my shoe and removed it. She examined the tender foot. "I don't think anything is broken," she said as she gently felt along each of the bones in my foot and the ankle joint. "It's pretty swollen already. I'll have you soak it, then I'll wrap it, but you'd better stay off of it for few days."

She brought a pan of cold water and a box of Epsom salts. "I'm happy to hear Roseanne is employed," she said, "but sorry about your poor experience." She was trying to hide a smile.

"Mumma, this is not funny," I said. She didn't reply, but I could hear her chuckling from the bedroom as she went to fetch a bandage.

By the time she was finished with her ministrations, I had taken up residence in her rocking chair with my foot wrapped and elevated on the hearth stool.

"I'm sorry, I'm not much good to anybody with a lame foot," I said, feeling frustrated at being stuck in a chair.

"There's plenty for you to do while you're laid up. That stack of mending, to start with," she motioned to the corner near the fireplace a short reach from where I sat.

Happy to have something to occupy my hands, I grabbed a shirt and the tin box of buttons and went to work. I sat there sewing and rethinking my fall, and I began to laugh out loud. What a clumsy lummox I was. Then I pictured a pair of vivid blue eyes and wondered if I'd ever see him again.

* * *

By the fourth day of my confinement, I was tired of being waited on like a baby—even being accompanied to the outhouse. I was bored silly. With the exception of the days it took to travel from New York to the thumb area of Michigan, I was completely unused to sitting around. I had so much pent-up energy and no place to put it. I decided to walk around a bit, doing the dishes and some of the cooking, but by that evening I was back in Mumma's chair with my still-swollen foot elevated on a stool, darning socks by lamplight.

After supper we were winding down for the night. Emma was finishing the kitchen chores, Dick was out tending the animals, and Mumma was tucking the younger children into bed. Papa had sat down and lit his pipe when suddenly we heard footsteps on the porch. We were all surprised to see Tommy walk in the door. He sat at the table talking with Papa for a few minutes.

"How are your brothers doing?" Mumma asked, coming back into the room.

"They're fine, working hard," he said.

"And how is it going at the quarry?" My brother was a strong, muscular man and worked as a stone turner at the grindstone mill.

Listening to their conversation with half an ear, I pulled the wooden darning ball out of a sock, now that the hole was repaired, and pushed it through to the toe of the next one from Mumma's basket. I heard my name mentioned and looked up from my work.

"I hear you had a bit of an accident a few days ago," Tommy repeated.

I looked back down at my sewing. "You saw your friend, Mr. Kilpatrick?" I guessed.

"Yes, I did. He said you'd done yourself an injury."

I motioned to my foot, still shoeless and elevated. "I wasn't watching where I was going."

"It looks like it hurts." He came over and looked at the bruising, which had turned a yellowish-green.

"I wish it would get better," I said. "I'm getting tired of being laid up."

"What were you doing walking on the road all alone?"

"Roseanne and I had gone to Port Hope looking for work. She was hired, and I was sent on my way." I breezed lightly over the story. "I had only gone a mile or so when I stepped in a hole and did this."

"And Mr. Kilpatrick came to the rescue?" he grinned.

"It was lucky that he came along. I was wondering how in the world I was going to get home. He kindly gave me a ride. He said it was right on his way."

He coughed and rubbed his nose awkwardly. "Um, the man is quite taken with you."

I looked at him blankly. "Pardon me?" I said. I looked over to Mumma.

"He's quite taken with you," my brother repeated. "He's interested in courting you, Eliza, if you're willing," Tommy said. "He'll get Papa's permission first, of course."

"He was a very pleasant young man," Mumma said, smiling at me encouragingly.

"Oooh," Emma said, "Eliza has a beau."

My cheeks felt hot, and I shot Emma a look of annoyance. "Aren't you supposed to be drying the dishes?"

"What's going on?" Georgie called coming down from the loft.

"Eliza has a beau," Emma sang in a teasing voice. This time I ignored her.

I didn't know what to say. My first impulse was to say no. Or even better, run out the door. I glanced at Mumma again.

"It's completely up to you," she said.

My mouth felt very dry. Part of me leapt at the chance to see him again, but the rest of me shied away from the idea of courtship. I shrugged my shoulders.

"He's quite a good guy, Liza. You might consider giving him a chance."

I thought about those intense eyes and his teasing smile. He was a very nice-looking young man. I had butterflies in my stomach. He was the first man who'd ever shown any interest in me.

"Of course he hasn't met Roseanne yet," Tommy goaded.

That was the incentive I needed. It would be nice to have a chance to get to know someone before he met my beautiful sister. But the thought of being courted made my stomach flip-flop. Then I heard Grandma's voice whisper in my ear, *It's time to start your own stories, Eliza Jane.* I made up my mind.

"Please tell Mr. Kilpatrick," I paused and swallowed, embarrassed at having to say this in front of the family, "I am laid up at the moment, but yes, I would be interested in having him call on me."

"All right then," Tommy slapped his thigh, visibly relieved. "I will give him your message."

And just like that, in the blink of an eye, my boring, workaday life changed. Relishing the sweet, sweet feeling of wonder, I smiled to my-self. I had a beau. At last. And I felt like throwing up.

The door opened again, and in walked Roseanne.

"What are you doing home?" Mumma asked.

"Mrs. Stafford doesn't need me over the weekend. I don't have to go back until Sunday evening," she said. She looked around, correctly guessing she had missed something important. "What's going on?"

This time, at a warning look from Mumma, Emma held her tongue. Georgie, not the least bit interested in affairs of the heart, climbed back up the ladder.

"I don't like the idea of your walking that distance in the dark," Mumma told Roseanne. "Have you had anything to eat?"

"Yes, I ate before I left, and it wasn't dark the whole way, just the last little bit," Roseanne said. She noticed my foot on the stool. "What happened to you?"

"I sprained my ankle," I said, "on my way home from Port Hope."

"Oh," she gave me two seconds consideration and then said, "I have some good news for you. The upstairs maid just got engaged and will be leaving her position. Mrs. Stafford asked if you would be interested in taking her place."

"Oh, my goodness," I said. "How soon?"

"In a few weeks, I think. The girl is getting married before Christmas, and she's working till the end of the month." She looked around at everybody. "Have I missed something? I mean besides Eliza's ankle?"

"Eliza has a beau," Emma burst out, voice pitched high and twirling the dishtowel around.

"What? When did this happen?" Roseanne said.

Tommy stood up. "Time for me to leave." He kissed Mumma's cheek and gave my shoulder a squeeze. "Take care of yourself, Eliza."

Just as he went out the door, Dick came in, finished with his chores.

"Eliza has a beau," Emma made her announcement yet again.

"Oh, for heaven's sake, Emma, get back to work," Mumma scolded and put the kettle on for tea.

Dick looked at me and smirked, "Congratulations, I guess."

Roseanne rolled her eyes at him then turned to me. "Tell me every little thing, Eliza."

Not interested in girl talk, Papa tapped his pipe on the hearth, gave Mumma's hand an affectionate squeeze, and went into his bedroom. Dick climbed up the ladder to the loft.

I hobbled to the table to join Mumma and my sisters, holding up a hand to halt any further questions.

"When I left Stafford House the other day, I wasn't looking where I was going, stumbled in a hole on the road, and twisted my ankle. I was miles from home and couldn't put any weight on my foot. I sat there on the side of the road wondering if I would have to crawl the rest of the way, but a young man in a wagon came by to help me. His name is Mr. Kilpatrick, and he's a friend of Tommy's."

"What does he look like?" Roseanne said.

"He has blue eyes and curly hair, and he knows the boys," I said.

"Does he work with Tommy at Grindstone?"

"No, I don't think so," I said. "I'm not sure how he knows the boys, but he did say he plays cards with them. He works on his family's farm. He's the oldest son and I think he's about the same age as Tommy."

"Do you like him?" she asked.

"I guess so," I said. "He was very polite and kind. I don't know what I would have done that day except sit there in a heap and wait for Papa to wonder where I was and come looking for me."

"Someone else would have come by," Mumma said from the stove.

"Probably some grizzled old man," Roseanne said. "Thank goodness your rescuer was young and single." She exhaled a dramatic sigh of relief as if I'd dodged a bullet.

"I didn't know he was interested in me until Tommy came over tonight," I told her.

"Testing the waters for his friend," Mumma said bringing the cups to the table and filling them with scalding hot tea.

"Did you and Papa meet him?"

"I was here when he brought her home. Papa hasn't yet, although it sounds like the young man intends to ask permission to court Eliza."

"I can't believe your luck. I'm positively green with envy. I wish something like that would happen to me."

"No, you don't. I haven't been able to walk ever since." Secretly, I was happy Roseanne hadn't been there. I had no interest in competing with her for Mr. Kilpatrick's attention.

"That's not what I mean," she said, leaning her cheek on her hand. "It's just so…"

"Romantic," Emma interjected. Mumma gave her a stern look and she went back to drying dishes.

"I thought you'd be happy. You're always telling me to find a suitor," I glared at her.

"Oh, I am," Roseanne said, but her smile didn't reach her eyes. "I just wish someone would ask to court me too."

"Maybe you'll marry him," Emma said.

"Emma, I don't even know him."

"You know he's handsome and gallant. He's like a knight on a white horse rescuing a damsel in distress," she said.

I shook my head, still with that feeling of wonder and disbelief. I was afraid to dream, to hope for the future. I didn't understand what he saw in me. I recalled his words: *You have a really nice smile, Eliza Jane.*

"Are you excited, Eliza? I mean, are you interested in him? Is he handsome?" Roseanne pressed.

"I'm too nervous to be excited," I said. "I suppose he's good-looking."

"And that's the least of your concerns," Mumma said sagely.

"What do you mean?" Emma asked.

"You girls need to keep your feet planted firmly on the ground. When you do decide to settle down, I want you to choose someone who is a good person, and kind, and a hard worker," she said, making a list of required attributes. "Handsome is not a necessary quality."

Roseanne and Emma looked at each other and giggled.

"The fact that he's handsome doesn't hurt," I admitted with a grin.

"There may be hope for you yet," Roseanne said, then she completely changed the subject. "What do you think of taking the job at Stafford House?"

"That's really good news. I'm happy she thought of me. After we had tea the other day, I thought I'd made a bad impression."

"You sat there like a dunce and didn't say a word the whole time," Roseanne said.

"Roseanne, that's enough," Mumma scolded. "I won't have you calling your sister names."

"You should have seen her," Roseanne continued. "I know you're shy, Eliza, but for Pete's sake, you were there trying to get a job."

"I know," I moaned. "I just kept thinking about what happened when I met Miss Stafford on the ship. It was so embarrassing."

"It wasn't embarrassing," Roseanne said. "It was hilarious."

"And stinky," Emma chimed in.

"I'm going to bed," I said, not wanting their teasing to spoil the delicious and hopeful feeling I had. I hobbled off toward the bedroom. Roseanne was right, I had to admit. I did make a terrible impression. But if Mrs. Stafford was willing to take a chance on hiring me, she would find out for herself what kind of worker I was.

I limped quietly into the room where the little ones were sleeping, changed into my nightgown, and lay down on my bed. I thought again with wonder how my luck had changed. A beau and a new job all in one day.

Chapter 12

I was lighter of heart. With my ankle improving, a potential suitor, and a new job, I was overjoyed. I felt more energetic and gladly helped Mumma gather the apples that were so ripe they were falling to the ground. Mumma, who couldn't abide wasting food, had Georgie, who was quite a tree climber, go up to pick the fruit on the higher branches while she pulled the ones she could reach. Ben and I sifted through the ones on the ground that weren't too bruised.

I peeled and cored and cored and peeled. By the time we were only a quarter of the way through what we had picked, I had blisters on my right hand. It was certainly worth the effort, though, to have sweet dried apples the rest of the year. When Mumma decided we finally had enough to last till next fall, the rest of the apples were put into the press that we'd borrowed from the Bruces for cider.

As the days passed with no word from Mr. Kilpatrick, I started to feel nervous. I had been on tenterhooks since Tommy brought me the news that he was interested in me. What if he had changed his mind?

Finally, on the Sunday afternoon just before I had to go to Stafford House to begin my new job, he arrived to ask Papa if he could court me. We had just finished the noon meal, and Papa was finishing his coffee. Mumma and I were clearing the table when we heard the wagon pull up outside.

Georgie burst in the door. "Eliza, guess who's here."

Dick, who'd been chopping firewood, came through the door with my handsome rescuer.

"Good afternoon, Mr. Kilpatrick," Mumma said.

I had instant butterflies in my stomach but managed a tentative smile.

"Good afternoon, Mrs. Ludlow," he nodded to Mumma.

"This is the gentleman who brought Eliza home when she got hurt, dear," Mumma said to Papa.

Papa stood up, taking the pipe from his mouth. "I'm very grateful, young man," Papa said, reaching out to shake hands.

"You're very welcome, sir," he replied. "It was my pleasure." He stood there awkwardly fiddling with his hat. No one spoke. I half expected him to turn around and bolt out the door. Then he cleared his voice. "Mr. Ludlow," he started, then cleared his voice again. "Sir, I would like your permission to court your daughter Eliza Jane." He said it boldly and maybe with just a bit of a wobble in his voice.

Papa set his pipe down, smoothed his short, graying beard with one hand, and finally said with all seriousness, "Yes, you have my permission, as long as my daughter approves." Papa turned to me.

I nodded my head, speechless.

Roseanne, who'd been out in the garden, swept into the house followed by Emma, Georgie, and Nellie, and smiled her most charming smile. I had a moment of fear that, once he took a look at her, my courtship with Mr. Kilpatrick would be over.

"You must be Mr. Kilpatrick," she said smiling in that charming way I could never hope to match.

He nodded to her but gave her no more attention. "Miss Ludlow, would you like to go for a ride down to the lake?" he asked.

"I'd like that very much," I said, anxious to be away from this uncomfortable situation.

Emma, Roseanne, Georgie, and Nellie all turned toward Ethan. "Could we come along?" Roseanne asked. Emma smiled hopefully.

Oh, my goodness, I thought. As if I didn't already feel self-conscious enough. I turned pleading eyes to Mumma.

She put a halt to their begging. "Emma, you have chores to do. Roseanne, I need your help before you return to Port Hope. Georgie and Nellie will be enough of a chaperone, I think."

I gave her a quick, grateful hug, grabbed a shawl, and went out the door.

"I see you're walking again," Mr. Kilpatrick said as we approached his wagon.

"Yes," I smiled back, "both my ankle and my pride have healed up nicely." He gave me a hand up to the wagon. The children clambered into the back.

The autumn sun was warm as we drove down the lighthouse road. Ethan parked near the lake and let the reins trail so the horse could munch grass. He helped me down and grabbed the blanket he'd brought along for us to sit on. The children ran ahead to the water's edge and in no time had removed shoes and socks to go wading.

"You have a very big family," Ethan said as he spread the blanket on the grass along the edge of the sand. "Have I met them all?"

"You have," I smiled.

He began counting on his fingers. "There are the three older boys, you, your sisters Roseanne, Emma, and Nellie, and your brothers Dick and George. Did I get them all?"

"And the baby, Ben," I added, "Although he isn't really a baby any more. He's three years old."

"So, ten of you," he said.

"How many brothers and sisters do you have?" I asked.

"I'm the eldest of six. Next there are four girls and my baby brother."

"How old are they?" I asked, although it was his age I was curious to know.

"Kathleen is fifteen, Bridget is twelve, Mary is ten, little Maggie is six, and my little brother, Johnny, is one."

"And how old are you, Mr. Kilpatrick?" I dared to ask.

"I'm twenty, almost twenty-one," he said. "There was another sister born between Kathleen and me, but she passed away when she was very young. Please call me Ethan," he added, "we are courting, so I think it would be all right."

"All right, Ethan," I said with a smile. "Your parents are probably younger than mine."

He nodded. "My mum had me before she was twenty."

"Do you work with your pa?"

"Mostly, but I also work at the mill with Tom when I have time. I've been trying to save up money to buy the land adjacent to ours."

So that was how he knew the boys, I thought. "John has a place just up the road from ours," I said. "Will is his farmhand."

"Yes, I know. We get together once in a while for a game of cards."

I recalled what he had told me during our first meeting. "They do like to play cards," I said, "although Mumma disapproves."

Ethan shrugged. "There's no harm in playing cards as long as there's no gambling."

"They don't gamble?" I asked, surprised.

He ducked his head and chuckled. "Well, there's no serious gambling. Mostly penny ante."

"Where did you live before you came here?" I asked.

"I was born in New England, and both my parents were born in Ireland. They came out here when Maggie was two. My brother was born here. What about your family?"

"Mumma and Papa both came from Ireland when they were very young. Papa's family came over to Canada when he was just a baby. Mumma's family farmed on Prince Edward Island. The older children—including me, Roseanne, and Dick—were born in Ontario."

While we talked I rubbed my blisters. He took my hand, laying it palm up in his, and touched the spot where a blister had popped.

"How did this happen?" he asked.

"Paring apples," I said, rolling my eyes ruefully. "After months of helping Papa in the field, I still got blisters from a paring knife."

"A little hard to wear gloves in the kitchen, I suppose," he said.

His touch was gentle and so distracting. I looked at his eyes again and felt suddenly warm all over. I took my hand back and looked away. I could feel his eyes boring into me and looked back at him. He was smiling roguishly and reached out again, but I folded my hands in my lap. I could just hear my sister tut-tutting at me for being a prude.

"Oh, I have some news," I told him, changing the subject. "I'm going to be working at Stafford House after all."

"Was there ever a doubt?" he asked. "I mean, your sister probably put in a good word for you."

I shrugged. "Maybe, but after the impression I made that first time I met Miss Stafford, I'm surprised her mother was interested in me at all."

"Are you ready to tell me the story then?" he pressed.

I told him the entire deplorable story. He laughed uproariously at my expense.

"Seriously, it wasn't funny, Ethan. It was awful. She was dressed so richly, and I'm sure some of the sick may have splashed her." Then I began to giggle. "And I spent the entire rest of our trip smelling like vomit. Truly it was the worst experience of my life."

"Even worse than the day of your accident?" he asked.

"A completely different situation," I said. "We'd gone to Port Hope at Miss Stafford's invitation to Roseanne. She and her mother were very cordial to Roseanne. I didn't say a word, I was so nervous. I just kept thinking of the first time I'd met her and the horrible impression I'd made and that she'd probably told her mother all about it. It was like reliving the shame all over again."

Ethan was watching me, his gaze penetrating deep into my soul. I realized I was speaking earnestly, for I wanted him to understand the humiliation I'd felt, but I was afraid I'd said too much and stopped speaking abruptly, looking away.

"I'm sorry," I said.

"For what? None of that was your fault," he remarked.

I smiled at him gratefully.

"You have the most beautiful smile, Eliza Jane. Don't ever stop smiling."

I swallowed hard. I thought perhaps I'd found someone who really understood me. I blinked as tears sprang to my eyes. Thankfully, Georgie and Nellie came running up just then and plopped down on the blanket with us.

Ethan said, "So Georgie, how do you like living in Michigan?"

Georgie wrinkled his forehead in thought, pulled on his socks, and said, "I like the farm. But I don't have a dog anymore. And I hate school."

Ethan looked surprised. "What happened to your dog?"

"He was too old to make the trip," I told him. "He's living with Grandma and Grandpa."

"I really miss him," Georgie hung his head.

"Well, a boy needs a dog," Ethan agreed. "Maybe you'll be able to get another one."

"That's what Eliza says," Georgie said, trying to pull on his shoes without untying the laces.

"What's the problem with school?"

Nellie answered for him while doing up her own shoes. "The teacher doesn't like him. He gets in trouble a lot."

I knew Georgie didn't like school, but I didn't realize he was having problems with the teacher.

"Hmmm," Ethan said thoughtfully, "what's the real problem, George?"

Georgie ducked his head ruefully and admitted, "I don't pay attention."

"I had that problem too," Ethan told him.

"You did?" He looked at Ethan in disbelief.

"Yes, I did," Ethan said, "and had many a punishment because of it. One time the teacher got so mad at me she made me sit under her desk."

I looked at him closely to see if he was telling the truth.

Georgie laughed out loud. "I've never had to do that. What did you do?"

Clearly enjoying the retelling, Ethan continued, "I pulled the hairs out of her legs."

"You didn't!" I laughed. "What did your Mum say?"

"Did you get a whipping?" Georgie questioned, longing for the gruesome details.

Ethan ducked his head for a moment. "Well, I did get a spanking. But the next day, my dad took me hunting, and we talked things over. He said everyone has a job to do in this world and mine was going to school, that even farmers need to know how to read, write, and figure numbers. He told me he expected me to always do my best and be respectful."

"So, did you?" Georgie asked, eager for more tales of the classroom.

"I did. I'd like to tell you I was really good after that, but that wouldn't be truthful. I can tell you it gets easier the older you get."

I was so pleased with Ethan. He knew just what to say to a young boy like Georgie.

"Are you going to marry Eliza?" Georgie blurted out.

"Georgie," I cried, dismayed. "You are being inappropriate." I couldn't look at Ethan, afraid of what I might see in his face.

He chuckled, stood up, and said, "Come on, let's go for a walk." He offered a hand to help me to my feet but let go of it as soon as I had stood.

We wandered down by the lighthouse and along the lakefront.

"See the little boats?" Ethan said, pointing toward the water.

I looked at him, confused.

"The rocks poking up out there, just above the surface of the water in the waves? They look like little boats. That's what *barques* means in Pointe aux Barques. But they really should call this part of the lake 'shipwreck alley.'"

"Are there a lot of shipwrecks?" I asked.

"There's a reef under there, dangerous to ships. There have been shipwrecks in bad weather because it's so shallow and rocky through here. That's why they finally built the lifesaving station."

Georgie and Nellie collected feathers, rocks, and flowers as we walked, which I ended up carrying for them. Then Georgie pulled up some grass and chased Nellie to sprinkle it over her head. She shrieked and laughed and ran away from him, but he soon caught her. Their antics were entertaining and made Ethan talk more about his family.

"One of these days you'll have to come and meet my sisters," he said.

"I'd like that," I smiled.

It was late afternoon when we got back to where we started. We shook out the blanket, folded it, and started home. I was more excited coming back than when I had left because I knew I liked Ethan. I hoped he felt the same.

When we pulled up the drive and stopped, the children ran ahead into the house. Ethan walked me to the door. He shook my hand politely and said, "Thank you for a very pleasant afternoon. I hope you enjoyed yourself, and I look forward to seeing you again."

"I would like that," I told him, smiling, "and thank you so much for taking me."

In bed that night, before I fell asleep, I thought about that blue-eyed boy. I still felt that feeling of wonder and surprise that he was interested in me. That we were actually in a courtship. Life was so unexpected.

CHAPTER 13

At daybreak, Dick harnessed the horse and delivered us to Stafford House in the wagon. I was a bit nervous but also excited at the prospect of finally having a job.

"Welcome, Eliza Jane," Mrs. Stafford greeted me. I was surprised she knew my name. "Roseanne may show you to the room you'll be sharing with her upstairs. You'll find your uniform up there, and then Katie can take you through her tasks and teach you what needs to be done."

"Yes, ma'am," I answered. Upstairs was really up two floors to the attic bedroom. It was very tiny but had two cots with pillows and quilts and a small table between with an oil lamp on it. In one corner was a rocking chair, and on the wall opposite the tiny window were some hooks where several petticoats, a black dress, and a starched white apron awaited me. They were plain and serviceable and not the least attractive. Dressing for my new job would take some getting used to. My foundation garments now included a corset, a very uncomfortable article, but required nonetheless.

My sister laced me into it. "At least it's the soft kind," she said. "It won't be too restrictive."

I added three petticoats, topped them with the black dress buttoned to the neck, and looked down at myself. Clearly, the person whose uniform this had been was more robust than I, but after putting the starched full-length apron on and tying it around my waist, I decided it would be all right. I brushed my hair, pulled it flat against my scalp, and wound it tightly into a bun and pinned it securely to my scalp, then covered it with the required white cap tied under my chin.

"Tie it to the back," Roseanne recommended. "It will drive you crazy under your chin all day."

I did as I was told, then we went to find the young woman who was going to train me for my new job.

"This is Katie," Roseanne said.

We were of a similar type, both short, freckled, and Irish. We probably looked enough alike to be sisters except she was a redhead. We grinned at each other.

"I'm pleased to make your acquaintance, Eliza," she said.

"Congratulations on your upcoming marriage," I said. "Will you be living nearby?"

"No, I'll be moving to Sebewaing. My fiancé's family is German and has a large farm there."

Katie gave me a tour of the house and explained that Mrs. Stafford was very particular about how the cleaning chores were to be done. When dusting tables, I was to be sure to dust every single square inch right down to the floor.

"She's a fair employer, though," she added. "It does get a bit busy when the girls are home from school or there are houseguests."

I paid attention as she took me through each of her tasks and the schedule she followed to get everything completed in a timely manner. There were many daily tasks, some weekly, and others once a month. My days would certainly be busy, but that was how I liked my days to go—busy and fast. It made the time fly.

Down in the basement, there was a large laundry room. She explained how the modern boiler was worked. It had a metal drum with holes in it. The clothes went into the drum, and then you just rotated it through the hot water by turning the crank on the side. There were also lines near the ceiling made of an intricate system of pulleys for hanging the wash to dry indoors during bad weather. All of this was necessary to handle the linens and clothing of a large household. I wouldn't have to handle the laundry alone. There was a washerwoman who came in two days a week.

Life at Stafford House was not all work. I enjoyed sharing the attic bedroom with my sister, and the evenings were my own. I had a bit of time to read, sew, or write letters to Grandma. There was a large library, and Mrs. Stafford gave us permission to borrow books as long as we didn't remove them from the premises. I was thrilled.

My favorite room was the kitchen, also down in the basement, which was a cool respite on the remaining warm days that fall. Kind and funny, Cook quickly became my second mother. When I first met her, she took one look at me in my hand-me-down maid's attire, clicked her tongue, and shook her head.

"So, you're the new girl," she said. "I can see I have my work cut out for me."

"Excuse me?" I said.

"You're going to need some fattening up," she smiled. Almost as round as she was tall, I was to learn she was at her happiest when feeding the family and the staff.

I smiled self-consciously. True to her word, she tried her hardest to get me to eat. The food was so wonderful; she was a wizard in the kitchen. Eating almost the same as the family, we had meat, poultry, or fish at most meals. She tried unsuccessfully to get me to have second helpings, but I didn't have so large an appetite.

I finally began to put on some weight, even with the nonstop house-keeping and laundry. After a few weeks, I could no longer count my ribs, and I began to fill out. I was so relieved that I was finally developing a woman's figure.

Life settled into a routine five to six days a week. Most of the time Roseanne acted as personal secretary to Mrs. Stafford. She did her writing and accompanied her on shopping trips. To fill in the rest of the time, she did the mending and small sewing projects that, at our house, Mumma would have done. My chores were completely menial: sweeping, dusting, polishing, scrubbing, washing, ironing, changing bedding, all of which occupied every daytime hour of the workweek. I had weekends off, unless there was a dinner party on Saturday night when Cook needed help preparing a meal with several courses. Then I would serve and help with clean-up.

I bathed and washed my hair on Saturday nights and attended church with the family on Sundays. Weekends would have been a good time to walk home for a visit, but the fall weather finally arrived with a vengeance, bringing wind and rain and unusually cold temperatures. In early November, we had already had the first freeze and some snow flurries. It didn't bode well for what was coming in the next few months.

"I think we're in for a cold winter this year," I said to my sister while we dressed one morning after the first freeze.

"It sure became cold all of a sudden," she agreed.

"It's good that we brought our warmer clothes with us," I said.

"I wish we'd had a chance to go home," she sighed, looking morosely out our little attic window.

"Maybe over the holidays?" I suggested, tying my apron snugly around my middle.

Later that morning, Mrs. Stafford came to find me with a letter in her hand. "This came for you yesterday, Eliza Jane," she said briskly.

"Thank-you, ma'am," I said and put it into my pocket.

"Aren't you going to open it and find out who sent it?" she asked.

I pulled the envelope back out of my pocket and looked at it. There was only one person who might write to me. Grandma.

I looked at the envelope, shocked to find the writing was not Grandma's. Definitely a man's handwriting. Ethan had written me a letter. My heart began to pound. What a wonderful surprise. I looked up at her, my cheeks hot from embarrassment.

She remained there looking at me. Did she expect me to tell her who it was from? I hesitated then said, "It's from Ethan Kilpatrick, a young man I met a few weeks ago."

Her face was unreadable. I wondered if she was angry that I would be receiving mail from a suitor at her residence.

"Does this mean I'm going to lose another maid to marriage?"

I was startled. "Oh, n-no, ma'am," I stammered, "I mean, w-we just met. I barely know him."

She gave me a crooked, knowing smile. "Very well," she said and walked back down the hallway.

That night I took the letter from my pocket and, in the dim light of the lamp next to my bed, read:

Dear Eliza Jane,

I hope this letter finds you well. I'm doing fine. With the turning of the weather, my chores have become less time-consuming, and I'm spending more and more time in the house or barn. I'm going to talk to the foreman at the stone mill to see if I can work some extra hours. How is your job coming along? Did you get settled in all right? I walked over to your brothers' place last weekend. John Bruce and his sister, Annie, were there. Annie made us some eggnog, and we played cards. By the time I left, it was freezing. When I got back home, I had to thaw out my hands by the fire. I'm not sure if you have any time to write, but I would sure like to hear from you.

Yours,
Ethan

I read the letter over several times, savoring each word, then tucked it away in my dresser drawer. When Roseanne came in, I shared the bit about everyone getting together to play cards.

"Annie Bruce?" she said. "I think she's sweet on John."

"Yes, she is," I said. "She said so, in so many words, at the barn raising."

Unshed tears shone in her eyes. "Everyone will be getting together, and I'm stuck here," she complained.

"It wouldn't be any different, even if we were home," I told her. "Besides, if it's meant to be…"

"Oh stop, Eliza, you sound just like Mumma, or worse, like Grandma."

She got out of her uniform with a lot of exasperated sighs, put on her nightgown, and climbed into bed. I put out the light and rolled over with my back to her. I didn't want her bad mood to spoil the delicious feeling I had inside from reading Ethan's letter.

"How am I going to get Billy to fall in love with me if I never get to see him? He's probably forgotten all about me by now," she said mournfully.

I could tell she was crying now. I rolled back over.

"Roseanne, you're not exactly forgettable," I said soothingly.

She ignored my comment. "I know he likes me."

I wondered who she was trying to convince, me or herself. "How do you know?" I asked.

"I just know," she said. "How can you tell that Mr. Kilpatrick likes you?"

I laughed self-deprecatingly. "If Tommy hadn't come over that night, when I was laid up from my ankle, I would never have known that Ethan was interested in courting me."

"Well, you were probably preoccupied by the pain in your foot."

"Maybe," I said. I rolled back over. "If we get a chance, we need to go to town to buy some paper and ink."

Roseanne continued to toss and turn. I would just as soon lie there thinking over my time at the lake with Ethan and every word of his letter, but I was distracted by her restlessness. I threw off my covers and sat up in bed.

"Did I tell you about that afternoon Ethan and I went down to the lake?"

"No," she sniffed. "How did it go?"

"It was a very enlightening experience," I said, piquing her curiosity.

She sat up and faced me in the dark. "What happened?"

"Don't ever take Georgie as a chaperone," I warned with mock-seriousness.

She started to giggle. "What did he do?"

"He asked Ethan if he was going to marry me."

"Oh, my goodness, Eliza! What did you do?"

"I was so embarrassed," I said, chuckling. "But do you know what? When I finally looked at Ethan, he was blushing too."

"That little monkey," Roseanne said. "Somebody needs to teach him some manners."

"He's only eight," I said. "He doesn't really know any better. And he's never been in that situation before."

"When it's my turn, I'll be sure to take Emma. She'd know better."

"Maybe, but even she was ridiculous the night Tommy came over. She kept saying over and over, 'Eliza has a beau.' It was annoying," I said.

"But also exciting, wasn't it? Especially because you didn't expect anything?" she said. "It's going to be different with Billy and me. He's a bit younger than Ethan, so he might take some encouragement."

"He's not that much younger, Roseanne. He's older than me, and Ethan's only twenty-one."

"I wish he'd figure it out," she said, "because I sure like him."

"Look at it this way, when it does finally happen, it'll be that much more exciting," I told her. *All good things are worth waiting for,* I thought, but I didn't say it aloud because she would tell me I sounded like Grandma again.

"I suppose," she said sighing and lying back down. "We'd better get some sleep."

I snuggled back into my covers and must have fallen right to sleep, because the very next thing I knew, it was dawn.

Chapter 14

My prediction of an early and fierce winter came to pass. The days became shorter and darker, and before we knew it, there was ice on the ground more often than not. The flurries of snow turned into the first real snow weeks before the solstice. It wasn't very deep, but it was so beautiful. I had that excited feeling everyone gets at the first snow of the year. Like a small child, I felt like running outdoors to play, but the closest I came to enjoying it was a glance out the window between chores. The snow didn't last long and melted away overnight when the temperature came back up.

As December arrived, there was a new hustle and bustle of getting Stafford House ready for the holidays. Roseanne came into our attic bedroom one night later than usual. She had been working with Mrs. Stafford behind closed doors all day long. She flopped down dramatically onto her bed.

"I may never be able to move my hands again," she moaned.

"Why? What in the world happened?" I asked, torn between concern and amusement.

She held up her hands; the right one was stained with black ink. "I have been writing Christmas greetings for hours on end. And they have to be perfect. I mean flawless," she exclaimed. "But, oh my, you should see the beautiful cards the notes are for. Mrs. Stafford spent the whole summer painting the coziest winter family scenes with watercolors. Then these special Christmas greetings go inside of them, and she sends them to her friends and family. The ones going to New England are finished already because they'll take some time to get there."

"Christmas cards," I said. "I'd love to see one."

"I'll see if you can tomorrow. I still have loads more to do. She must send one to everyone in the village."

"They probably know everyone in the village," I said.

While she was slaving over the inkpot at a desk in a comfortable room, I was put to work after my routine tasks were complete, shining all of the silver, including dinnerware, serving dishes, and tea service, until they were spotless. I lined the finished pieces along the cupboard in the dining room where they awaited use on Christmas Day.

Next I was given the job of unpacking all of the decorations, most of which were imported from Germany. I loved unwrapping these, for each was a beautiful surprise. Some were made of wax, and each was unique in its intricate beauty. These ornaments, I learned, were for the Christmas tree, which the Staffords cut and brought into their house each year on Christmas Eve. They even put little candles in special holders, Mrs. Stafford explained, that clipped to the ends of the branches. This was hard for me to imagine, since I couldn't understand why anyone would put fire on a tree.

Finally, there was the deep cleaning. I waxed and polished all the woodwork and floors and cleaned each fireplace and hearth in the library, master bedroom, and drawing room, and then did the usual washing of all the bedding. I was familiar with spring cleaning at home, when we washed all of the windows then opened them to let in the fresh air, beat the rugs, changed the bedding, and swept and dusted every square inch of the house. I had no idea big houses went through a similar routine, minus opening the windows, more frequently. It was a tremendous amount of work. The one thought that kept me going during those weeks was the fact that I could go home to celebrate the holiday with my family. Not having been home, even for a day, since beginning my job, I missed Mumma and Papa and all the children.

Ethan and I had settled into writing to each other twice a week.

My heart quickened each time another letter arrived. Our missives had become more personal, sharing our hopes and dreams about the future. He was quickly becoming the central person in my life, occupying my thoughts while I cleaned and scrubbed as I imagined what we would say when we saw each other again.

In our free moments, Roseanne and I worked on gifts for each member of our family. We crocheted woolen scarves for the older boys and knit mittens for the younger children. For Papa, I made a rum cake under Cook's tutelage. Mrs. Stafford's dressmaker gave me some scrap material, which I tore into strips and tied together to crochet into a rag rug for Mumma to put next to her bed.

The day before Christmas Eve, the north wind began to blow, and with it came our second major snowfall. The temperature dropped to well below freezing, and the drifts began to pile up. I wondered if we would be able to go home after all. When I awoke the next morning, the first thing I did was look out through our little window, which was frosted all around, creating tiny patterns of ice crystals on the pane. I blew onto the frost and wiped a spot clear. In spite of the morning darkness, I could see that everything was shrouded in white. The branches of the pines were hanging low, heavy with a blanket of snowfall. Disappointment settled over me. There would be no getting home in this.

Roseanne joined me at the windowsill. "I wonder if Mr. Stafford has a sleigh?" She sounded despondent.

"He probably does," I said, "but remember, this is the day they cut their Christmas tree. If there is a sleigh, it'll be in use by the family."

Mary Ellen and her sisters had arrived home for the Christmas holiday earlier in the week and were looking forward to their yearly trek to choose the most perfect tree.

"Maybe they have a second one?" she asked hopefully.

Sadly, I thought of the small pile of handmade gifts, each one wrapped in a remnant of fabric scavenged from the seamstress's trunk and tied with string. I envisioned my family engrossed with their own last-minute tasks, finishing up gifts or possibly decorating the house with fragrant pine boughs. Mumma would already be planning a special dinner for Christmas Day, I was sure. And we were going to miss it all.

Feeling dejected, Roseanne and I went down to the kitchen where Cook had prepared sweet buns as a special treat for the family. She put one for each of us on the table, hot and sticky, with melted butter and sugar icing dripping down the sides. My eyes closed dreamily on the first bite as the sweet sugar and rich butter melted in my mouth. I opened my eyes to find Roseanne hadn't even tasted hers.

"I wonder what Mumma is cooking for Christmas dinner?" she said, leaning her cheek on her hand, clearly feeling the same pangs I was of homesickness.

"Roasted goose. Or duck. Or ham," I said, my mouth watering, "stuffed with bread and dried herbs from the garden."

"Potatoes and gravy," she added. "And apple pie."

"Or squash pie with whipped cream," I said.

"But we're going to miss all of it," she said, choking up with unspent tears.

"There's no need to be worried," Cook said with a kind smile. "You'll have a fine Christmas meal right here with me. Nobody ever goes hungry if I'm around." Her pleasantly plump pink cheeks and jolly laughter did much to diminish my sadness. A middle-aged woman who had lost her husband during the Civil War, she always found the silver lining. By working as a cook and housekeeper, she had managed to raise her four children alone.

A bell chimed, signaling someone at the back door. I quickly climbed the stairs to answer it, thinking it was the gamekeeper bringing the meat for the day. But when I opened it, there was my oldest brother, John. On the drive was a sleigh with two fine horses stamping their feet, shaking their manes free of the snowflakes that had started falling again, and breathing out white clouds of vapor. Annie Bruce was sitting in the front seat, snuggled under a pile of blankets and merrily waving a mitten-covered hand.

"Surprise!" my brother said, grinning as he removed the woolen scarf from around his nose and mouth.

I threw my arms joyfully around his neck and hugged him tightly. "Where did you get the sleigh?"

"It belongs to Annie's family. I can't take credit for the surprise. It was Annie's idea. She couldn't bear to think of you two stuck in Port Hope for Christmas, so she and Billy drove over first thing this morning."

Roseanne dashed up the stairs upon hearing John's voice. "Is Billy here?" she asked hopefully, poking her nose out the door past him.

"He's with the boys at our house, having my pancakes and hot coffee."

I hugged him again. "Thank you, thank you for coming for us," I said. I stepped out onto the porch and waved Annie to come into the house.

I led them downstairs to the kitchen to be warmed by the stove and hearth fire. Cook gave them each a sticky bun and a much-needed cup of hot coffee with fresh cream to make up for the breakfast they'd missed. Roseanne and I hurried up to our room to gather our things. We packed our extra set of clothes as well as the Christmas presents we had made. I remembered to grab my money, which I had saved from my weekly wages and tied into a handkerchief hidden inside my pillow-case. Most of it would be handed over to Papa to help with the farm costs. After working for several weeks at fifty cents a week, Roseanne and I each had a nice little sum to contribute.

Before we left, Mrs. Stafford and Mary Ellen came into the kitchen with gifts for us. Quickly removing the ribbon and paper, we each found one of the beautiful hand-painted Christmas cards containing a heart-felt message of thanks for our hard work and a soft woolen scarf, red for Roseanne and dark green for me.

"Thank you so much," Roseanne and I said at once.

"You're very welcome." Mrs. Stafford waved us off. "Have a very Merry Christmas, girls. Don't forget to come back."

I wore my wool cloak, put my new scarf over my head, wrapped the ends around my neck, and tied them behind. It was a windy, cold ride home. The frigid air was crisp, and I enjoyed listening to the sound of the sleigh's runners as they cut through the snow. There was no time for a heated brick to warm our feet, but I didn't mind at all. For this moment in time, I hadn't a care in the world.

At the back of our land, I caught sight of the house, smoke curling from the stone chimney. As we neared I could hear the raucous noise of several boys having a snowball fight. There was such laughter and excitement. I'd barely set foot on the ground when I caught one in the chest, spraying snow in my face. I dropped the scruffy carpetbag and picked up snow with my mitten-covered hands. With no aim or throwing experience, it was a wasted effort and an invitation to get pummeled by Georgie, who was out without scarf or mittens. I don't know how he tolerated the freezing snow on his bare hands.

Mumma opened the door to let Ben out, all bundled up. But poor Nellie, who had a cold, stood sadly in the doorway wrapped in a blanket. I handed Mumma the carpetbag.

"George Ludlow, you'll catch your death," she said. "Get in here and put on something warm."

Roseanne, cheeks flushed from cold, glowed with pleasure at seeing Billy Bruce. She chased him round and round with her arms full of snow until she could splat it across his back and shoulders. Then she ran away screaming as he chased her back across the yard. She didn't try very hard to outrun him.

Their antics lifted my spirits, and for several minutes I didn't even notice the cold. Papa was coming up from the barn, and I ran to him and gave him a hug.

"So, daughter, you made it back in spite of the weather," he said wrapping his arm around my shoulder. "It's good to have you home."

"I'm so happy to be here," I said, smiling up to him.

"Hello," I heard John call out.

I turned to see him waving at two men trudging through the deep snow and up the road to our drive, one of whom was my brother Will.

"Who is that with him?" I asked, squinting my eyes against the bright glare.

"I think that's your young man," Papa said with a twinkle in his eye. He left me and continued walking the short distance to the house.

Hampered by my skirts and cloak dragging through the snow, I walked part of the way down the drive and waited for them to close the gap between us. I reached out toward Ethan, somehow wanting to touch him.

"Hello, Eliza Jane," Ethan said, taking my soggy mitten in his. It felt so good to see him. He had grown a full beard since I had seen him last, but those brilliant eyes, with their mischievous gleam, I would recognize anywhere.

"Hello, and Merry Christmas," I said. I hadn't realized how much I had been hoping to see him until that moment. I turned to Will. "I thought you were sick."

"I am," he said, grinning.

"He's been doctoring himself with your pa's special tonic," Ethan said and winked at me.

"I didn't want to miss out on all the fun," Will said.

Stomping the snow off our shoes, we trooped into the house and hung our wraps on the pegs along the wall. We moved the chairs and benches nearer the fireplace to warm our frozen fingers and toes. Mumma had heated some cider and poured it into cups. There was lots of laughter and excitement for our homecoming. Ben and Nellie climbed up onto my lap for attention. I hugged them tightly and kissed them on the tops of their heads.

Roseanne and Billy sat together at the end of the table. She was in high spirits, talking with her hands moving as fast as her words. Billy looked at her with an awestruck expression. Clearly, he didn't mind at all that she'd set her cap for him.

Ethan leaned down and said softly into my ear, "Eliza, I have something I would like to give you for Christmas before I head home."

"Oh, do you have to leave so soon?" I asked.

"Yes, I told my folks I'd be right back. I wanted to give you this."

He pulled a small parcel wrapped with brown paper and tied with a ribbon from his jacket pocket. Everyone's eyes were on us as I moved the children off my lap and untied the ribbon. It was bright red, and I would save it to wear in my hair on Christmas Day. Inside the paper was a beautiful white handkerchief sewn with a delicate hand around the edges and embroidered with purple violets.

"Oh, my goodness, Ethan, it's beautiful," I said. "Thank you so very much. I have something for you too." I retrieved the pile of gifts from the carpetbag and handed one to Ethan. It was a scarf I had crocheted in stripes of leftover woolen yarn. Immediately, he wrapped it around his neck and, looking at me with a smile, struck a dandy pose.

"Am I dashing, Eliza?" he asked, looking right into my eyes.

Everyone laughed at the figure he made, but my heart skipped a beat when I looked at him, even with his silly expression.

Later that night, after John and Will went home and most of the family had gone to bed, Roseanne and I were helping with some last-minute preparations for the next day.

Mumma said to me, "Your Ethan is quite a fellow."

I smiled. "He is, isn't he?"

"So is Billy," Roseanne said. "I just know he's the one for me."

I stopped what I was doing and turned to her. "How do you know? How can you be so sure he's the one for you?" It was the same question I'd asked her before. She always seemed so sure of herself. I didn't understand it.

She shrugged her shoulders. "I just know."

I turned to Mumma. "How am I supposed to know if Ethan is the one for me?"

She wiped her hands on her apron and sat down at the table. I poured each of us another cup of tea. Mumma looked thoughtful for a moment, then said, "First of all," looking pointedly at my sister, "there is no hurry to marry anyone. The longer you get to know someone, the better. Then, of course, you have to think about how he makes you feel."

"I like him," I said, thinking of the butterflies in my stomach whenever I saw him or got a letter from him.

"That's good, but more importantly, does he make you laugh?"

"He does have a good sense of humor," I said.

She nodded, smiling at me. "Because life is hard enough, with all of its ups and downs, without being able to laugh with somebody."

"That's a good point," I agreed.

"I think if you keep seeing him, in a few months you will know one way or the other."

"Know what?" I asked.

"If he's a keeper," Roseanne said, nodding her head knowingly.

The next morning all three of my older brothers arrived to spend Christmas Day. Will was still pretty sick with a cough, as was Nellie. They went up into the loft where the air was warm from the fireplace and played cards together in-between their coughing fits.

Roseanne and Emma took care of the cleanup while Mumma and I began preparations for the big holiday meal. We worked all day, but it was worth our effort. In the late afternoon, we sat down to stuffed roasted goose, baked potatoes with fresh butter and sour cream, some of Mumma's pickled green beans, and squash pie for dessert.

After dinner, we exchanged our gifts and Roseanne, with her sweet soprano voice, led the caroling. We sang all our favorites: "The First Noel," "Good King Wenceslas," and "The Holly and the Ivy." The men enjoyed coffee, to which Papa added a shot of something stronger, and the rest of us had hot apple cider.

Each of us was able to head out into the cold the next day wearing new scarves and mittens on our way home. Billy Bruce brought the sleigh over to pick up Roseanne and me and drive us back to Port Hope. Roseanne smiled and chattered the whole way, even though she knew it would be a long time before she saw him again. I hunkered down in the back, wrapped tightly in my cloak and a blanket, and relived the laughter and carol singing from Christmas. I, too, had a smile on my face that I hoped would hold me for a good long while.

Chapter 15

With the winter of 1880 came a bitter cold spell. The north wind blew in more snow and ice, and we kept all of the fireplaces stocked and burning to keep Stafford House warm. Luckily, I was so busy with the laundry and housekeeping I didn't have a lot of time or energy to worry about the weather.

Ethan and I continued to write to each other weekly, although the mail delivery was spotty. Some weeks I would have no letter and other times two or three. I learned more about him with each letter. I began to think it might be possible to have a future with him, even if it was a long time to come. I wasn't about to let anyone know how I felt about him though. I kept his letters tucked away in my drawer and took them out to reread in those rare times when I had a moment to myself and was missing him.

By February we'd had snow on the ground for over a month. It seemed ages since I'd been outside. I was beginning to feel discontent. Growing up, I had been outside all the time, rain or shine. This seemed to affect Roseanne even more than me. Not her usual vivacious self, she became sullen and quiet. Then, all of a sudden, the temperature rose, and everything melted all at once.

Having missed Georgie's ninth birthday, I suggested to Roseanne that we try to get home for a visit. We set off early on a Sunday morning bundled up in cloaks, scarves, and mittens to make the miles-long hike back to the farm. It was a forlorn kind of day. Mirroring my sister's mood, the clouds hung low and threatened rain. The shore road was a muddy, mucky mess, but we were determined to make the trek. Roseanne, who was taller than me by several inches, tromped her way quickly along the side of the road as I struggled to keep up.

"Slow down," I begged.

"Stop being such a baby. I want to get home while there's still daylight," she spat.

"You don't need to yell at me," I said. "Maybe we should turn around and go back. You don't seem in any kind of mood for a visit."

"I'm not like you," Roseanne wailed. "You go along your merry way, day after day, as if nothing ever bothers you. And even if it did, you'd just pretend everything is fine."

Stung by her words, I thought she was being quite unfair to me. Tears sprang to my eyes. When I didn't respond, she paused from her determined march and looked at me.

"I'm sorry," she apologized, although her tone clearly indicated she cared not a bit about hurting my feelings. She let out her breath in a huff. "I'm just frustrated! I don't want to go back to work. I don't like it there. I mean, I'm happy to have a job," she amended, "but I don't wish to spend the rest of my days slaving for a rich family."

"If you hadn't started out thinking Miss Stafford was going to be your new best friend," I retorted, knowing exactly how to get back at her.

"I didn't think that," she said, but we both knew the truth. My sister had spent too long thinking she could move in circles to which she'd never belong. She was the same as me—a servant girl from a poor Irish farm family.

"Well, if it wasn't for your getting acquainted with Miss Stafford, we might not have jobs at all," I allowed. "Someday, I'll get married and have a family, but right now I'm content with having to work for a living."

"You're never going to marry unless you find a husband. And you won't be finding a husband unless you begin to notice the young men in your life," she said pointedly. "Aren't you the least bit interested in Mr. Kilpatrick? I mean, gosh, you haven't said a word about him in weeks. Aren't you afraid he's forgotten all about you?"

I bit my tongue and ducked my head. I didn't want to talk about Ethan with her. "For Pete's sake, Roseanne, I'm barely old enough to even think about getting married. Why the big hurry?"

"Listen to me, Eliza. You're going to be eighteen next month, and I'm going to be seventeen shortly after that. We have a family that can't afford to keep us under their roof. We have two choices. We can slave away emptying other peoples' chamber pots or find a husband and get married."

"Emptying chamber pots?" I almost yelled at her. "How many chamber pots have you had to empty?"

She turned away in a huff and strode ahead of me. I kept my mouth firmly shut the rest of the way home, hoping her disposition would improve.

When we got to the farm, Roseanne couldn't get away from me fast enough. She went directly to the barn in search of Dick and Emma.

"Hello, my girl," Mumma said when I walked in the door.

I hung up my cloak and gave her a big hug. "It's so good to be home," I said. "I've had a bit of the doldrums."

Mumma always made a fine meal on Sunday. There was already a ham in the oven. She sent me to get some potatoes out of the root cellar to peel while she mixed the corn flour, eggs, and milk for cornbread.

"Nothing beats eating at home," I said, my mouth watering.

"How are things at Stafford House?" Mumma asked.

"Busy, as usual," I said, "but I've been stuck inside forever it seems."

"How is Roseanne doing?" Mumma asked. She knew full well how Roseanne could get during the winter months.

"She's such a joy," I said, my upper lip curled in distaste, "and I always seem to be the object of her torment."

"She does get restless," Mumma said. "Always in a hurry, that girl."

Restless. That's one way to put it, I thought. "Well, I wish she wouldn't take it out on me. She's in a hurry all right, and always pushing me along ahead of her."

"I'm not pushing you, Eliza," Roseanne said, coming through the door. "I'm just trying to wake you up."

I sighed. I didn't want her to berate me again. "I heard you the first time, Roseanne. There's no need to beat a dead horse."

"Yes, but it never seems to sink in," she retorted.

"What doesn't sink in?"

"The fact that, until you are settled, I can't be settled. Until you are married, I can't get married. I'm going to be a wrinkled old maid before you get around to settling down."

I stopped what I was doing and turned to look at her. "Roseanne, you have years before you're even old enough to think about getting married."

"I'm almost seventeen. I should be in a courtship by now. But I'm not. And why? Because of you."

"I have a beau. What more do you want?" I said.

"How can you have a beau when you never see him or talk to him? And even if you did, look at yourself, Eliza. The least you could do is something with your appearance," she accused.

And then what? Become an insufferable flirt like you? I railed silently to myself. I nervously touched my hair, which was pulled into its usual bun, and ducked my head. *What does she expect me to do?*

"I'm just saying you need to try, Eliza, instead of acting like an old dishrag all the time."

Out of the corner of my eye, I noticed Nellie standing there, watching us with her hands over her ears. Wiping my hands on a towel, I said quietly, "Leave me alone." I grabbed my cloak and walked out the door, slamming it shut behind me.

I didn't know where I was going except away from Roseanne. The wind was cold and damp. Having neglected to put on hat or scarf or mittens, I turned up my collar and pulled it tightly around me. I decided just to walk as far as my brothers' house. Tommy would be there, and I could talk things over with him, maybe find out how Ethan was.

When I arrived, I strode quickly up the drive, wishing to be out of the cold wind. The little house stood at a short distance. The place had the neglected look of the winter months, all the fields turned to weeds and flattened by the snow and rain of the past several weeks, waiting for the warm sun to bring them back to life in the spring. As I approached the door, I heard their voices within. I knocked, and John opened the door.

"Eliza Jane!" he exclaimed in surprise, welcoming me inside. "What brings you here? I thought you were in Port Hope for the duration of the winter."

"I was feeling cooped up and chanced a walk home, but Roseanne is being cantankerous so here I am. Who's here?" I asked, looking around him.

"A bit cold for a walk, don't you think?" Will said from the table where he, John, Tommy, and Ethan had been playing cards.

When I saw Ethan, my heart went into my throat. I don't know why seeing him there made me feel like crying. All the accusations Roseanne had yelled at me came pouring back into my mind. I reached up and smoothed my hair back, which had mostly escaped its bun. I felt embarrassed knowing what I must look like; that I had barely put a comb through my hair that day. It was no use. I wasn't good enough. I was never going to be good enough for Ethan or any other man. I was trying hard to swallow around the lump in my throat so as not to cry. Ethan jumped up and came forward to hug me.

"Sh-sh-sh," he soothed, rubbing my back. "What's the matter, sweetheart?" he whispered into my ear.

The endearment sounded so wonderful, but was my undoing. I shook my head back and forth. He pushed my hair gently back and lifted my chin, looking into my flushed-with-cold, tear-streaked face. He took out his handkerchief and gave it to me to wipe my runny nose then led me to the table and gave me his chair.

Tommy handed me a cup of hot coffee, and I took a sip, grimacing. It was the foulest tasting coffee I'd ever had, very strong plus another flavor I didn't recognize. I looked up at Ethan, and he winked at me.

Alcohol. My brother had put a shot of alcohol in it. I tossed caution to the wind and took a gulp and swallowed. I immediately felt the heat go down my throat to my stomach.

Ethan chuckled at the look on my face. "It's all right, Eliza, it won't kill you. It'll just make you feel better," he said.

"How much did you put in it?" John asked. "She's too small to drink very much."

"She'll be okay," Tommy said.

I took a couple more swallows of the coffee and set it down on the table. I sniffed and smiled at them, wiping my eyes and nose again with Ethan's handkerchief, shaking my head ruefully. I was making quite a scene, and I had interrupted their game.

"So what's the matter?" Will asked.

"Roseanne and I had an argument. It got pretty heated."

My brothers looked at each other and feigned surprise.

"Are you sure it was an argument, Liza?" John teased. "You have to actually participate to make it an argument, you know."

I let out my breath and smiled at them. I wasn't known for my temper. I probably was as much of a dishrag as my sister accused me of.

"What was the argument about?" Will asked.

I shrugged my shoulders. "You know what she's like," I said quietly. I couldn't explain with Ethan standing there.

"Eliza, you need to learn to speak up for yourself," Tommy said. "I don't know why you always let her bully you."

I didn't respond, just looked down into my lap, where I was twisting Ethan's handkerchief into a knot. I took another drink of the coffee and then decided to drain the cup. I knew the alcohol was having an effect on me. I felt warm and tingly all over.

"Give her another cup," John said, "without anything extra."

"No, I need to get back," I said. "Supper's almost ready, and I have to go back to Port Hope tonight."

I stood, feeling a little off-balance, but Ethan was there with his hand on my elbow to steady me. I looked at him. Our eyes met.

"I'll go with you, sweetheart," he told me and pulled on his jacket, hat, and gloves.

"I'll probably just head home after I drop her off," Ethan said to the others.

We went out the door and back into the dismal, cold day. "I've got my horse," he said. "Just give me a minute to put her saddle back on."

He led me to where the mare was stalled. Once inside the quiet, dim barn, out of sight of the house, he turned to me and pulled me into his arms. I went willingly, all inhibitions gone. He kissed me then, first just a taste of lips and then deeply and longingly. I lost all sense of where I was, it was so dizzying. If his arms had not been wrapped around me, I was sure I would have floated up off the ground. When the kiss ended, we just stood there in each other's arms, foreheads together, breathing each other's breath. Then we pulled apart and smiled shyly at each other.

"Don't ever let anyone tell you that you are anything less than the most special person in the world," Ethan said, his voice deep and husky.

He left me off at my home, and I walked back in to where my family was already seated at the table, grace having just been said. Silently, I hung up my cloak and took my place next to Georgie. I leaned over and gave him a kiss on the cheek and whispered a happy belated birthday into his ear.

"We'd almost given up on you," Mumma said.

"I'm sorry," I told her, feeling self-conscious. Mumma was watching me. Could she tell? Did she know that I had just experienced my very first kiss? Or that I'd been drinking alcohol? It was all I could do not to wriggle.

The dishes were passed around and conversation resumed. I ate my dinner in silence, savoring the luscious feeling of being in Ethan's arms and being really and truly kissed. Reliving it revived the delicious feeling from my stomach to my abdomen. Suddenly, I looked up. Everyone had stopped eating and talking and were staring at me.

"What?" I asked.

"You're smiling like the cat that got into the cream," Roseanne said.

"It's nothing," I lied. "I was just over to John's visiting with the boys. They were joking around. Got me out of my bad mood."

"I wish I'd gone with you," Roseanne said. "I could use something to laugh about."

I refused to respond. Having her with me this afternoon would have been the last thing I would have wanted.

After supper, Mumma shooed us off without having to clean up the dishes. Dick hitched up the wagon and delivered us back to Port Hope.

Upstairs at Stafford House, in the little attic bedroom and getting ready for bed, Roseanne said, "Eliza, I'm sorry for acting so awful toward you today."

"Don't worry about it," I told her. I was not going to let anything interfere with the wonderful feeling I had inside of me. I wanted it to last as long as I could make it.

She tilted her head to one side and regarded me quizzically. "Something's different about you."

I avoided her eyes. "What do you mean?"

"You've had that look on your face ever since you walked back in the door at supper. What is it? Has something happened?"

"I'm not sure I want to tell you," I said, buttoning up my nightgown and climbing into bed.

"That's not fair," she whined. "I told you I was sorry."

I regarded her a moment, pulling my covers up to my chin. "Ethan kissed me today." I said it quickly then pulled the covers over my head.

My sister squealed, pulling at the blankets to uncover me. "What was it like?" she demanded.

I considered a moment, savoring the memory of that one kiss. "A lady doesn't kiss and tell," I said.

Roseanne bounced up off my bed and went over to her own. "Never mind," she said. "I know everything I need to know by the look on your face. There may be hope for you after all. And that means there's hope for me."

Chapter 16

The long, harsh winter looked like it was finally giving up its hold. We received a letter from Annie inviting us to a maple sugaring party at the Bruce farm. The sap was running, and her pa had tapped the trees in their sugar bush.

The morning we were to leave, I looked out our little attic window with dismay. More snow had fallen during the night. Not wanting to miss a chance to see Billy Bruce, Roseanne insisted we make the walk anyway. Wearing woolen cloaks and our Christmas scarves, we departed with high spirits toward home.

The snow was wet and slushy, which made it challenging to stay on our feet, but it was going to be a pristine day. There wasn't even any wind. When we got as far as our farm, we stopped in for a hot cup of tea, to warm our feet, and to collect Dick, Emma, and Georgie, who walked the rest of the way with us.

It was a big outdoor party. The older boys were already there, plus Annie's brothers, which made fourteen. Mr. Bruce, having put the spiles into the tree trunks earlier in the week, already had a cast-iron pot of sap hanging over a fire to boil. He sent us back into the bush to check the sap buckets and pour the clear, watery liquid from each into a barrel that was tied to a sledge.

Billy and Dick had volunteered to be the workhorses pulling the sledge through the slushy snow by way of a leather strap across their chests. There were dozens of sugar maples. Each tree had three or four spiles in it. There was much laughter and chatter as we went from tap to tap, lifting the small buckets and pouring them carefully into the barrel. When we were finished, the big boys hauled the barrel back to the clearing with the younger boys behind, pushing to help the sledge along.

Mr. and Mrs. Bruce were stoking the fires, and two more pots had been hung. Emma and George Bruce held a piece of wool cloth over each kettle to filter out the bits of dirt, bark, or twigs as Annie and I poured dippers of the sap over the top. Mrs. Bruce, her curly hair tied back and covered with a scarf, tossed a piece of pork fat into each cauldron to help clean out the smaller bits of dirt that would be skimmed off as the sap boiled down.

The original kettle, which had been boiling since the early morning, needed constant stirring. Annie had taken that job over from her mother, and her fair cheeks were already flushed from the heat of the fire.

"Oh, my goodness, Eliza," she said to me after a while, "my arms are already getting tired. Do you want a turn?"

"Sure," I said. "This is fun." I hadn't been to a sugaring since I was a little girl. "Mmmm, this smells sweet already," I added, taking a whiff of the liquid, which had become a pale amber.

Georgie and Andrew were watching. "My favorite part is at the end," Andrew said, his eyes dancing merrily.

My brother looked at his friend. He'd never seen the process of making the syrup. "Why?" he asked.

"Because that's when Mum makes candy."

At the mention of candy, Georgie's eyes brightened, and he looked gingerly into the pot. "How do you turn it into candy?"

"When we're finished for the day and the syrup has been poured into jugs, there will be a little bit of the hot, sticky syrup left," Annie explained. "We spoon the remains out onto the snow where it hardens into candy."

The boys looked at each other and rubbed their stomachs. Georgie licked his lips in anticipation, then said in a loud voice, "No peeing in the snow." Everyone laughed their agreement.

I continued to stir as the syrup bubbled merrily in the pot. I saw Roseanne and Billy standing together, talking and laughing. Annie and John were doing the same. I smiled a secret smile. My Ethan was not here, but that was all right with me. I had the memory of our last meeting to sustain me.

"Hey," Will, said, "you know what day it is tomorrow?"

We all looked at one another, and Dick piped up, "February twenty-ninth, leap year!"

"That's right," said Will, grinning wickedly.

"And we all know what that means," Annie said in a teasing voice looking pointedly at Billy.

"What's going on?" Billy asked.

Roseanne, looking pretty as usual with her long, black, wavy hair pulled back from her face and rosy cheeks, knew very well the significance of leap year. She smiled sweetly back at him. "Leap year is when girls wear the britches and get to ask the boys to marry them."

"Wha-at?" Billy yelled and took off running with Roseanne hot on his heels.

"By St. Brigid do you think one of these days he'll slow down long enough for her to catch him?" Mrs. Bruce said cheerily.

"What does St. Brigid have to do with it?" Will asked.

"St. Brigid was the one responsible for making the rules about leap year, granted by our own St. Patrick."

"Is that true?" John Bruce asked.

"Why yes, it is, Johnny my boy," said his mother. "But I don't think you are the one who needs to worry."

Billy and Roseanne were walking back toward the group, her arm linked through his with a big smile across her face. His hands were shoved deeply into his pockets.

"It's not just February twenty-ninth," Roseanne was saying, "it's for the whole year!"

"I told you, Roseanne, I'm too young!" Poor Billy's cheeks were stained bright red, but Roseanne strode confidently alongside him.

"That's all right," she retorted, her mood unusually buoyant. "I can wait."

"Roseanne, you are shameless," I said, but I laughed with the others at the scene they were making.

In the afternoon, Mrs. Bruce took her youngest son back up to the house. I walked home for a spell with Emma, who had gotten cold. I returned toting an empty jug to be filled later with syrup, and a sack with some sliced bread, ham, and cheese for sandwiches. Georgie and the younger Bruce brothers, tired of waiting for the candy-making, had wandered off to play. Only the oldest were left. Mr. Bruce raised a hand to wave at someone out on the road. To my surprise, trotting up on his chestnut mare was Ethan.

My heart beat faster at the thrill of seeing him. I walked over to greet him. In his heavy sheepskin coat and a dark-blue knit hat pulled down onto his forehead, he looked so fine to me. He smiled and put an arm across my shoulders as we walked over to the group. Tommy stood up and moved to the bench next to Will, giving us his place on the log by the fire. We sat close to each other. Ethan stretched a booted leg out in front of him and pulled off his gloves.

Annie and her mother returned with cups and two jugs, one of hard cider and one of apple juice, and a pot of steaming tea. Tommy and John Bruce grabbed the cider and started pouring. Ethan and I made sandwiches and passed them around. Mr. Bruce squatted down to use a twig to light his pipe. He looked up to check the sky, something I noticed he did quite often.

"We've been lucky with the weather today," he said.

Roseanne and Billy were stirring the sap, which was still bubbling away, the steam rising into the cold air.

"Eliza," Roseanne called to me, "are you planning to ask Ethan an important question?"

Ethan looked at me. I shook my head at him and ignored my sister, sitting back down to enjoy my sandwich. Will filled him in about the talk of leap year. Ethan nodded and winked at me.

The sun sank low in the sky, creating long shadows. Everyone was content to keep vigil over the simmering cauldrons and take turns stirring. Ethan leaned over to whisper in my ear, "Care to take a walk with me?"

I nodded. We stood up hand in hand and started to wander away from the group.

"Take a torch with you and make a last check of the sap pots," Mr. Bruce said. "Give a yell if it looks like they need to be emptied."

Ethan had no intention of checking sap pots. He led me into the bush until we were hidden by the trees. After sticking the torch into the ground, he put his arms around me, and I leaned back against one of the trees.

"Well, Eliza Jane, my sweetheart, are you going to exercise your womanly rights on me this leap year?" he asked, voice deep and soft. Then he kissed me. The ground fell out from under my feet.

A long moment later, when next I caught my breath, I answered, "No. No, I don't think I will."

His smile wilted, but I quickly added, "I prefer my man to be the one to wear the britches." That put a smile back on his face, and he kissed me again slowly.

"Well, where's the sap?" Mr. Bruce called out in a loud voice when he spotted us coming out of the trees empty-handed.

Ethan cleared his throat and said, "It was too dark to see, um, even with the torch." Mr. Bruce gave him a knowing grin.

As we had done earlier in the day with the first kettle, two of the strong young men, with hands covered in thick mitts, poured the syrup through a funnel into the waiting jugs and bottles. As promised, Mrs. Bruce spooned the leftovers onto a clean patch of white snow. The thick, dark amber liquid quickly cooled into a taffy-like candy, which we all enjoyed, especially Georgie, who had a sweet tooth.

Mrs. Bruce insisted we take some of the maple candy along for the little ones and one of the larger syrup jugs and reassured me there would be plenty more before the sugaring was finished for the year. We all said our good-byes and went our separate ways heading for home. We'd all had a wonderful time. Even Roseanne could find nothing to complain about. Such a sweet day, in more ways than one.

Chapter 17

I turned eighteen on March 7, and Cook made a cake for me to mark the day. The weather continued to warm up. Time for spring cleaning. At home, Mumma would be doing the same, although it would take considerably less time to accomplish. For a few weeks, on every beautiful, sunny spring day, I turned Stafford House inside out, taking advantage of the wonderful breeze that came off the lake for airing out quilts and draperies and rugs. I used a rug beater to remove months of dirt embedded in the carpets, which strangely enough was a very satisfying task. Windows were washed and everything looked cleaner, brighter, and lighter.

One day in late in April, Roseanne dashed into the house and burst with news from town. She'd accompanied Mrs. Stafford on a shopping trip to Sand Beach. While there, a crowd had gathered at the dock, and Mrs. Stafford had sent her to find out what was going on. I was in the laundry, elbows deep in washing sheets.

"You'll never believe what happened," she said, when she found me. "A ship ran aground near Pointe aux Barques early this morning!"

I dried my hands on my apron and sat down to take a breath. "What happened to it?" I asked.

"Nothing," she said. "It ended up getting free of its own accord and came into Sand Beach while we were there. It was the McGruder hauling a load of timber, and the captain had his wife and little ones on board. For the longest time, it was stuck, and they signaled distress, so Captain Kiah, the keeper of the lifesaving station, and six of his men made their way out to help, but their boat was overturned. I don't know what happened to them though."

"That's dreadful," I said. I felt like a shroud had just fallen over me.

"I've got to go right now, but if I hear anything more, I'll let you know."

Mr. Stafford had the rest of the story that evening. My sister, coming into the kitchen for supper, told Cook and me what she'd found out.

"The crew of six men went out in a surf boat with Captain Kiah when he saw the *McGruder*'s flag was turned upside down and the light onboard signaled distress," Roseanne said, slumping into her chair at the table. "Their boat overturned in the surf. A farmer on the bluff was wondering why his dog was barking and carrying on. When he went to investigate, he found Captain Kiah on the beach."

Cook put a fist to her mouth and turned toward the stove. I swallowed hard. "Oh, my goodness, that's so sad," I said. "Was he dead?"

"No," she said, "he's not well but is expected to recover."

"What happened to the others?" Cook asked.

"All lost, I'm afraid," she responded.

I swallowed hard. Six men lost. Six men trained to save the lives of others with no one to save them. "Those poor men. Some of them have families, I'm sure," I said, voice low.

Cook sniffed and wiped her eyes with her handkerchief.

"Maybe the newspaper will run a story," Roseanne said, "or we'll find out the rest the next time we go home."

I prayed for the lost souls that had made up the lifesaving crew that day. The news certainly took the wind out of my sails. Before I fell asleep, I thought about what Ethan had said about the frequent shipwrecks in Lake Huron. It occurred to me that anyone traveling on that lake could lose their life. I belatedly added a prayer of thanksgiving that we'd arrived safely in Port Hope.

***

When the Stafford girls returned from their school term, the family decided to close up the house for an extended vacation, and my sister and I returned home for a few weeks. It was the second week of May when we trudged along the shore road, toting the threadbare bag and a pillowcase full of our meager belongings. Summer term had not yet started, so the children were home and helping with the farm work. Mumma and Papa were happy to have the extra hands and I was happy for the change of pace and to be closer to where Ethan and I might be able to spend more time together.

Papa and Dick had teamed up with John, Will, and the Bruce men early in the spring to plow and plant all three farms. Doing so spread out the workload, and Dick said it seemed like things got done faster. Many more acres were still a scraggly mess. That meant more trees to chop down and stumps to pull in hopes of breaking more ground. From sunup to sundown, we toiled doggedly with the intention of doubling the arable land. It was strenuous work but early enough in the year that the sun was not extreme. In fact, we worked more in the rain than sun that month. The wet ground made it easier to pull up grass roots and brush.

A few days after I was home, I began to notice that Mumma was not well. She was pale, her face lined with fatigue. She usually had the energy of two, and I began to be concerned for her. One morning, when she took Ben with her and returned to the house from the fields, I decided to follow her.

I hurried across the field, up the path to the barn, and across the yard to the house. Mumma was sitting in the shade of one of the trees in the yard, leaning back with her eyes closed. Ben sat nearby, happily playing in the dirt.

"Mumma?" I said, wondering if she'd dozed off. Like a child caught daydreaming, her eyes popped open and she sat up. "Mumma, are you all right?"

She slumped back against the tree. "Yes, Eliza, I'm fine."

"I'm sorry," I said, "but you don't look fine."

She regarded me for a moment. Then she said, "You're eighteen now, a grown woman, and you'll probably be married in a short time, so I suppose there's no harm in telling you."

I listened without interrupting. I was startled that this conversation, which I had thought was going to go something like, "no, I haven't been sleeping well," or "I just have a backache," had turned suddenly serious.

"I'm pregnant."

"Oh," I said lamely. "Is there anything I can do for you?" I searched my memory for when she'd been pregnant a few years ago with Ben, but I couldn't recall her not feeling well. I sat down on the ground next to her.

"No, dear. I'm fine." She smiled at me and patted my hand.

"Maybe you should go lay down. Ben can come with me, and I'll keep an eye on him while I work."

Mumma smiled. "No, Eliza, I just needed a little break. This is what early pregnancy is like. It's usually the first sign for me, the fatigue. And sometimes I feel nauseated for the first few weeks."

"So all this is normal, then," I said.

She smiled again and nodded. I regarded her momentarily. Something crept around in the back of my mind and a knot of worry settled in my stomach. She really did not look well.

"I'm fine, Eliza," she insisted, but the tone didn't match the look in her eyes.

"All right then. I'd better get back to work. I want to take some cider back with me."

I carried a pitcher, cups, and some bread out to the field where we were working.

"What did you do? Press the apples to make the juice?" Roseanne huffed.

I ignored her, which wasn't an easy task. I poured a cup and handed it to Emma, the next to Nellie. I had to bite my tongue to keep from saying anything else. If Mumma had wanted everyone to know, she would have said something. By the end of the day, Mumma wasn't the only one under the weather. Emma went to bed with a fever and, by the next morning, had started to break out in spots.

"Chicken pox," Mumma quickly diagnosed.

It never rains but it pours, Grandma, the old soothsayer, sounded in my mind. With Mumma not feeling her best, I stepped up my efforts to help. Emma remained in bed, and after the noon meal, both Georgie and Nellie threw up. I checked their foreheads to find both had fevers as well. Ben was the only one who hadn't gotten sick. The other three had probably been exposed at school.

I got them into pajamas and tucked them into bed then heated some water to wash the soiled clothing. Having little patience for complaining children, Roseanne went back out to the field with Dick and Papa. Mumma took Ben with her and went out to weed the garden.

By evening, my legs were tired from the countless trips up and down the stairs. At least I didn't have to navigate the ladder that used to lead up to the loft. During the long winter, Papa had built a staircase and railing against the back wall.

By the end of the week, Ben broke out in chicken pox as well, and although he was a model patient, the rest of them had begun to itch. They were miserable. Tired of being in bed and too sick to read or play, they began to whine and complain. Emma was by far the most uncomfortable.

"Whatever you do," I told her, "don't scratch them." I shivered at the memory of when the older children in our family had the disease when we were young.

"But they itch," she whined and continued to rub the ones on her forehead near her hairline.

"Please stop," I begged her. "Emma, you'll get scars. If you want to scratch, do it somewhere else, not on your face." My bedside manner was certainly lacking, as she began to cry. My skin was prickling just looking at the red pustules.

Nellie and Ben started to cry, fitful and inconsolable. Nellie's high-pitched cry was like fingernails on a chalkboard. I was instantly overwhelmed. *Do something, Eliza Jane,* I ordered myself.

Georgie put his hands over his ears, sat up, and yelled, "Be quiet!"

The cacophony of cries turned to a puppies-in-a-basket whimpering. I ran down the stairs and found the bottle of witch hazel, which I quickly made into a paste with baking soda. Then I filled a basin with cold water and put some washrags in it. Back up the stairs I flew with my supplies. I wrung out the washcloths and placed one across each child's forehead. Then, starting with Emma, I put some of the paste onto her worst spots. I continued to Nellie, Georgie, and finally Ben. By the time I was finished with Ben, Emma and Nellie were asleep.

"Whew!" Georgie whispered and mimed wiping his brow.

I ruffled his hair and kissed him on top of the head. "Try to get some rest."

A couple of days later, Nellie's and Georgie's spots started to dry up, and they felt like getting out of bed. Although Ben had started to break out later, he had a much lighter case of the disease. Poor Emma was miserable though. I filled the metal tub with water and made it just slightly warm by adding some hot. I sprinkled in some baking soda and had her soak for a few minutes, pouring water over her head and down her back, watching the soothing water flow through her wavy blonde hair, which fell to her waist. I knew it wasn't a cure, but it would give her a break from the constant irritation. Then I put some calming chamomile in Mumma's tea ball and steeped it. I added some honey and had her sip it slowly while she soaked. Then she put on a fresh nightgown and went back to bed.

Time creeps slowly when you are stuck in the house and not feeling well. Once the children were on the mend, my most demanding task was to entertain them. We played countless games of hangman on the little slate they used for playing school. I told them another story about Reggie Rabbit and the Purple Polka Dots, embellished with voices and as much drama as I could muster. Georgie, Nellie, and Ben loved these stories and, when they were finally feeling well enough to play, reenacted Reggie's antics. It was wonderful to hear them laughing again.

"How do you ever remember your stories?" Emma asked me.

I smiled at her. "They're never exactly the same. That's the best part about storytelling. With each telling, something changes for the better—or for the worse."

Just as all of the children were mostly recovered, Mumma took to her bed. I knew something was seriously wrong. In all my years of growing up, I had never known her to lie down in the middle of a day, except when she had a baby.

I went into her room and closed the door. "What the matter?" I asked.

"It's the baby. I don't think I'm going to keep it," she told me tearfully.

"I'll make you some tea," I said.

"No tea, Eliza."

"I don't know what to do," I said, feeling panic begin to rise and make my hands shake.

"Make the noon meal, and ask Papa to see me when he comes in to eat."

I got right to work and did as Mumma directed, and called everyone to the table. I gave Papa Mumma's message. When he came back out of the bedroom, he did not stop to eat but went out the door. After the children ate, I told Roseanne to keep them outside as long as possible.

Mumma's pain was intense, and she labored through the long afternoon. Afraid to leave her, I sat by her side. She gave birth a few hours later. The baby, so very, very tiny, had been a boy. Mumma instructed me on what to do. I wrapped him in a clean linen towel and set him carefully into her arms while I cleaned her up. Then I took the soiled bedding and towels out to soak in the washtub.

I found Papa in the barn with hammer in hand. He'd built a tiny coffin from leftover wood. He looked up when I came in.

"Is it over then?" he asked.

I nodded. Then slowly, as if he carried a heavy yoke across his shoulders, he turned from the small wooden box and walked to the house. Later that evening, Mumma and Papa went out to bury the baby.

It was the saddest thing I'd ever seen. The house was so quiet. The joyful laughter of children on the mend became hushed whispers. When I went to bed, I curled up in a ball with my head buried in my arms and cried for the loss of what might have been.

Chapter 18

The longest days of the year were upon us when I was finally able to relax. I felt like I'd been holding my breath all through May. By June, the sun seemed to have come out to stay. Mumma bounced back fairly quickly after the miscarriage, in time to bake a cake to celebrate Roseanne's seventeenth birthday. It was good to have everyone healthy at last. Emma's spots were mostly gone. She had the longest case of chicken pox anyone in the family could remember. Mumma said it was because she was so much older getting them.

By the time the children returned to school for the summer term, Papa had a second field to plant. The huge kitchen garden, lovingly tended by Mumma, was flourishing. Georgie had a new batch of piglets to care for; Papa bred our cow to the Carsons' bull, and she miraculously had a set of twins. He took this to be a good omen and said he felt like we were finally getting on our feet with the new farm. We'd been in Michigan almost a year. Roseanne helped me with the deep cleaning of the house. She sang, making the work more enjoyable. Mumma opened the windows and the door to let in the lake breeze. We removed the quilts to be aired out and hung them on the extra lines Dick had strung.

In the afternoon, Roseanne walked up to meet Emma after school and pay a visit on Mrs. Pottinger, whose husband was one of the men lost from the lifesaving station. She was left alone to raise her young family and tend the farm. Mumma sent along two loaves of bread. While they were gone, I picked a large batch of peas from the garden. I was sitting outside shelling them when Ethan drove up.

He jumped down from the wagon and came over to see me, smiling. I had missed him so much. Beardless and with a recent haircut, he looked so handsome to me that I couldn't take my eyes off of him. He looked quickly around to make sure nobody was nearby and then stooped to kiss me.

"I can't stay," he said. "I'm just running an errand down to Port Hope. Is Georgie back from school?"

"You aren't here to see me?" I feigned a pout and then chuckled. "He's out behind the barn with the pigs. I'll get him. What's going on?" I asked.

Ethan smiled devilishly. "You'll see."

I walked across the yard yelling for Georgie, and he came running with Nellie and Ben trailing his footsteps. "Ethan is here to see you."

"Me?" Georgie asked.

"Yes, and don't ask me why. He's got something up his sleeve but won't tell me what," I said.

Ethan was at the wagon getting something out from under the seat. It was a bundle wrapped in a small baby blanket. Georgie and the other children ran up to him. Mumma came out of the house to see what was going on. Ethan put the bundle, which had started to squirm, into Georgie's arms.

A small yellow head with floppy ears, black nose, and pink tongue poked out and started to lick Georgie's face. "A puppy!" Nellie exclaimed.

"Is it for me?" Georgie asked.

"Yep. A boy should have a dog," Ethan said. "He's eight weeks old and looking for a new home. I thought of you."

"Thanks, Ethan," Georgie said. "What should I call him?"

"That's up to you," he told him.

Georgie put the puppy on the ground, and he immediately scurried off to explore his new surroundings. The children followed him, laughing and exclaiming at his antics.

"Thank you, Ethan," I said, looking up to him with my heart full of gratitude.

Mumma smiled and went back to her work in the house. I walked with him to the wagon, and he kissed me again before he climbed back onto the seat.

"Would you be interested in coming to dinner next Sunday after church?" he asked.

"You want me to go to church with you?"

"Yes, if you'd like. Then come over for Sunday dinner at my house."

"I'd like that. What time will you be by to get me?" I asked.

"About eight o'clock. We'll probably have to walk up to Huron City, and then we can ride home with my folks."

"I'll see you then," I said. He released the break, slapped the reins against the horse's neck, and drove off with a smile and a wave. I went back to my task with the peas.

Mumma brought a chair out after he left and sat down for a rest. "That young man of yours is very thoughtful, isn't he?" she said.

I smiled and looked at her. "I really like him, Mumma. I think he is someone I could spend my life with."

"Well, if that's the case, we'd better get going on your hope chest, or you won't have much to take with you when you marry."

"Oh, I don't know if he's going to ask me to marry him. I was just saying he has all the qualifications."

"Either way, you need to get busy. Sooner or later you'll be getting married, whether it's Ethan or somebody else. You're eighteen and should be thinking about your future," she said.

"You sound like Roseanne," I said, rolling my eyes.

"No, I sound like your mother," she retorted, then she grinned and went back in the house.

When the girls came back from their visit with the Pottingers, they were very excited to find the new floppy-eared member of our family. Georgie was over the moon with happiness. I hadn't seen him smile so much since before we'd moved to Michigan. Emma ran off with the others to get to know the puppy and help decide on a name.

"How are things going at the Pottingers'?" Mumma asked.

"She's very sad, but things are looking up," Roseanne said. "She has a farmhand helping her in exchange for room and board. He's been a huge help. They've gotten the fields planted."

"That's good news," Mumma said.

"So, Ethan brought Georgie a puppy?" Roseanne asked.

"Yes, and I'm going to go to church with him on Sunday and then to dinner with his family," I told her.

"That's good news," she said, "I mean, you're going to meet his family. Do you think you'll marry him?"

"That's up to him," I shrugged.

"No it's not. You need to encourage him to pop the question," she said.

I rolled my eyes. "I'm not in that big of a hurry. Right now, it's moving along as fast as I want it to."

Chapter 19

On Saturday, I painstakingly cleaned my shoes, pulled out the laces to wash them, and polished the leather right down to the heels. I had clean drawers, camisole, and petticoats, but my one good dress needed repair. With needle and thread, I closed up a couple of spots where the seams had come loose and reattached the ruffle on the collar where it had pulled away. Lastly, I stitched in a fresh set of shields inside the underarms. I loved that dress, although it had been worn into the ground in the last three years. It was blue with tiny white flowers. The blue had faded over time but still looked very nice. Roseanne said it matched the pale blue of my eyes. It had long sleeves with ruffled cuffs, and the bodice buttoned up to the neck in the front. I wouldn't need a jacket, but Mumma lent me her shawl, and Roseanne insisted I wear her bonnet because it was in much better condition than my own.

Lastly, I took a bath and washed my hair. It was still wet when I went to bed, but I had combed it out and put a towel on my pillow so it would finish drying during the night. Normally I'd just braid it or pull it into a tail or bun, but I wanted Emma to fix it special for me. The next morning, I donned all of my undergarments, and she put my hair into a French knot at the back of my head but left some curls down to frame my face. After placing the hat and tying it under my chin, she let me look in the mirror.

"Eliza Jane," Emma smiled, "you look so pretty."

I smiled back. "Thank you, Emma," I hugged her.

When I was completely dressed, I came into the big room. Roseanne was doing the breakfast dishes, and Mumma was washing Ben's face and hands. Everyone else was already outside tending the animals and usual chores.

Roseanne turned to look at me. "Eliza Jane?" she looked at me surprised. "You look so nice. Do you want to borrow my gloves and handbag?" She dashed upstairs to get them.

I didn't like wearing gloves but pulled them on anyway. Then I placed the embroidered handkerchief Ethan had given me at Christmas into the little purse and wrapped the crocheted drawstring around my wrist.

I had butterflies in my stomach and didn't have much appetite for breakfast, but I forced down some bread and a small cup of coffee with milk. It did help a little. Ethan came by to pick me up right on time as planned, and his eyes lit up when he saw me, restarting the whole butterfly-in-the-stomach revolt that I thought had been settled. Then he smiled that charming smile with the twinkling eyes, and I felt like the luckiest girl in the world. I placed my arm in his, and we set out walking the shore road toward the church at Huron City.

"My family doesn't attend church regularly," I confessed.

"Your family has been pretty busy all year," he said, "but I think you will like the minister here. He has some good sermons. Didn't you tell me you and your family are Methodists?"

"I was baptized Methodist as a baby when we lived in Canada, and when I'm at Stafford House I'm required to attend church with the family on Sundays."

The weather was cool that morning with a breeze coming off the lake. The lack of clouds, though, promised a warm afternoon. We arrived at church just as the singing began. Ethan held the door open for me, and we found that his family had saved us seats in their pew. There wasn't time for introductions, so I just smiled at his parents and sisters, who were beaming at me.

The service lasted over two hours. As ill at ease as I felt, I couldn't say what the sermon was about. The sun shone through the eastern windows, and the air was warm and still. I found it difficult to concentrate and couldn't wait to pull off the ridiculous white gloves and shawl, which were too warm for this time of year. Even my scalp was prickling with perspiration.

Afterward Ethan introduced me to his mother and father, his four sisters, and his little brother. There was a strong family resemblance between Ethan and his sisters.

"Kathleen, Bridget, Mary, Maggie, and little Johnny," he said pointing each one out, oldest to youngest.

"I know Emma and Nellie," Mary said. "Emma and I are the same age. We're in the same grade at school. Your brother Georgie gets in trouble a lot. I don't think the teacher likes him very much."

"I know," I said, smiling ruefully. "School isn't his favorite place."

"It's so warm this afternoon," Bridget said, pulling the ribbon on her bonnet and removing it.

"Yes, it is," I said. I removed the gloves and put them in the little purse and untied the ribbons of Roseanne's hat. Ethan removed the shawl from my shoulders and placed it over his arm. I was so relieved I let out an audible sigh.

"How many brothers and sisters do you have, Eliza?" Mrs. Kilpatrick asked.

"Three brothers older, two younger, and three younger sisters," I said.

"Oh my, your mother must be busy," she said.

"My older brothers work and live on their own. Dick works with Papa on the farm. Roseanne, my next youngest sister, and I work at Stafford House in Port Hope. Three of the children are school age, so only Ben is left at home most of the time," I told her. "And yes, she is very busy," I added, smiling.

The Kilpatrick home was much nicer than my own. I could tell by the furnishings that they had been here much longer than my family had. The house had an upstairs where the bedrooms were, so the whole downstairs was living space. It had many windows and was very light and bright inside. There was even a rug on the floor of the living room.

While Ethan's mother and sisters were making dinner preparations, Ethan and I took a short walk, and he showed me the rest of the farm. Then we walked along the fields where the spring plants were growing, through a copse of trees, and across a small stream where we stopped and he gestured widely with his hand.

"This is the place I was telling you about. I just made arrangements to purchase it."

I looked at him, surprised. "It's yours?"

"Yes, except for making payments. I can start working on clearing the land this year, and I want to build a house and barn. Where do you think we should put the house?"

Startled, I stared at him a moment. The implication of a life together hung between us. He cleared his voice and took me by the hand pulling me along. The land was not in any better shape than Papa's had been when we'd first arrived, although there were a few more standing pines and not as much evidence of the treetop fire of a decade ago. There were large piles of slash from logging that had been done on part of the acreage. I knew he wanted me to see the potential there, but all I could see was the daunting amount of backbreaking work that would have to be done.

"Well, what do you think?" he asked.

"Will your pa be able to help you get started?" I asked.

"Yes," he said. "All of our fields are producing. The farm is running pretty smoothly. That's why we thought it would be a good idea to buy the land now. We'll work both pieces of land together. Where do you think the house should go?"

"Hmmm," I said, turning around thoughtfully. "Are you going to plant some fruit trees?"

"Yes."

"And you'll need room for a large garden," I added.

"Yes," Ethan said, looking at me intently and smiling.

I felt weak-kneed and looked away. "Where are the boundaries?"

"Well, roughly, Kinde Road on that side," he pointed to the east,

"Pa's place that way, where we crossed the creek," he added, pointing southward, "the Lakeshore Road to the north, and the old Stewart place to the west."

"How many acres?" I asked.

"Forty, same as my dad's."

"The house should be placed near the road," I said, thinking aloud. "Maybe over there." I pointed toward the northwest corner of the property, not far from where we stood.

We walked that direction. It would take quite a bit of clearing to be able to put a house on that part of the land. Ethan surveyed the surroundings.

"All right then, that's where I'll build it," he said and my eyes met his penetrating gaze. A moment of time passed. The butterflies were flitting through my stomach again.

"Could you see yourself living here then?" he asked huskily.

I tore my eyes away from his and looked around me again, trying to remember to breathe. I tried to imagine a house and garden, a barn, and chickens.

"I think so," I said to him.

He dropped down on one knee and took both of my hands in his, "Marry me, then, Eliza Jane Ludlow, for I want to spend my life with you."

Tears gathered in my eyes. *It's happening. It's really happening,* I thought.

"Ethan, do you love me?" I asked.

"Yes, my darlin' girl, I'm in love with you. I have been since the moment you first smiled at me."

I took a breath. The single most important decision of my life. I gave the gravity of the situation not one single more thought but said, "Yes, Ethan, I'll marry you, for I love you too with all my heart." And at that moment I knew it was true. I had been falling in love with him for months. I could see a future with him as my husband.

He took my face in his two strong hands and kissed me long and hard, the passion we felt for each other welling up between us and igniting like the sparks of a fire. When the kiss finally ended, we stood there, our foreheads pressed together, breathing hard as if we had run a distance. I hadn't known how tense I'd been until that very moment when all my cares in the world had slipped away, and for one lovely moment, it was just the two of us.

"Oh my God, I love you, Eliza," he said.

"And I you," I said. We hugged and then laughed, giddy with the excitement of finally declaring our love for each other.

We walked back arm in arm, crossed the little creek, and followed the path the plow had left along the fields of corn and beans sprouting from the ground.

"When do you think we can marry?" I asked.

"After the house is built, I think," Ethan said. "I would like us to have a home of our own."

"How long do you think that will be?"

He looked toward the sky thoughtfully. "About a year, maybe," he said.

One year. Thank goodness. That will give me the time I need to get the proverbial hope chest filled.

When we returned to the house, dinner was on the table, but everyone was standing at the door waiting for us. Little Maggie was hopping from one foot to the other.

"Are you going to get married?" she asked, voice high with excitement.

Before her mother could tell her to hush, Ethan said, "Yes, Maggie, we are. Eliza has agreed to become my wife."

There was an outburst of congratulations, and the younger girls jumped up and down, clapping their hands delightedly. Mrs. Kilpatrick gave me a big hug, and Mr. Kilpatrick shook his son's hand. Kathleen, who was the closest to my age, also gave me a hug.

"Welcome to the family, my girl," Mr. Kilpatrick said. "What do you think of the land?"

"It's wonderful," I said, "but there's a lot of work to be done."

"Ah, but he has real motivation now, you see," he said with a wink. He had a lilting Irish voice and loved to tease, so different from my pa, who was a quiet man.

The supper was delicious, but like the sermon during the morning's church service, I was unaware of what I was eating. I was so excited and overwhelmed that the meal passed in a blur.

I tried to help with the cleanup, but Ethan's mother told me no as I was the guest of honor that day. "Next time you come, we'll treat you like one of the family," she grinned.

Ethan and I used the wagon to return to my home. We were excited to tell my folks the news.

"You'll have to ask Papa for my hand," I said.

He nodded knowingly. I wondered if he was nervous. He didn't seem to be. Maybe for him, the hard part was over. I had been excited announcing our engagement to his family, but it was nothing compared to the anticipation I felt thinking about telling my own family, especially Roseanne, for whom my engagement would be the realization of a dream.

"Congratulations!" my family yelled as we opened the door. Even John, Tommy, and Will were present. There was much hugging and hand shaking.

"You knew?" I asked.

"Ethan came by a couple of weeks ago and asked my permission," Papa said.

I turned to find him grinning victoriously. I poked him in the ribs. "You had this well planned, didn't you?" I teased.

Roseanne hugged me and said, "Eliza, I'm so happy for you." She had been so sure I would never find someone to marry. She hadn't been the only one. I hadn't thought it would ever happen for me either, but it had. I was filled with awe that Ethan loved me.

"I had a feeling about the two of you," Tommy said, hugging me and kissing the top of my head.

"Thank you for the part you played in getting us together," I said, hugging him back.

Mumma had made Johnny cake with fresh berries to celebrate. I told them about Ethan's farm and that the wedding would be in about a year or so.

"You mean our farm, darlin'," he reminded me.

Papa, my older brothers, and Ethan talked over the plans for clearing and building.

Mumma was pleased that I would have a home of my own when I married, rather than living with his parents like so many young couples had to do when just starting out. Ethan had planned and saved. It was his dream I was caught up in, and I was so happy that he had chosen me. It truly was a dream come true.

Chapter 20

THAT EVENING, AFTER ETHAN AND MY BROTHERS LEFT AND THE YOUNGEST children were tucked in bed, Dick and Georgie went out to help Papa with the evening chores. Mumma, Roseanne, Emma, and I sat down around the table for a cup of tea and talked about the wedding.

"You don't have much to offer as a dowry," Roseanne said.

The dowry, I thought, as a small piece of my excitement ebbed away. It was such an antiquated custom, like the father paying someone to take his daughter off his hands. I didn't like the idea, especially because it was one more thing that pointed to how poor we were. I certainly didn't have much to offer.

I looked to Mumma, who said, "Don't worry," and patted my hand, "we'll get to work on your linens and a wedding quilt. I'm sure in a year, Papa will have some pigs and chickens for you."

"And she can save up her earnings from work, can't she, Mumma?" Roseanne said. I looked gratefully at her. I had forgotten about the money I turned over to Papa every month.

"I'll talk it over with Papa. Now that you're betrothed, you'll want to put your earnings toward the home you'll make with your new husband."

My husband. My new home. I smiled to myself.

"And you'll need a trousseau," Roseanne said.

A trousseau? I wondered how she knew so much about this. "I thought a trousseau was just for rich ladies," I said and looked at Mumma.

"Your linens and quilt are part of your trousseau, but you will also want to sew new undergarments and petticoats, a nightgown, and maybe a new dress," Mumma said, "a dress that is nice enough to be married in and for church on Sundays."

"I really do need a new dress," I said, looking down at the faded blue dress I still wore and had been wearing since I was fifteen.

"I do wish it was happening for me," Roseanne said. "I need a new dress too."

"It will happen for you in due time, Roseanne," Mumma said. "And you don't need to get married to sew a new dress."

"Billy isn't much older than I am," she said morosely. "It's going to be forever before he can marry me."

"If he's the one you have your heart set on, then you must be willing to wait," Mumma said.

"But shouldn't I be saving my earnings as well?" she said, suddenly realizing that she could be working on her own dowry.

"You have plenty of time, Roseanne. Let's concentrate on getting Eliza Jane married and settled, and then we'll start thinking about you."

"May I help with the sewing?" Emma asked.

"Of course you may," I told her. "I will need all the help I can get to sew all of this in a year. Mumma, may I take your dress pattern back to Port Hope with me?"

* * *

The summer was coming to an end. I'd been able to help Mumma with preserving vegetables from the garden, although we hadn't gotten to the apples and pears yet. Soon the fields would be ready to harvest. It was time for us to return to work at Stafford House.

The day before we had to go back, I managed one more outing to the lake with Ethan. It could have been a very romantic time together; however, we had many chaperones: my brothers and sisters, the Bruces, and the puppy that Georgie had finally decided to call Finnian, or Finn for short. It was a fun-filled day and the water was warm, so we all spent some time in the shallows in bare feet, splashing each other and cooling ourselves off. Roseanne was in heaven being able to see the object of her affections before heading back to Port Hope. Annie and John spent the whole time in each other's company as they were courting at long last.

We organized ourselves into teams for a game of baseball. Between my family and Ethan and the Bruces, there were fourteen of us. John Bruce had brought along a sturdy stick to use as the bat and a stitched leather ball.

Most of us knew the rules of the game, but there was a lot of bending those rules. The men could all hit the ball a distance, and they got pretty raucous. There were times I was laughing so hard I could scarcely breathe, like when Billy Bruce was running the bases and had to go through Roseanne, who was covering second base and wouldn't let him pass. He didn't seem to try very hard to get free of her either.

Ethan and I were on opposite teams. He was very thoughtful, pitching me the ball so I was able to hit it easily, for which he took a lot of ribbing from his teammates. Unfortunately, in spite of having a pitcher who was determined to see me succeed, my first hit wasn't even as strong as the nine-year-old boys'. Ethan caught it easily and tagged me out, but then followed the tag with a quick kiss, for which he underwent even more teasing.

I had no idea which team won, nor did I care. I was a girl in love on a beautiful day having a wonderful time with my fiancé, my family, and my best friends.

After the game, we spread blankets on the ground and unpacked bread and cheese, fresh vegetables from the garden, and cold fried chicken that Annie had brought. There was cider and cold tea to drink and an apple pie for dessert. After we ate, Emma played tag with the younger children while we lazed around on the blankets. Georgie and Andrew took their dogs down by the lake so they could play fetch with them, throwing sticks into the water. Making the most of her time with Billy, Roseanne talked him into taking a walk with her. Annie and John went with them. The other boys were back to horsing around in the lake, which left Ethan and me alone for a few minutes.

There was nothing for me to do but enjoy being with Ethan on this fine day. He glanced around to make sure we were unnoticed, then kissed me longingly, gently pushing me back until I lay on the blanket. I reveled in his attention.

"I'm going to miss you," I said.

"I know," he replied, "but we'll stay busy. It'll make the time go faster."

"I know, but I'll still miss you," I told him.

"Will you be able to come home on the weekends?" he asked.

"Until the weather gets too cold and rainy." I nodded. "Could you come to see me?"

"I don't know, Eliza," he replied. "I'll be trying to get as much clearing done as possible on our place this fall. Might not be much time."

"Let's just wait and see," I said, a little sadly.

He kissed me again. After several minutes, he pulled back and gazed down at me, eyes deep and passionate in the moment.

"I love you, Eliza Jane," he said gruffly. "I wish we could be married now."

I sighed. "I love you too," I said, then pushed him gently away and sat up. "We should get this stuff picked up," I added.

"You get started. I'll go chase down the others," he said and jogged off toward the lake.

As I walked back to my job the following day, I savored the moments I'd had with Ethan. Already I was missing him. It was a good thing I'd be busy over the next weeks and months. I sighed to myself, *Absence makes the heart grow fonder, or so they say.*

Chapter 21

As I was freshening up Stafford House in preparation for the family's return, and knowing Ethan was hard at work on the farm and planning our future home, I was actually content to be back in town after a long absence. Cook sent Roseanne and me to the store to pick up her list of groceries. Mr. Stafford's groom brought the wagon so we didn't have to carry the heavy supplies back.

We promised ourselves that the next trip to the store, after we got paid, would be to buy fabric and get started on our new outfits. I also needed more remnants for my quilt, as well as yards of linen for pillowcases, towels, napkins and tablecloths for my new home. To keep from getting overwhelmed by how much I had to do before next fall, I took a page out of Mumma's book and made a list of everything I would need for my trousseau. Once I did that, I made marks by the ones I should be working on now and which could wait until later.

The largest project was one I had actually started years ago. "This will be for your hope chest," I remember Mumma saying to me when I was learning to make my nine-patch quilt. I hadn't taken her very seriously at the time because I'd been so young. I took the pieces out of the bag I'd stored them in. I only had three blocks sewn. Each one had nine squares sewn together into a larger square. There was no artistic pattern to them. I had just used whatever scraps of material that came my way. *I could make half the squares plain white muslin, maybe applique a heart or a tulip. I do love tulips…* I stopped myself. Thinking too far ahead made me nervous.

Roseanne and I pored over Mrs. Stafford's old copies of *The Queen* fashion journal looking at the latest styles for women. The fashionable outfits advertised were draped with yards of fabric and lace details and bustles. I thought they looked uncomfortable and not the least bit practical. The drawings were of women who obviously laced their corsets tightly—the one article of women's clothing I absolutely abhorred—and the hoop skirts looked like a birdcage one was required to wear under the full skirts to help them stand out. Even Roseanne, who longed for sophisticated fashions, in the end agreed with me on the more useful clothing.

We would use Mumma's dress pattern, and although we weren't of the same height or size, we would be able to adjust it to fit both of us. After weeks of saving our money, we walked to Leuty's, looked through the bolts of fabric, and made our decisions. Roseanne helped me choose a pretty blue-and-green print for my dress. I tended to want brown, which wouldn't show the dirt as much, but as my sister was wont to point out, I was already in enough brown with my hair and freckles.

"Which one do you want for your dress?" I asked.

"I can't decide between the violet floral and this one." She indicated a black and white pinstripe.

"Oh, I really like the pinstripe," I said, "but maybe that would make a better blouse for your skirt."

She held the bolt up near her face. I was envious. Her striking hair and eyes and creamy complexion made everything look good. I considered the pinstripe to go with the skirt I wanted but settled on simple white cotton. I decided on a lightweight gray wool for the skirt, with black velvet to go around the waist for special occasions. Roseanne did get the stripes, a dark corduroy for her skirt, and the violet floral for her dress. I gathered all the other notions we needed for our project: thread, bias tape, hooks and eyes, buttons, and extra needles, and I splurged on some lace to spruce up my collar and cuffs.

"You should have a little lace on your dress when you're a bride," Roseanne told me.

While I was about my chores the next day, I stared longingly at the treadle sewing machine in the seamstress's room. I wondered if Mrs. Stafford would let me use it. *It wouldn't hurt to ask,* I thought. If I was lucky and she said yes, the long seams of our dresses would go much faster, and we would only need to do the basting and finishing work by hand.

As it turned out, the seamstress gave us a lesson using the treadle as soon as we had our dress pieces cut. We did the sewing on Sunday afternoons and sometimes in the evenings if we finished our work early enough. The pin tucks and hand-stitching the button holes on my blouse took quite a bit of time and effort, but when they were finally completed, I was thrilled with the results and could hardly wait for Ethan to see me in my new outfit.

I was so in love. Each day I eagerly awaited the arrival of the mail, hoping for a letter from him. When one arrived I would tuck it in my pocket and count the minutes until my day ended so I could read the precious words he had written to me, treasuring each one as a tender caress. He told me about clearing the land and his plans for the barn and house. I knew he was working hard every day for our future. How he had enough energy to write me sweet love letters, I don't know. Often writing long into the night, I poured my heart out to him in my return letters. Like a flower blooming in the spring when the ground warms up in the sunshine, my love for him blossomed. My thoughts were consumed with him as I scrubbed floors, polished furniture, and worked in the laundry. No longer bored with the drudgery, I looked forward to the monotonous tasks as a chance to daydream. I imagined living with him in our own home and starting our family. I even tried to decide which names I liked the best for our children, of which I was sure we'd have many.

I was working on a quilt square by the light of our small lamp one night when Roseanne came in and sat down on her bed.

"What are you smiling about?" she asked, a tired edge to her voice.

I looked up, annoyed at the interruption to my reverie. "Nothing, why do you ask?"

"You always have that same look on your face lately. Half the time you don't even hear me when I talk to you. And I'm not the only one who notices."

My cheeks grew hot, but I shrugged my shoulders.

"She's in love," she said with a sneer. "That's what Cook says."

I dropped my sewing into my lap impatiently. "I thought this was what you wanted me to do," I said, "to be courted, fall in love, and get married."

She skirted the subject. "I don't know how you get anything done when your mind is wandering all the time."

"My chores are different than yours. They're mindless," I said.

She sighed and lay back on her cot. "We haven't been home in weeks," she complained. "Maybe we should go before the weather gets too cold. Then you could actually see Ethan instead of just thinking about him."

"I don't suppose you're thinking the same thing now?" I looked at her and grinned. "Maybe to show off your new dress for someone special?"

A small smile tugged at the corners of her lips. "Oh, could we, Eliza? I'm just so pent up. I really want to see Billy again. And it's so hard being stuck here in town so far away from him."

The very next Saturday, early in the morning, we dressed in our new skirts and blouses. We packed an overnight bag and headed north. The wind was blowing the last of the brown leaves from the trees, but luckily the rain held until we arrived so the mud on the road did little to damage the new hems. I had my shawl wrapped about my shoulders. I promised myself I would bring my winter cloak back to Port Hope with me on Sunday. Like my sister, I was hoping to see my lover while we were home.

Life was comfortingly the same as ever when we walked through the door of the small house. After Mumma admired the new clothing, Roseanne went to find Dick. I dropped right into the routine of helping Mumma with her tasks. She had a borrowed apple press out in the yard to bottle cider from the abundance of apples that had grown this year. Remembering my blistered hands from last year, I was relieved that she had already dealt with the drying of sliced apples. Emma had gone up the road to help Mrs. Pottinger, and Nellie and Ben were playing with Georgie and Finn, who had grown so much in the past few months that he could hardly be called a puppy any longer. I grabbed a full-length apron off the hook by the stove and put it over my head, tying it in the back.

We worked the remainder of the morning until we had to go in to fix the meal. I kneaded the bread dough for the week's bread while Mumma warmed up leftovers from dinner the previous night.

"Have you heard from your Ethan?" Mumma asked.

I smiled. "Of course. We write letters each week. They're finished with their harvest, and now he's working hard on clearing the land. His pa is a big help."

"Will you be seeing him while you're here this weekend?" she asked.

"I'm not sure. I didn't have a chance to write him to tell him I was coming."

The door opened and Roseanne dashed in. "Eliza, do you want to go with me over to John's tonight after supper?"

"Why? What's going on?"

"Dick says they've all been getting together on the weekends at John's house."

"Who?" Mumma asked.

"Everybody," she said airily. Mumma gave her a piercing look. "I don't know—just some people."

"This is like pulling teeth," Mumma said, exasperated. "Which people, Roseanne?"

Roseanne looked sheepish. "The boys and some friends," she said vaguely.

Mumma pursed her lips then said, "I don't think the two of you need to be going over there at night. It isn't respectable. They'll probably be playing cards and drinking."

Mumma didn't approve of gambling or alcohol, although she didn't complain too much when Papa took a drink now and then. Card games were fine, but the thought of my three brothers and their friends sitting around a table playing a lively game of Go Fish was comical, and I almost laughed out loud.

"Maybe we could just go over and say hello," I said hopefully. "If Ethan's there, I'd like to see him. And Roseanne could go with me to chaperone." I knew she wouldn't deny me a chance to see him, although it was likely my sister would be the one who needed a chaperone.

Mumma looked at me thoughtfully and then gave in. "Go together and come back together," she said, glaring at Roseanne to make her point. "And don't stay too long. I know it isn't far, but I don't like the idea of you girls out on the road at night."

Bursting with excitement, Roseanne danced a little jig and clapped her hands. I shook my head at her behind Mumma's back. If Mumma caught on that Roseanne wanted to see Billy Bruce, she'd renege on the permission.

* * *

It wasn't until after the supper dishes were done that we were able to get away. Clouds had gathered and rain threatened when we set off walking the short distance. We carried a lantern to light our way in the dusk. I pulled my woolen cloak tightly around myself and hoped the rain would hold off.

We were both giddy and chattered the whole way to John's house. When we arrived, we walked right in the door without knocking. The house was filled with tobacco smoke and wild laughter. I'm not sure what I'd been expecting, but it certainly wasn't what we found. Like a soap bubble floating in the air, my innocent vision of the wonderful get-togethers during the maple sugaring and our picnic at the lake last summer burst. I felt like an intruder. John, Tommy, and Will, along with Billy Bruce and Ethan, were sitting around the table playing poker, smoking cigars, and drinking an amber liquid I knew must be whiskey. My first impulse was to turn around and go right back out the way we came, but foolishly I didn't.

I stared through the smoky haze, transfixed as Ethan tipped his glass and drank the whole thing at once. And then he noticed me.

"Eliza," he shouted overly loudly as he scooted his chair back noisily against the floor. "Come here and give me a kiss."

Nobody else seemed to hear him, as they were bickering loudly about their game. Roseanne and I weren't the only girls in the room. Besides Annie, whom I'd known would probably be there, my brother Tommy had a young lady friend sitting next to him. She was attractive and very young, probably younger than me. Another girl, also very young, was standing behind them with a drink in her hand and watching Billy Bruce. She was tall and slender with long auburn locks pulled back from her face and tied with a green ribbon.

I grabbed Roseanne's hand to pull her back out the door, but she was standing as still as a statue staring at the young woman whose attention was fixed on Billy Bruce. If people were cats, my sister's claws would have been out, her back arched, and her tail puffed up.

Uh-oh, I thought. *Please, please don't make a scene.*

But I needn't have been concerned. I have often said my sister was much wiser than I in situations involving the heart. She gracefully removed her cloak, placed it on a hook, and walked into the midst of the gathering as if she were the guest of honor. Rather than throwing a fit, as I thought she might, she decided to become acquainted with the usurper. Hanging my cloak as well, I remained near the door, wishing I hadn't come. I had an impulse to leave, with or without my sister, but my chance to escape was cut off as Ethan ambled over to me.

"Hello, darlin'. I wasn't expecting to see you tonight," he said, grabbing me and pulling me to him. He was flushed and glassy-eyed. I caught a strong whiff of alcohol and tobacco on his breath and jerked my head back. Unfortunately, his kiss missed my lips completely. His face fell, and the drunken smile faded from his lips. Then he chuckled and crooned, "What's the matter, sweetheart?"

I didn't answer. My disgust seemed to have gone unnoticed. I allowed Ethan to pull me by the hand over to his place at the card game. I stood there awkwardly while the next hand was dealt.

Annie came to my rescue. "Eliza!" she exclaimed. "I'm so happy to see you." She gave me a hug. Annie had not been drinking, I was happy to see. "I'll make us some tea." I smiled at her gratefully and followed her to the stove but continued to watch Roseanne.

My sister placed herself right next to the new young woman who dared to flirt with Billy. "Hello," she said sweetly, offering her hand, "Have we met? I am Miss Roseanne Ludlow."

The girl, dragging her eyes from Billy, took her hand by the fingertips in a limp handshake. "No, we haven't," she said, neglecting to give Roseanne her name.

"I'm so happy to make your acquaintance," Roseanne gushed. "Do you still attend school?" My sister's syrupy voice did not match her dangerously snapping eyes.

The girl laughed loudly and looked Roseanne up and down. They appeared as two wild animals stalking each other. I could tell the girl was slightly tipsy, which meant she would be no match for Roseanne.

"Bess," Billy called, completely ignoring Roseanne, "come over here and keep me company."

The girl giggled and said in a stage whisper, "He thinks I'm his good luck charm."

Before Bess had a chance to move, Roseanne was at Billy's side and placed a possessive hand on his shoulder. He looked up, expecting to see Bess, but there was Roseanne with her vibrant red lips curved in a teasing smile. "Oh, Billy," she said playfully, "isn't that a full house?"

All the men groaned aloud, and Billy threw his cards down in the middle of the table. He stood up and put his hands on the sleeves of Roseanne's lovely lace-trimmed, pinstriped blouse as if he was going to shake her. "Roseanne," he said warningly, then he let his breath out in a long sigh. She placed her hand on his chest and looked up at him with wide, innocent eyes. The look on his face softened. I saw Billy lick his lips as Roseanne held his gaze. If the rest of us had not been in the room, I was sure he would have kissed her.

For the time being, it looked like the game was over as they all abandoned their cards and left the table. John and Will stepped outside, and Tommy and his young lady friend were having a tête-à-tête. My jaw dropped, and I quickly looked away. Annie placed the cup of tea in my hands, and I mumbled a thank-you.

"What's the matter, Eliza?" she said.

"I didn't know Tommy was courting."

"I didn't either," Annie said, rolling her eyes.

Ethan was coming my way, but instead of stopping to talk to me, he walked right past me as if I wasn't there, poured himself another glass of whiskey, and walked away. He went over to Bess and clinked glasses with her in a mock toast, and her face lit up. She took his hand in hers, and he whispered something into her ear that made her giggle.

I watched, frozen in place, as he smiled his crooked, charming smile with his bright, twinkling, teasing eyes. At another girl. A very pretty girl. I stopped breathing. I blinked in disbelief. I was standing not six feet away from him. She continued to laugh at something Ethan had said. Then she leaned in to him. His hand was at the small of her back.

I became invisible. Plain Eliza Jane, in an ordinary white blouse and drab gray skirt. The tea cup rattled on the saucer as my hands began to shake. I felt so foolish. I didn't want to see any more. I pushed the tea back into Annie's hands and ran to the door. John and Will were coming back in, but I pushed past them, forgetting to grab my cloak, and out into the night where the clouds had let go their rain.

Tears mixing with the raindrops streamed down my face as I ran heedlessly through the dark toward home. The painful memory of my sprained ankle forced me to slow down. Unable to see the mud puddles, I tramped through them, soaking my shoes and stockings and the bottom of my new skirt.

Numbness set in. What had just happened? Just who was that girl to Ethan? Horrified and humiliated, I felt like throwing up. I so wanted him to come out the door behind me and see me safely home. The Ethan I knew and loved was kind and good-hearted. He would never want to see me so upset. But he didn't come after me. He probably didn't even know I'd left.

When I reached our farm, I went into the barn instead of the house. It smelled strongly of wet animals, but I went in anyway, looking for a place to hide. In the back corner of an empty stall, I slid down to the floor strewn with straw and manure. I shivered and drew my knees to my chest, covered my face, and sobbed as if my heart were breaking. My hair had escaped its pins, hanging wet and cold down my back and sticking to my face, soaked with rain, tears, and runny nose. I had trusted him. In my mind's eye, I had always pictured him pining for me as I did for him. *I'm just not good enough or pretty enough for him.* The self-pitying thoughts came with a new onslaught of bawling. With each tear my foolish dreams of love and marriage dropped into the dirt and grime of the barn floor. My future was over, there was nothing more to look forward to. I slumped over into the straw and cried myself to sleep.

I awoke to find Papa pulling me gently up by the shoulders into a sitting position. I looked at him through my mess of tangled hair and saw his caring eyes clouded with concern.

"Oh, Papa," I said and buried my face in his chest.

"There, there, daughter. What's this all about now?"

I just shook my head back and forth. I couldn't say the words. I couldn't tell my pa that it was over.

"Everyone is up at the house and worried about you."

"I don't want to see him," I said. "I can't."

"Who?" he asked, waiting patiently while I wiped my nose on my sleeve. "Eliza, I can't help you if you don't tell me what has happened."

"Ethan," I choked. It was all I could say.

"All right now, let's get you into the warm house," Papa said as I stood up. He opened his coat and wrapped it around my shoulders to shelter me from the still-pouring rain.

We returned to the house where Roseanne, Tommy, and Ethan, were sitting at the table waiting. I looked down at the floor to avoid their stares and made a beeline across the room. Mumma followed me into the bedroom to get me out of my wet things and under some warm quilts. I heard Papa telling Ethan to leave, that I didn't want to see him. There was no argument, just a shuffling of chairs and the closing of the door. Then the house was quiet. I was grateful to Papa and Mumma for not pressing me. Safe and secure in my own bed, I rolled over, curled up in the layers of blankets, and fell into a deep, dreamless sleep.

CHAPTER 22

THE FOLLOWING MORNING WHEN I AWOKE, DAYLIGHT WAS STREAMING through the window. The little ones, whose room I always shared when I was home, were already dressed and out of the room without disturbing me. I stretched my arms over my head, feeling groggy and hungry. The events of last night came crashing back to me in a wave of humiliation. I cringed. My stomach curdled. Then I saw my clothing. My beautiful new skirt was ruined. It hung on a hook wrinkled and soiled with mud and remnants of filth from the barn floor. And Ethan never even noticed me in it. I felt the tears coming on again and promptly rose out of bed. I wrapped one of the lighter blankets about myself and went out to the kitchen.

"Good morning, sleepyhead," Mumma greeted me.

"What time is it?" I asked.

"Almost lunchtime," she said. "Are you hungry?"

I shook my head and plopped down in a chair. All of my brothers and sisters were outside somewhere. Even Roseanne was nowhere to be found.

"Do you want to talk about it?" Mumma asked.

I looked down at my hands and tried to wipe some of the dirt from them onto the blanket. I would never be able to figure this out on my own. I wasn't sure how to proceed.

"I should have listened to you," I told her. "Ethan was drinking last night." I took a breath and let it out again. Mumma didn't say anything but just stirred her tea, watching me.

"There were a couple of girls there I didn't know," I went on. "Ethan was very friendly with one of them."

"Oh," Mumma said. "How friendly?"

"He was looking at her like he used to look at me," I said. "And he was whispering in her ear. And they were smiling at each other. I felt," I hesitated, "I felt really awkward, like I saw something I wasn't supposed to." Then I cried out in anguish, "I thought he was in love with me."

Mumma laid her hand on mine. "Sometimes when men drink they don't know what they're doing. They don't act like themselves. Some men get mean, like my pa did when I was young. Others get affectionate, like your pa," she said. "Is he a drinker?"

"I don't know. I didn't think so. But one time he said something about playing cards with the boys. He didn't say much, just looked sheepish." I decided not to mention that other time when I had interrupted one of their games.

Mumma was quiet for a moment.

"What should I do?" I asked her.

"I don't think you should do anything," she said. "Go back to Port Hope. Get on with your business. If he loves you, he'll make it right. If he doesn't make it right, you are better off without him."

I stared at her, unable to respond. *Better off without him?* I stopped crying and sniffed, staring at her. I swallowed and tried to breathe. Then I nodded and went out to the basin and mirror to survey the damage. I didn't feel very well. My stomach churned, my throat was scratchy, and my cheeks were flushed. I wasn't in the habit of putting on such an emotional scene and chalked it all up to the results of my upset.

I put on my old clothes and stuffed the new ones, still damp and soiled, back in the bag. Roseanne and I left shortly thereafter. For a while we walked along in silence.

"Eliza, what happened last night?" she finally said.

"You were there," I said. "You should know."

"Well, yes, I was, but I was a bit preoccupied."

"You remember that girl who was flirting with Billy?" I asked.

"Apparently she knows Ethan quite well," I said with a bitter note in my voice. "They were very, um, cozy together. He didn't even look at me. When I saw them I…" my voice began to tremble.

She came to a dead stop and turned to face me. "Eliza Jane, snap out of it! That girl doesn't have anything you don't have, except maybe knowing how to get what she wants."

I looked at her intently. "What do you mean?"

"If it had been me, and my fiancé had treated me that way, you can bet your sweet life I would have set him straight, right there, in front of everyone. He's supposed to be marrying you in a few months, for Pete's sake. I certainly wouldn't let him get away with it and go running away crying like a baby."

I hung my head shamefully. She was right. I knew it.

"No self-respecting girl would put up with it. Learn to speak up for yourself. If you don't like what he's doing or how he's acting, you'd better tell him now before you marry him. You're acting like an old dishrag. You need to get a backbone, Eliza, and stop blubbering like a schoolgirl."

Her tirade finished, she turned around and continued walking down the muddy road.

I followed her, taking her words to heart. The way he'd been playing up to that girl was only part of the problem. I didn't like that he'd been drinking. If he hadn't been drinking, all of this might not have happened. I began to feel angry and decided that if Ethan did come to his senses and apologize, I was going to tell him how despicable I thought he was. I wrapped the anger around me like metal armor, but it didn't make my stomach or my throat feel any better.

We trudged on. What could have been a delightful, fun-filled weekend had become sour and unsettling. I hated that feeling, like the world had been knocked off its axis and needed a shove to put it right.

A few minutes later, Roseanne turned to me and said, "I'm sorry, Eliza. I shouldn't have yelled at you. Last night was a total fiasco all the way around. And today I don't feel very well."

"I don't either. I just want to go lie down and sleep for a while," I said.

I took a close look at Roseanne then. She too was flushed and had dark circles under her eyes. I was startled, as my sister was seldom sick. She usually glowed with good health. We walked the remainder of the way in silence, and I was relieved when we walked up the back steps to our second home.

The house was dark and eerily quiet. There was no meal being prepared, nor fires in the fireplaces. Neither Cook nor Mrs. Stafford were anywhere to be found. I wondered if they might be sick. I knew illness would be the only reason Cook would not be at work in the kitchen. Mr. Stafford wasn't present either, but he was away on his last business trip before winter set in.

Roseanne went straight up to our room, but my sense of duty impelled me to check on our employer. I knocked lightly on Mrs. Stafford's bedroom door and entered the room cautiously. If she was sleeping, I didn't want to wake her.

"Eliza Jane," the woman said to me, her voice weak. She stretched a hand toward me.

I went quickly to her bedside and took her hand. I laid my other hand on her forehead and said, "You're burning up." I poured a glass of water from the pitcher on the bedside table and offered it to her, but she pushed it away. She put her hand to her throat and swallowed hard then began a racking cough.

"Has the doctor been in to see you?" I asked.

She shook her head no. I left the room then and brought back a basin of cold water and a washcloth. I wrung the cloth out and laid it across her forehead. Then I went to Cook's room, found her in similar straits, and did the same. I knew the sickness must be serious to make Cook take to her bed in the middle of the day. I suspected Roseanne and I were coming down with the same thing. A feeling of dread crept into the back of my mind.

I donned my cloak and went out the door. Dr. Dickinson's residence was only a few blocks away. I walked with urgent quickness, in spite of the fact that I didn't feel well myself. When I arrived, I rang the bell, and his servant opened the door.

"Is Dr. Dickinson available?" I inquired. I was let into the foyer. A stout, bald, elderly man wearing spectacles and dressed in his Sunday suit came down the staircase.

"How may I help you, miss?" he said.

I curtsied and said to him, "I'm sorry to disturb you on your Sunday afternoon. I am servant to Mrs. Stafford. When I returned to the house today, I found her in bed with a fever. Her cook is also ill. I thought perhaps you should examine them."

"And what is your name, miss?"

"Eliza Jane Ludlow," I responded, "one of the maidservants at Stafford House."

"Very nice to meet you, Miss Ludlow," he said. He put on his overcoat and grabbed his black bag. We went out the door, down the front steps, and back the way I had come.

On the way he asked me what Mrs. Stafford's symptoms were. I told him only those things I'd observed and that I had just returned to Stafford House that day.

"How are you feeling, young lady?" he asked.

"I'm not at my best," I confessed. "I had a busy weekend."

"No sore throat?"

"Yes, my throat is a little sore," I admitted. "My sister Roseanne, who also works there, took ill and went right to bed as soon as we got back."

"Do you have younger siblings at home?" he asked.

"Yes," I replied, that worrisome feeling creeping back into my mind.

He said no more. We arrived at the house, and I led him to Mrs. Stafford's room. I stood back but paid attention to his examination. He looked in her throat, checked her temperature, and felt her neck and belly. Then he turned to me.

"You've done a good job with the cool compresses on her forehead. You can also give her a sponge bath to help bring her fever down."

He reached into his bag and handed me a paper envelope. "Steep these herbs in hot water and have her drink several cups a day for the next few days, as well as some bone broth. Let me know if she worsens or if you notice a rash develop."

I nodded at each instruction. "Would you have time to check on Cook and my sister?" I asked.

He went to the servants' quarters and then to the attic bedroom, doing a quick appraisal of each patient. "I think we have different stages of the same illness here," he told me. He gave me another envelope of the herbs. "That should give you enough for all three women while they are recovering. Take some yourself if you continue to feel ill. Keep your hands clean, and change their bedding as soon as they are on the mend. When they begin to be hungry, you can give them some bread soaked in milk and more of the bone broth."

I nodded and led him to the door. "Thank you, Dr. Dickinson," I said. "I'll try to do everything you told me."

He patted my hand. "You'll do fine, young lady. Oh, and don't go home until you are sure you and you sister are well."

"Yes, sir," I replied as I closed the door.

I went right to work. As I'd seen Cook do in the past, I requested a chicken from one of the men to prepare the broth. It arrived momentarily, cleaned and dressed, so I had to assume they had an icebox somewhere on the premises. I placed it into a stockpot full of water and heaved the heavy pot onto the stove to boil. After the meat fell from the bones, I sieved everything except the bones and added some cider vinegar. I located Cook's stash of dried herbs and put in some rosemary, bay leaf, and salt, then left it to simmer again until the minerals had time to leach from the bones. I thanked my lucky stars that Mumma was such a good healer and had taught me long ago to prepare the healing broth.

For the next few days and nights, I was so busy tending my patients that I had no time at all to think of what might be going on elsewhere. I so wished I had resolved things with Ethan. Thinking of him brought about a thin stream of fear trickling through my mind. *Worrying won't change anything,* Grandma used to say. In any case, I had no extra energy to devote to thinking about what I might have done differently, and sadly I hadn't heard word one from him.

Slowly the older two women recovered. Roseanne was a different story. The rash the doctor had me checking for showed up on her a few days later. I ran down the road to Dr. Dickinson with my report, and once again he paid us a house call. By then Mrs. Stafford and Cook were up and about, regaining some strength. But Roseanne wasn't. She scarcely awakened unless it was to drink some tea or broth. Her fever had lingered, although it ceased to be as extreme as it was at first.

"Scarlatina," the doctor announced after looking at my sister. "This house is under quarantine until she recovers."

Scarlatina? Children die from scarlet fever. What if the little ones get it?

I was shocked. "Doctor, how serious is this?" I asked.

"She's not a young child, so it's not as serious as it might be, but she is very, very ill."

"I'm worried about our family," I said. "We were both under the weather when we were home last week. My brothers and sisters are quite a bit younger."

"I'm sorry, Miss Ludlow, there's nothing you can do about it. You must remain here for the duration of this illness. By the way, how are you feeling?"

I hadn't given my own condition any thought all week, but knew I looked a sight. The last time I had peered into a mirror, I'd had dark circles under my eyes. I swallowed. "My throat isn't as sore as it was, but I'm tired, probably just from taking care of the others," I said.

"You'd make a good nurse," he told me and patted my hand again. "Now that the women have turned a corner, you should be taking better care of yourself. You and the other two women have probably had mild cases. But make sure you eat properly and get enough rest." With that he turned and walked out the door.

After he was gone, I quickly scribbled a note to my parents about the quarantine and asked how everyone at home had been doing. Then I called out the back door to the groom, explained the quarantine, and asked him to deliver my letter. He took it from me without coming too close, and a few minutes later I heard the sound of a horse trotting down the drive. Later that same evening, there was a knock on the back door. The groom passed a note through to me.

Dear Eliza Jane,

Thank you for your letter. Yes, I'm afraid you were correct to be concerned. All of us came down with a sore throat and fever for a few days and are doing better now, except for poor Georgie. Just today he developed the rash. I sent Papa to Huron City for the doctor.

Love,
Mumma

Poor Georgie. Oh my God, don't let him die. I gave myself a mental shake for the dreadful thought. I pulled the rocking chair up to my sister's bedside. With my shawl pulled around my shoulders for warmth, I prayed for a speedy recovery for both my sister and my little brother.

Roseanne's recovery seemed slow. It was probably because I was chomping at the bit to get the quarantine lifted so I could go home and check on how Georgie was doing. She started perking up a few days later, and at the end of the following week, the doctor came to the house and declared everyone healthy.

The next day was Sunday, and I awoke early in the morning to walk home. The weather was miserably cold with rain and sleet. Determined to see for myself how Georgie was doing, I bundled up in my heaviest clothing.

"Are you sure you want to do this?" my sister asked.

"Yes, I'll come right back, I promise," I said.

"You might catch a chill, and then you'll be the one sick in bed," she complained.

"I was hardly sick this time," I retorted. "A little fresh air never killed anyone."

Roseanne glanced out the window. "This is not a little fresh air. This is an icy, windy storm."

I did not reply but ran quickly down the two flights of stairs to the main floor and out into the weather before she could change my mind. It was a miserable walk, with the frigid wind coming out of the north cutting right through to my skin in spite of my extra clothes, cloak, scarf, hat, and mittens. I ducked my face into my scarf and walked intently into the blustery weather. If I walked fast enough, maybe I would keep from freezing. *Oh, for a ride,* I wished. *Where is Ethan when I need him?* My silly wish triggered a stream of thoughts about him that I'd been tiptoeing around for the past few weeks. I wondered how he'd been. Most of my anger and disappointment had faded over time, but the hurt remained. He had never tried to write or come to see me. Maybe it really was over.

CHAPTER 23

HUNKERED DOWN INTO MY SCARF AND THE NECK OF MY CLOAK, I HADN'T heard the sound of a horse and rider approaching. I looked up to see Ethan bundled up and hunched over the reins of his mare. I was shocked. It was as if by thinking his name I had conjured him out of thin air. His eyes mirrored my own shock and surprise. Dismounting, he moved quickly toward me.

We stared at each other for a long moment, and then were in each other's arms.

"I'm sorry, Eliza Jane. I'm so very sorry I hurt you. Please forgive me," he cried in anguish.

In answer I kissed him long and hard.

"What are you doing out in such a storm, sweetheart?" he asked.

"Georgie is very ill. I want to go see him," I explained.

"Everyone has been sick at my house as well," he told me.

"And at Stafford House," I said. "Roseanne was the worst, but is better now. We're no longer under quarantine."

"Quarantine? What happened to cause quarantine?" Ethan asked.

"Scarlet fever," I said, "but nobody's sickness got that bad. Roseanne was the worst, and the doctor said she had Scarlatina. It's very serious for children."

"Let's get to your house and see what's going on," he said, mounting his horse and helping me to climb up behind him. He kicked the mare, and we trotted down the road, splashing through puddles, until we arrived at my house. He lifted me down and went to put the mare into the barn.

Georgie was in bed and isolated from the rest of the family in the downstairs bedroom. I gave Mumma and Papa hugs and the little ones clamored around me. I was so happy to see them.

"How is Georgie?" I asked.

"His fever finally broke, although he's still covered in rash. I think he's finally going to get better," Mumma said, putting the kettle on the stove. "He's still very weak. He just started eating more yesterday. It was touch and go for a while, really had us scared."

I went down the short hall and into the room. Finn was curled up on the foot of the bed. He raised his head, whined softly, and beat his tail against the quilt. I opened the curtains, and a little light penetrated the cloudy day to illuminate the small form of my brother. I sat down on the edge of his bed and smoothed the thick brown hair off his forehead, which was cool to the touch. I waited for him to awaken. He yawned and stretched, his long, thin arms reaching out of the sleeves of his nightshirt. Opening his eyes, he saw me and smiled. I was so relieved I almost cried. Instead, I scooped him up into a big hug.

"You had us all scared, young man," I said, mock-scolding him.

He looked confused. It crossed my mind that he didn't know how sick he'd been.

"A doctor came here," Georgie said, "because I have some spots." He lifted his shirt to show me his speckled stomach.

"Yes, I heard about it from Mumma. Guess who else was sick like you."

"You?" he asked.

"Nope. I did have a sore throat, but it didn't last very long. Roseanne got very sick. The doctor in Port Hope came to see her."

His eyes grew wide.

"And Ethan's sisters were sick too," I added.

"Emma and Nellie had it, and Ben, but they got better before me."

"Yes, it was very contagious," I said. "So how are you feeling now?"

"I want to get up, but Mumma says no." He moped with a long face.

"She wants to make sure you are really better before you start running around," I told him. "Otherwise, you could get sick again, and that would not be a good thing, would it?"

"No," he agreed, "but I'm bored. There's nothing to do."

"Well now that your fever has gone away, maybe Emma or Nellie can play a game with you. Would you like that?"

He nodded an emphatic yes.

"Are you hungry?"

"Yes, but I just had breakfast."

"That was hours ago, Georgie. You were sleeping when I came in. You probably slept the morning away."

I left the room to see if Emma would entertain him for a little while, to which she gladly agreed. Ethan and Papa were discussing the harvest, and I went to the stove to see if I could help prepare the noon meal.

"Have you and Ethan made it up then?" Mumma asked softly.

I smiled. "We made up, but we haven't talked any of it over yet."

"Don't be tempted to sweep it under the rug, Eliza. You two need to clear the air. It might prevent something similar from happening in the future."

I hadn't thought of that. I was just happy that the sick feeling in my stomach had gone away. It was hard to find a place to talk. With the weather so brutal, we wouldn't be able to go outside and take a walk.

"Could we use your room?" I asked Mumma.

"Yes, if talking's the only thing you have in mind," she said with a wink.

My face grew hot. I reassured her, "Just to talk." I gave her a kiss on the cheek and went to collect Ethan. I turned back around to her and added, "Georgie's hungry."

Interrupting the conversation between Ethan and Papa, I took Ethan by the hand and pulled him to his feet. I led him into Mumma and Papa's bedroom and closed the door so we wouldn't be disturbed. I sat down on the edge of the bed and pointed to a chair in the corner.

"We need to talk things over," I said. He nodded his head, and I continued, "The last time I saw you, you really hurt my feelings."

"I know, Eliza Jane. I told you how sorry I am."

"Just who was that girl?"

"What girl?" he asked. Was it possible, with all the alcohol he had drunk that night, that maybe he really didn't remember? But surely since then my brothers would have told him what had happened.

"You know very well what girl, Ethan. The one you were cozied up to when I left."

He shrugged. I couldn't tell if he really didn't remember or if he wasn't willing to admit to doing anything wrong. Then I recalled Roseanne's words. I wasn't about to be an old dishrag. He was supposed to be my fiancé, and he needed to act like it. I straightened my back with resolve.

"I don't think you're ready to get married," I said with conviction.

He leaned over and took my hands in his. "I am ready. Please, forgive me," he begged. "I love you and want to marry you."

I took my hands back and folded them in my lap. I couldn't think clearly when he touched me. "You were different, Ethan. What would you have done with that girl if I hadn't been there?"

"You acted differently too," he said defensively, "I tried to say hello to you, and you brushed me off. It made me mad."

I looked at him then. I felt scared. If I said too much, would he walk out of my life? I didn't want that. I loved him. I just wanted everything to go back to the way it was before that horrible night. But Mumma said this was something we needed to settle before we were married.

"I've never seen you angry before, or drunk," I said. I was on the verge of crying, regardless of the promise I made to myself.

"Jesus, Eliza, I work hard every single day, from sunup to sundown, so we can have a start when we get married. I deserve a drink once in a while. What's wrong with that?"

"You were so different. I hardly recognized you," I said.

"Your brothers all drink, your pa drinks. Everyone drinks sometimes," he said forcibly.

I sighed. "I know, but I've not seen much of it. And from what I saw, I don't like it."

"So what are you going to do? Forbid me to have a drink?" he said sarcastically.

"Of course not," I said and looked him right in the eye. "You still haven't told me who that girl is to you."

He looked away from me then. "She's nothing to me. We were just joking around. I hardly remember her."

Relieved, I did start to cry then. It didn't occur to me not to believe him. He approached me and wrapped his arms around me.

"Do you forgive me?" he asked.

"Yes," I said. "I don't want us to be cross with each other. It makes me feel sick to my stomach. But I also don't want to ever find you looking at another woman the way you look at me, drunk or not."

He stood up and pulled me into his arms. I wanted him to promise me he would never look at another woman, but then he kissed me and my resolve crumbled like a house of cards.

When we came out of the room, Papa didn't look up. He continued smoking his pipe and oiling a leather harness. Noting the look on my face, Mumma smiled at me.

Ethan drove me back to Port Hope using Papa's wagon. We made plans to see each other before the holidays if possible, even if it meant him coming out to Port Hope just to take me for a walk. We agreed to make a more concerted effort to see each other.

When I related the whole story to Roseanne, she started clapping her hands. "Well done," she said. "There might be hope for you yet, Eliza Jane."

I smiled to myself, satisfied with what I had accomplished that day. I was no longer worried about Georgie or Ethan. A great weight had been lifted from my shoulders. That night, before I went to bed, I took out my wedding quilt and did a little sewing by lamplight. I had not touched a single part of my trousseau since the falling out with Ethan. Rifling through my dresser drawer, I found the list I had made months ago. Overwhelmed at the length of the list, I sighed, knowing there would never be enough free time, and sewing an entire quilt was an enormous task. I promised myself, no matter how tired I was, I'd sew for a little while every single night.

* * *

My good intentions started to take their toll after a few weeks. One night close to Christmas, Roseanne awoke, sat up in bed, and looked at me.

"For heaven's sake, Eliza, when are you going to bed? It must be well past midnight."

I was hunched over my sewing near the lamp, trying hard to keep my stitches small and even. I set the fabric down in my lap and sat up straight to stretch the muscles in my back.

"I have so much to do," I replied, rubbing my eyes. "I'm never going to get it all done."

"You have months and months yet," my sister continued in her sleepy voice. "You don't have to get it all done at once."

I sat back and said, "But I'm so far behind."

"That's what you get for putting it off for so long."

"I know," I groaned. "After my ill-begotten plan to surprise Ethan that night, I wasn't even sure I would be getting married. And then you and the others got sick. I simply haven't had any time."

Thinking about that woeful night, I reminded myself that I hadn't dealt with the fate of my beautiful woolen skirt. Upon returning to Stafford House, I had removed it from the satchel, stuck it on a hook, and never looked at it again, so great was my disappointment in that night. I added it to the ever-growing list of tasks. I'd surely have to sew another new skirt to replace it. That was the trouble with wool—it wasn't very forgiving.

Roseanne laid back down and rolled on her side to look at me. "We can have a quilting bee in the spring," she said encouragingly.

I didn't answer. I wasn't sure I'd have the quilt top completed before that. A few minutes later, I set the finished block carefully upon the growing pile in the corner and stuck my needle into the pincushion. Finally, I blew out the light, crawled into bed, and pulled my covers up to my chin. I lay flat on my back on my hard cot and stared into the blackness. My shoulders, back, and head ached. Unwilling to put out the effort to roll over to a more comfortable position, I fell asleep to the sound of sleet pattering in windy waves against the windowpane.

The following morning, I crawled reluctantly out of bed, dressed, and found my way to the kitchen. It was our day off, and the harsh weather would keep us in Port Hope. I wanted to get an early start sewing again. Cook handed me a cup of strong coffee to which I added liberal amounts of fresh cream. I finished a breakfast of hash and eggs, the coffee awakening me from my grogginess. I hadn't uttered a word to my sister, who, having finished her own breakfast, was watching me from across the kitchen table, her head leaning on her hand.

"Would you like some help with your sewing projects?" she asked. "I've finished the holiday cards for Mrs. Stafford, and my hands aren't sore anymore."

"Oh, Roseanne, would you?" I said. "I would really appreciate it."

"What is the quilt going to look like?" Cook asked.

"It's a nine-patch alternating with an appliqued heart, or maybe a tulip," I said, covering a yawn with my hand. "I've just been working on the nine-patch squares."

"Tulips sound pretty. Are you going to scallop the border?" Cook asked.

"Probably not. Right now, I'm tempted to skip the appliques completely. I'd have a devil of a time turning in the edges when I'm bleary-eyed."

"Oh, don't be hasty. You should make it the way you want it to look. You could sketch it with hearts and tulips to help you decide," Cook said.

I thought about it for a moment. I could see the quilt in my mind's eye and decided on the tulips. "That won't be necessary. I'm going to make the tulips," I said decisively.

"Any special instructions so I don't mess it up?" Roseanne asked.

"I have all the little squares cut," I said. "Just try and keep the colors mixed up a bit."

"You might ask Mrs. Stafford about using the sewing machine," Cook suggested.

Roseanne and I looked at each other. Neither of us had thought about the sewing machine.

"It would make sewing the big blocks together much quicker," Cook added.

"What a good idea," I said, giving Cook a quick hug. "Do you remember the gray woolen skirt I made this fall? I'm afraid I've completely ruined it."

"How did that happen?" she asked.

"The night she got upset with Ethan, she ran all the way home in the rain," my sister tattled, "and sat in animal excrement on the floor of the barn," she added with disgust.

"You can try to wash it," Cook suggested. "Make sure the water is cool and put it in to soak. You can't scrub wool."

My sister and I went back up to our room and had a look at the skirt. She shook her head in dismay.

"Eliza, what were you thinking?" she asked.

"I wasn't thinking." I shook my head sadly, examining the dried mud around the hem and splattered up the back. I had felt about that skirt the way I had felt about my relationship with Ethan, excited at the newness and hopeful for the future. As I gazed at it, I realized it still looked like my relationship with Ethan—bruised but hopeful. I knew I must try to fix it. It would never be like new again but was worth salvaging.

"Brush the dried mud off first," she suggested.

"No, I'm going to be gentle with it," I said. "I'll put it to soak and see what happens. If it doesn't come clean, it just wasn't meant to be."

Roseanne turned her gaze on me. "Are we still talking about the skirt?" she asked.

I looked back at her, my lips set in a determined line. "Let's go ask Mrs. Stafford if we can use the sewing machine."

CHAPTER 24

TRUE TO OUR INTENTIONS, ETHAN MADE THE EFFORT TO VISIT ME AT Stafford House. He came every Sunday except when the weather was extremely cold. Most of our courting was done in the kitchen under Cook's watchful eye, but she always seemed to find some excuse to leave the room for a short time, allowing us to sneak a kiss in private. After the noon meal, he would get back on his horse and return home, leaving me smiling and feeling content.

The remainder of that winter flew by through the Christmas holidays and the beginning of 1881, the year I was to become Mrs. Ethan Kilpatrick. We had decided to marry after harvest in the fall, so I was able to relax into all of my sewing tasks. With my sister's help, about half the tulips had been sewn onto the muslin squares for the quilt. One Sunday in February, Ethan arrived with a note from Mumma.

Dear Eliza,

We received a letter from Grandpa on Thursday that informed us of Grandma's ill health. He is having a difficult time caring for her. He would ask one of your aunts to come, but she has been asking for you. We wondered if you would be able to travel to New York to nurse her back to health. A visit from you might be just what the doctor ordered. If you do decide to make the trip, be sure to let Mrs. Stafford know that this will be an extended visit.

Love,
Mumma

"Oh Ethan," I cried, burying my face in his chest.

"What is it?" he asked.

"Grandpa sent word that Grandma is sick. I'm to go to New York to take care of her. She must be dreadfully ill for him to send the letter."

"Don't borrow trouble," he said to soothe me, but we both knew, with such a distance between us, that Grandpa wouldn't send for me if it wasn't serious.

I pulled away from him. "I'll tell Roseanne and Mrs. Stafford and gather my things. Could you wait for me and take me home?" I asked.

Cook gave Ethan a cup of tea as I hurried off. Mrs. Stafford offered her sympathies and said Roseanne could help cover my chores while I was away. I grimaced at that thought, knowing Roseanne would not be thrilled at the thought of laundry, scrubbing floors, and all my other household duties.

I stuffed my things carelessly into the old carpetbag, including all of the money I had been squirreling away. I knew that if I used my own money, I would be able to travel by train.

* * *

Early the following Tuesday, I was filled with a mixture of trepidation and excitement. I dressed in my wool skirt, now freshly cleaned and pressed, if a little worse for wear, and my white blouse, starched and buttoned up to my neck. I borrowed all the necessities a woman needed for travel from Mumma, including her moleskin coat, a matching hat, and a pair of soft kid gloves. I placed a small amount of money, enough to pay for my train ticket, into Roseanne's crocheted purse, and the remainder of my precious savings I wrapped tightly in a hanky pinned to the inside of my waistband. I tied the little hat over my hair, which I had spun into a bun and pinned securely in place. Then I donned the short moleskin coat and gloves and wrapped the purse strings around my wrist. I picked up the tattered carpetbag containing my dress, change of underclothes, and nightgown and presented myself to Mumma for a quick inspection.

"I think I'm ready," I said.

"Are you sure you have enough money?" she asked, handing me my cloak and a lunch pail containing some salt pork, cheese, and biscuits.

"Yes. Hopefully I won't need it all," I told her.

"Don't talk to anyone. A girl alone on a train isn't safe," she warned. "Just keep to yourself. Don't invite any advances."

I smiled. "Don't worry, I'll be fine."

She gave me a hug and kiss and opened the door. Dick brought the wagon up to the house, helped me put my things under the seat, and gave me a hand up.

"Give them our love," Mumma said as I settled myself on the seat, "and don't forget to write so I'll know you've arrived safely."

"I will," I said and waved good-bye as Dick gave the reins a jiggle and the horse started off.

At Stafford's dock in Port Hope, I boarded the *Flora* on its return trip to Port Huron. I smiled to myself as I climbed the gangway. If not for the fact that I was so worried about Grandma and anxious to be in New York, I would have really enjoyed this adventure, traveling for the first time on my own. The *Flora*, not having picked up any more speed or efficiency since I had last been on it, took most of the day to get me through the first leg of my journey.

In Port Huron I walked over to the train station and visited the ticket master to plot my trip east. The first train would carry me south to Toledo, where I would change trains to get to Buffalo, and finally board a third train that would stop at Brockport. From there I would walk the three miles to Grandma and Grandpa's house. But for its usual drawbacks—the noise, the smell, the dirty soot, the numerous stops, and most of all the discomfort of remaining in a sitting position for days—I was very excited for my first train ride.

I didn't want to spend the money for the first-class ladies' car, so I purchased a second-class fare that left me in a car with plain wooden seats and mixed company. The car was closer to the engine, so the air quality was lacking, not to mention almost all the men were smoking.

It was stuffy and overwarm from the heat of a woodstove in the center of the cab. I would just have to make do.

The weather was fickle. Spring had not yet sprung, and there was snow on the ground most of the way. Mumma's moleskin coat kept me warm, and my cloak served as a cozy blanket when I tried futilely to sleep. At mealtimes, I nibbled the food I'd brought with me in the tin pail stashed in my bag and allowed myself to visit the dining car for a chance to stretch my legs and get a hot cup of tea.

Bearing Mumma's advice in mind, I kept to myself, not wanting to chance meeting someone annoying or unpleasant. The newspaper I bought at the stand in the Toledo station, the scenery during daylight hours, and my own thoughts were my entertainment.

I arrived in Brockport late Thursday afternoon and then walked the old Indian trail road through the cold wind off Lake Ontario to the little farming community of Sweden, New York. It was evening by the time I dragged myself and my belongings up the steps to the old Ludlow house and knocked on the door.

"Eliza Jane!" Grandpa greeted me. I dropped my bag onto the floor and went into his arms.

"I'm so glad to finally be here," I said. "How is she?"

"I'll let you see for yourself. Just be prepared," he said in a sad, low voice. "She isn't like her old self. The doctor says she had a softening of the brain. She can talk a little, but she tires very quickly."

I nodded my head solemnly, removing my coat, hat, and gloves. "Will she get better?" I asked.

He shrugged his shoulders. "I don't know," he said.

He led me up the stairs to her bedroom. There was a lamp by her bed and a chair pulled close. It looked like Grandpa had been reading to her, as a book was open and turned face down on the edge of the bed.

Her eyes were closed, and I thought she was asleep. But when I leaned over to smooth her hair from her brow and kiss her forehead, her eyes opened. She didn't immediately know me, but then I saw the light of recognition in her eyes. She tried to smile, but only part of her face moved, and she reached with one gnarled hand to touch my cheek. I placed my own hand over hers. It was cool to the touch and the skin paper-thin. There were tears in her eyes as she softly murmured, "Eliza Jane."

"Yes, it's me, Grandma. I've come to take care of you for a while," I said, trying hard not to weep at seeing her in such a state. No matter what I had imagined knowing that she was very sick, I was not prepared to see her like this. Such a drastic difference in the year I'd been away. "I love you," I said and pressed my lips to her hand. "I have so much news to tell you, but we'll talk tomorrow." I laid her hand back down and covered it with her quilt.

"Would you like something to eat, my dear?" Grandpa asked.

"Just some tea," I said, "I'm not very hungry." In truth, having missed supper, I'd been famished on the walk from Brockport, but after seeing Grandma so frail, I'd lost my appetite. I sat down at the kitchen table, and Grandpa put the kettle on to boil.

"How was your trip?" he asked.

"Long, but now I can say I've traveled by train," I said, smiling at him. "How long has she been like this?"

"A few weeks now," he said. "She started having headaches, bad enough that she would have to lie down. Then one day she took to her bed and hasn't been the same since."

"Has there been any improvement?" I asked.

Grandpa shook his head. He looked like he'd aged ten years himself. "People don't usually recover from this sort of thing, the doctor told me," he went on, "but I'm sure having you here will lift her spirits. How long will you be able to stay?"

I stirred my tea and blew on it to cool it off. "As long as necessary," I said.

His eyes welled up, and he patted my hand clumsily. "I'm very happy you're here, Eliza. Let's get your things to your room. You can tell me all about the family and the farm in the morning."

I brought my tea and followed him up to the bedroom at the top of the stairs, the same one I'd shared with my sisters. Grandpa put my bag and cloak on the bed and set the lamp down on the table.

"You remember your way around?" he asked, pointing vaguely in the direction of the outhouse. "Just make sure you take the lamp with you when you go." He patted my cheek. "Goodnight, dear, sleep well."

The following morning I was up at dawn, having slept soundly from the minute my head hit the pillow. I made a quick breakfast of bread and milk, then tried to get Grandma to eat some of the broth Grandpa had made.

"She hasn't had much appetite," Grandpa said, watching over my shoulder. "She's just wasting away." He shook his head mournfully. "Until this past week, she was still able to get up out of bed."

"Let's keep trying. No need to give up just yet," I said, ladling another spoonful of the warm liquid into her mouth.

As I fed her, she kept looking at me with wide, childlike eyes. Grandpa left us and went outdoors to tend to his chores. I took the bowl and spoon back to the kitchen and returned with two cups of strong, hot tea. I had added some milk and sugar, the way she and I both liked it. I placed the cups on the bedside table and settled myself into the nearby chair.

"I have so much to tell you, Grandma. Where should I begin?" I told her while the tea was cooling. I'd written her letters describing the trip to Michigan, the farm, my job in Port Hope, and having a beau, but I hadn't told her the more dramatic happenings. I started with my tale of the children getting sick all over me the day we met Miss Stafford and how, when I next saw her, I was so paralyzed with embarrassment that I could hardly speak. I had just finished telling her of my fall on the road back home when she fell asleep. I hadn't gotten to the part about my betrothal, but it could wait till later.

I smiled and pulled the covers up to her chin. She hadn't had the tea, but I didn't worry. I'd fix her a fresh cup later. I pulled the door softly closed and went to my room to find my stationery, pen, and ink.

I poured a little of Grandma's tea out, warmed it up with some hot water from the kettle, and sat down at the kitchen table to write home.

Dear Mumma and Papa,

I arrived safely, though quite tired, last evening. The train ride was uneventful, and I'm not sure which mode of transportation I prefer, having experienced both water and rail. Each has its share of discomforts, but traveling by train is certainly faster. In the time it took us to get to Buffalo on the canal last year, I was already here.

Grandpa is very happy that I have come to nurse Grandma. He has been trying to take care of her, the house and cooking, and all of his chores these past weeks. He has paid the toll with his own health. The doctor was in to see Grandma but is not hopeful since people seldom survive this kind of condition. However, she seems to be holding on for dear life and doesn't seem to be in any pain. I was very relieved she recognized me last night when I went in to see her.

This morning I was up with the birds, excited to get a start on my day. There are many chores that need doing, as you can imagine, so I will close for now. Please give everyone my love.

Your loving daughter,
Eliza Jane

That letter signed and sealed, I took out a new sheet and wrote to Ethan:

My Dearest Ethan,

I have arrived safe and sound to my destination and have found Grandma still fighting the good fight. She is very fragile and will need my most tender care. Grandpa is relieved to have me here, as he has fallen far behind on his own chores and is quite run-down himself.

I miss you so very much but know you are occupied with preparing our home. I am unsure how long I will be in New York, but I will persist until I have worn out my welcome and then return to you.
I will try to write often, as time allows, my love.

Yours always,
Eliza Jane

I gave both letters to Grandpa to take to the post office on his next trip to town, as well as a shopping list of items I found were needed. After fixing him a hearty meal, I asked him to help me get Grandma into a chair. Her bedding was in sorry need of cleaning, and taking advantage of the clear day, I intended to air out the blankets and change the sheets.

I enlisted Grandpa's help to get Grandma out of bed and into a chair with arms from the kitchen to help her to remain upright. I made quick work of stripping the bed and replacing the sheets. Grandpa kept an eye on her while I took the blankets to hang on the line in the fresh air. A sponge bath was next. She had been unable to wash herself for weeks, so she was quite ripe. She smiled at me as I washed her gently with soap and water and then rinsed and dried each part of her body. I combed her long gray-white hair lovingly and put it into a bun on top of her head. Not wanting any accidents, I had her use the pot. Refreshed and tucked back into bed, she fell asleep.

I continued with my chores—cleaning, sweeping, and dusting—while the sheets and her bedclothes soaked in a tub of hot, soapy water. Grandpa returned from town with the food items I had requested, and a chicken already dressed out by one of the neighbors. I roasted it, trimmed all the meat, and put the bones in to boil for some fresh broth. By the end of the day, I had a fresh, robust chicken soup simmering and the bit of laundry put through the boiler, rinsed, wrung, and dried on the line. Rather than head to bed, I went into Grandma's room and read to her until she was asleep for the night.

* * *

My days continued this way for the next month. I wrote my letters early in the morning, cared for Grandma, and kept up with the household chores and cooking. Grandpa, getting more rest, seemed to be returning to his old self.

Grandma, however, did not improve. And she never did speak to me after uttering my name the night I arrived. When I asked the doctor, who came weekly for a visit, if he thought she would ever get better, he patted my hand and looked me straight in the eye.

"Of course, miracles do happen, young lady, but I believe she will continue this way until she passes," he said gently. "You should prepare for the worst."

I nodded my head. I knew, in my heart of hearts, it was true. Grandma was reaching the end of her life. Swallowing hard, I resolved to make her remaining days as pleasant as I could. I kept her clean and comfortable, encouraged her to eat by feeding her endless chicken soup, and read to her by the dim light of the gas lamp each evening. Time passed. I don't think she knew who Grandpa and I were any more. She stopped trying to smile and rarely opened her eyes.

It was a stressful time, one I had not anticipated, for fear of tempting fate. I had for the past month tried to keep Grandma alive by the sheer force of my will alone, not wanting to lose her to death. But death came for her on April 23.

Chapter 25

"Eliza Jane." I woke up from a sound sleep to Grandma calling my name. Lighting the lamp, I tiptoed into her room to check on her. I knew as soon as my eyes beheld her that she was gone. I laid the back of my hand against her forehead. It was cool to the touch. I laid my ear against her chest. No heartbeat. Slumping back into the chair beside the bed, I took her hand in mine, crying my grief at losing the one person in my life who, I knew, had always truly understood me. She was gone. Gone forever. I had never felt so alone.

Grandpa shuffled into the room, having heard me moving around in the middle of the night. He saw me weeping and knew. Like butter as it melts, his body drooped, and he let out his breath with a small sob. He went around to the other side of the bed, leaned down, and embraced her still form. Then he kissed her forehead and stood up, regarding the woman he had loved for over fifty years.

"She passed in her sleep," he said, tears welling in his eyes. "That's good."

I kissed her good-bye. "I love you, Grandma. Godspeed," I told her.

Grandpa put his arms around me, and we wept silently. I had known in my heart, if not my head, as soon as I'd read Mumma's note telling me she was sick that this moment would come. It was the reason I had hurried to New York. The reason I had wanted to care for her. And now she was gone from this world.

No time to grieve; there was work to be done. I wrote letters to Papa and Mumma, and the aunts and uncles, informing them.

Grandpa took the letters with him to town when he visited the undertaker.

While he was away, I washed her body gently one last time, dressed her in her finest clothing, and fixed her hair. I did not cry as I did this task but rather talked with her, telling her all the things I wanted her to know and the cherished memories I had gathered from spending time with her throughout my short life. I wanted her to know how much I loved her.

Grandma had led a simple life, spending the past decades taking care of her family, attending church, and making an occasional trip to town to make necessary purchases. It was a life full of giving to her husband and family as she raised up her children, cared for their home, and tended to their meals, their clothing, and their illnesses.

I dressed myself in a black mourning dress I found in Grandma's closet, as I hadn't brought anything appropriate. The undertaker arrived and laid Grandma out in the living room as if she were ready to receive guests. He provided the black crepe and ribbon, which I hung on the outside of the door to notify the neighbors of her passing. I was obligated to accept each visitor as they came by the house to pay their respects.

The one ray of sunshine in an otherwise dreary time was when my best friend from school came by, the one who'd given me her very own copy of *Little Women.* I was able take a few moments of respite to catch up with her and tell her about my betrothal. I told her about my job at Stafford House. Unwilling to laugh out loud in the presence of the dead, we clapped our hands over our mouths and shared a silent chuckle when I told of my sprained ankle mishap and ensuing relationship with my Ethan. We could have talked for hours. I hadn't realized how much I had missed her until I saw her again. I took her hand in mine and promised sincerely to write often.

The bereavement did take its toll on Grandpa. By the end of the second day, his face was ashen, and the wrinkles and lines were deeper and more pronounced. I made him eat, then fixed him a hot toddy and sent him to bed. The following day we would lay Grandma in her final resting place.

Although I was very fatigued, I sat up with her through the night. I knew all the superstitions about people not really being dead and possibly coming back to life, or about protecting her against evil spirits. I knew it was all poppycock. I just couldn't stand for her poor, frail little body to lie cold and alone through another long night. I gathered the quilt from her bed, wrapped it around myself for warmth, and settled into the old squeaky rocking chair. While I sat there, I wrote her a letter, my final words to her:

Farewell my dearest Elizabeth, my sweetest Grandma,

Years from now I will still be missing you. I will think of you often. In my mind's eye, I will see you in the garden planting seeds or picking vegetables, in the kitchen cooking the supper, by my bedside comforting my fears or my ills. I will recall our many conversations as you explained life to me. I will repeat your many proverbs as I follow my own path. I am making my own memories now, Grandma. I will never ever forget the wonderful woman you have been to me.

Yours always,
Eliza Jane

I folded the letter and tucked it into the pocket of her skirt where she might find it in the afterlife. Maybe a silly thing to do, but I didn't care. Somehow it made everything better. I sat down again, folding myself into her quilt and inhaling deeply her scent that remained within its fibers. I laid my head against the back of the chair.

For the first time I could remember, as I sat in silence, I was fully aware of the passing of time. Life seemed so short, the tiniest fraction of a moment in the whole scheme of things. Our time on earth was spent working day in and day out, seldom noticing more than the changing of the seasons. I was nineteen years old. Grandma had lived to the age of sixty-seven. If I lived as long as she did, that meant I only had forty-eight years left. I felt sudden alarm that, if I sat there too long, my own life would pass by without notice.

I want to go home, I thought. *Home.* I smiled to myself in surprise. When had Michigan become home to me? I longed to be back in the arms of my lover, whom I missed most desperately. I didn't want to spend one more minute away from him. Filled with the memory of his strong arms around me, the touch of his lips against mine, I finally fell asleep.

We laid Grandma to rest in the church cemetery the following day. It was a cold and drizzly spring day. My aunts, uncles, and cousins who were close enough to travel, as well as many of the neighbors who had known Grandma for years, were present at her graveside. Later everyone came back to the house for the traditional Irish wake.

I went through the motions of the day, no longer feeling the dreadful sadness that had hung over me since her passing. Nor was I happy. It seemed like there was someone missing; every time I turned around, I would expect to see her or hear her, but no one was there.

Papa's two youngest sisters, Aunt Letitia and Aunt Rose, were there to play the part of hostesses. I slipped into the role of servant once again, seeing to the needs of our guests, taking their coats, and bringing a hot drink to each. I had placed a white linen cloth, napkins, plates, and silverware onto the table and arranged the many dishes of food brought by so many of the bereaved. Afterward, with help from the aunts, I washed and dried all those dishes and put the house back in order.

It was a long and tiring day, but I was filled with gratitude for all of the wonderful comments and stories, both funny and sweet, about everyone's experiences with Grandma. My aunts were going to stay for a few days to make sure Grandpa was going to be all right on his own. It was time for me to return to my own life.

CHAPTER 26

I HARDLY RECOGNIZED THE LANDSCAPE AS I WALKED THE SHORE ROAD TOward the Kilpatrick farm. Spring was in full bloom. I had left on a cold, dreary late winter day and returned to find summer knocking at the door. Already full of life, the fields swayed green in the breeze. Birds chirped, insects hummed, and my heart felt so full I wanted to sing out loud. It was so warm for this time of year, I was perspiring in the black dress I wore out of respect for Grandma. But my heart felt anything but black.

I found Ethan on our land, working with his dad and a team of oxen to pull stumps from the newly logged section. Mr. Fitzpatrick spotted me first and greeted me with a wink and a smile but kept his silence as I approached my beloved. The expression on Ethan's face when he looked up from his work changed instantly from creased brow to brilliant smile. He removed his gloves and swept me up in an embrace, swinging me in a circle before setting me down. In spite of the fact that we were not alone, his lips found mine in a deep, longing kiss that took my breath away.

Mr. Fitzpatrick cleared his throat and said, "It's as good a time as any for a break. Think I'll head up to the house."

We joined him after a time, walking with our arms about each other's waists, hardly able to keep our eyes—let alone our hands—from each other. *Absence truly does make the heart grow fonder,* I thought.

We sat down to the noon meal with Ethan's family and shared our news, although mine was not so uplifting.

"But now you're back, my lovely bride," Ethan said. The look in his eyes made me blush to my roots.

"I'm so happy to be back," I said.

"What are your plans?" Mrs. Fitzpatrick asked.

"Well, first I have to see if I still have a job at Stafford House. And I have many sewing projects to complete, although my sisters likely made some headway on those. And I might have time to make a new dress for the wedding. I'll be out of mourning by then and glad to trade the black for some color."

"We have the ground cleared at the building site," Ethan said proudly with a nod to his father.

"Could we take a walk over there before I go home?"

"Of course. I can spare a bit of time," Ethan said, standing up and taking me by the hand.

"I should help with the dishes first," I said.

"Nonsense, my girl. The girls and I can take care of the cleanup. You kids go on and have your walk." Mrs. Fitzpatrick walked to the porch with us. "I'm so sorry for your loss, but I'm very happy you're home."

I gave her a quick hug, and Ethan and I made our way down the edge of the fields and across the stream. The whole building site had been cleared and leveled.

"I'll dig the well here," Ethan said, pointing with the toe of his boot, "and the house will be over there, where we decided last year, and the barn a short distance away. The paddock will be fenced in, in back of the barn," he went on, "and I'll finish fencing the boundary before next year's planting."

He had a clear vision, I could tell. He had a far-off look in his eyes, as if seeing it complete in the future. I shared his enthusiasm, as this was to be my home for years to come, but was overwhelmed by the amount of work that still had to be done.

"I have only one request about the house," I said.

"Your wish is my command," he said solemnly, with a courtly bow.

I grinned at him. "I would like a window in the kitchen so I can see out while I'm working."

We walked the perimeter of our imaginary house. "Would you like a view of the road?" he asked looking toward where the drive would be. "The barnyard? Or the garden?"

I thought for a moment. "The garden," I said, smiling up at him. "Are you building the house first, or will you have a barn raising?"

"I'll keep using my dad's barn for the time being since we are working both places together. The house I will build this summer. Your brothers have said they will help with the construction. Maybe I can get some more of the fellows to volunteer from the mill and have a real work crew."

I was filled with such joy at the thought of going to my own home when we were married rather than living with his folks. He grabbed me by the hands suddenly and pulled me toward him.

We kissed again for a long moment. The kiss deepened, and I pulled away. I didn't want to make the waiting for marriage harder than it already was.

"I have to be on my way," I said.

He took a deep breath and blew it out. "Would you like me to drive you home in the wagon?"

"Oh, heavens no," I said. "It's such a beautiful day. I'm going to walk."

"When are you returning to Port Hope?" he asked.

"First thing in the morning," I told him.

"Then I will try to be out on Sunday after church. I'll stop by and say hello to your folks on my way."

"If you can't make it I will understand, Ethan. I know there is such a lot to be done," I said, starting to walk away.

"Sunday is a day of rest. I'll do my chores, go to church, then come your way," he said. Then he smiled his cocky smile and put his hat back on.

Oh, how I had missed him. I rushed back over to him and wrapped my arms around him in a fervent embrace. We kissed again. Then I pulled away and started to walk toward the road. I yelled back, "Tell your mother thank you for dinner."

He waved to me, and I looked back again to find him still watching me. I waved to him and almost skipped down the road, so full of happiness was I.

* * *

The only other person who rivaled Ethan's joy at seeing me was my sister Roseanne when I returned to Stafford House the next day.

"You're here," she shouted, coming out the back door of the house. "You're finally here."

We hugged and went down to the kitchen so I could greet Cook. Mrs. Stafford had gone to Sand Beach for a luncheon. Cook was having a late breakfast, and we sat down to join her. I told them all about my time in New York. Roseanne had read the letters I'd sent to the farm, so she knew most of the story already. Afterward, I went up to our attic bedroom, changed into my uniform, and put my things away.

It felt good to be back to my job, mind-numbing and muscle-wrenching though it was. As I fluffed up the beds and dusted the furniture, I allowed my mind to wander toward those pesky sewing tasks I'd been putting off for the past few months. Now that time was upon me, I was suddenly in a hurry to get back to them.

In the evening Roseanne showed me how much she had completed on the quilt squares.

"I finished the tulips," she happily announced. "I would have started sewing the squares together, but I thought you'd like to be here for that part."

"Oh my, this is wonderful," I said. "Thank you so much. I was thinking maybe of having a quilting bee early this summer."

"This isn't all that has been finished," she smiled coyly at me.

"What do you mean?"

"Mumma and the girls have some things ready as well," Roseanne said.

"But Mumma didn't say anything when I was there," I told her.

"I think they want to surprise you. So don't let on that I said anything and get me in trouble."

"Oh, I won't," I promised. "I saw Ethan yesterday. He has big plans to build a house for us this summer."

"Eliza, you are so lucky. I can't believe how lucky you are. I'm positively green with envy," she said.

"How's Billy?"

"Who knows?" she said. Her face fell from its beautiful smile and radiant eyes to a look of sadness. "I decided to quit chasing him. Mumma told me to let him go, and if it's meant to be, he'll come back to me."

I sat down on my cot. "So, the whole time I've been gone you haven't seen him?"

"Nope," she said with finality. "I stayed in Port Hope almost the whole time. Heaven knows I've had plenty to keep up with here. But really, Eliza, I'm all right."

I looked at her searchingly. She turned away from me and got into bed. I changed into my nightgown and blew out the lamp. Before I fell asleep, I thought I heard her softly weeping. I turned over on my cot, trying not to let her mood affect my contentment, and fell quickly to sleep.

My life settled into the old familiar routine. Some weekends I was able to get away and see the family or have Ethan come to see me. He came by almost every week through the spring, and as we were having such unusually fine weather, we were able to take walks down to the lake, sometimes putting our bare feet in the water. Roseanne, true to her word, did not go home on the weekends. Instead, she continued to work on my quilt, taking turns with me at the sewing machine until the top was completed.

CHAPTER 27

June arrived, bringing the long days of summer. I pressed and folded the finished quilt top and got ready to take it back to the farm to show Mumma. It was Roseanne's birthday the following week. Not wanting her to miss her own birthday celebration, I pleaded with her to come home with me, and she finally gave in.

We walked along the shore road, enjoying the early morning air of a day that promised to be warm. The leaves on the trees along the road were fully green now with the onset of the summer months. It had rained the night before, and I thought how joyful rain always made farmers as their fields brought forth new life from each crop they planted. Papa was happier this year, having finally cleared enough ground to start making a profit from his labors. Brother John's farm had been coming along as well.

Mumma and the children were happy to see us as we walked up the drive. She came out drying her hands on her apron and embraced Roseanne.

"Happy birthday, my sweet girl," Mumma said. "I was hoping we'd see you today. Emma is determined to bake you a cake. She said if you didn't come home, we should take it to you."

Roseanne smiled and her eyes lit up. "I wasn't going to come, but Eliza talked me into it. We've finished her quilt."

"Let's have a cup of tea, and you can show it to me. Are we going to have a quilting bee soon then?"

"We'd better," I laughed. "Otherwise it won't be much to keep Ethan and me warm on a winter's night."

"That shouldn't be a problem for newlyweds," Roseanne teased.

My heart skipped a beat, and I quickly changed the subject. "How's the farming?"

"Busy as ever," Mumma said.

We went into the house where Mumma put the kettle on, and I opened the quilt top up and laid it across the table.

"Oh," Emma breathed, "I like the tulips."

"I didn't think it would ever be finished, especially leaving it behind when I went to New York, but Roseanne did so much work on it while I was gone. We worked on it together with the Staffords' sewing machine to get it finished," I said, putting my arm around my sister and giving her a grateful squeeze.

"I'm going to go say hello to Papa and Dick," she said.

She left hastily and returned almost immediately. Mumma put out another cup.

"You didn't tell me the Bruces were here," she said accusingly.

"You didn't ask," Mumma retorted.

"What's happened?" I asked. "Roseanne, you've been acting so differently. I thought you were in love with Billy."

"Not anymore," she said angrily.

Mumma caught my eye and shook her head slightly so I dropped it.

"Who are you going to invite to the quilting bee?" Mumma asked.

"Annie and her mum, Mrs. Kilpatrick, and some of Ethan's sisters," I said.

"Can I help?" Emma asked.

"Of course," I said, "the more the merrier. And you sew better than I do." I smiled at her. "When should we do it?"

"On a Saturday? Maybe next week or the week after?" Mumma suggested.

"Let's plan it for the Saturday following the Fourth of July," I said. "The weather is sure to cooperate by then."

It was settled. I wrote out invitations to Mrs. Bruce and Annie, and Mrs. Fitzpatrick and her daughters Kathleen, Bridget, Mary, and

Maggie. I knew the younger girls wouldn't be sewing, but I didn't want to leave them out. I placed the letters in the mailbox and went back to the house to help Emma with the birthday cake.

The next day Ethan came by in the wagon to deliver Roseanne and me back to town. After we arrived, Roseanne said an abrupt good-bye and left us alone.

"What's the matter with her?" Ethan asked.

"You noticed?" I said.

"She certainly isn't her usual self," he replied.

"I'm not sure, but I think it has something to do with Billy Bruce."

"Ah," Ethan nodded knowingly.

"What do you mean?" I asked suspiciously. "Do you know something?"

"I know he's been seeing a girl from Huron City. Seems pretty smitten with her," he said.

My heart dropped into my stomach. "Oh dear."

Ethan shrugged. "I don't think it's anything serious yet, but she's a pretty girl. I can see why he's interested in her."

"Are you talking about Roseanne or someone else?"

He ducked his head and cleared his throat. "Um, the other girl, Eliza," he said. "Her family goes to my church."

"Do you like her too, then?" I asked, feeling suddenly jealous and a little worried.

"I'm not going to lie to you, Eliza, she's a good friend of my sister. I've known her for a while, but I've not been interested in courting her, if that's what you mean."

I was thinking back to our awful misunderstanding of last winter. I shook my head but didn't respond. My heart was racing. What was he saying? That the love of Roseanne's life had found another to love? And what about Ethan? Would he be tempted to find another as well?

"Eliza? Sweetheart?" He placed a finger under my chin, his eyes seeking mine. Realizing I was upset, he wrapped his arms around me and held me close. "Don't worry so much. We're fine, you and me, aren't we? I love you with all my heart. Did I tell you we started felling the trees for the house?"

It was the perfect change of subject. I pulled back and smiled up at him. "You have?" I said.

"Yes, we have. The timbers we're removing from the land I'll use for the house. There's quite a stack piled up already waiting to be hauled to the saw mill."

"Oh my, that's good news," I said, suddenly smiling. "I'm getting so excited for when we can finally be married."

"Now there's the smile I love so much," he said and kissed me long and deep. When the kiss ended, he said in a husky voice, "And I can't wait either. It's a good thing I have a lot of work to keep me busy."

* * *

My sister and I left Port Hope at daybreak on the ninth of July. The sky was clear and promised another hot summer day. It felt so good to be up and out, the sun barely peeking above the horizon over the lake. Our attic bedroom had been stifling—worse these days because it hardly seemed to cool off during the night. The countryside had lost that intense green of early summer, and the grass on the sides of the road had already started to bleach in the sun.

It felt so good to be outdoors. We walked with a lively step, chattering the whole way. Even my sister's doldrums seemed to have lifted with the anticipation of a fun-filled day at the farm.

When we arrived, we found Mumma's quilting frame set up under two old oak trees that would provide shade in the heat of the day. Georgie, with Finn at his heels, was carrying the ladderback chairs and then the benches one at a time from inside the house and placing them around the frame.

I still had to get the quilt layers put together before everyone arrived. Layering the backing, batting, and quilt top carefully on the floor, I recruited Emma and Roseanne to help me baste the layers together so they wouldn't shift about. This took a bit of time, and the smaller children sat nearby watching the process. When finished we ate a quick breakfast of bread pudding and milk then carried the quilt out like a guest of honor and laid it lovingly across the frame. It fit perfectly width-wise. It was wrapped around one end of the frame then stretched lengthwise to the other. Done in the nick of time.

My guests arrived carrying baskets of food to share in the evening when our project would—I hoped —be finished. Nellie, Robert Bruce, and Mary and Maggie Fitzpatrick were put in charge of Ben and Ethan's little brother and told to stay out of trouble. Mumma brought a pitcher of cool tea sweetened with honey for refreshment. There were nine of us altogether: Mumma, my new mother-in-law, Katy and Bridget Fitzpatrick, my best friend Annie and her mum, Roseanne, Emma, and me. There was room for six or seven to fit around the quilt at a time. Emma and Bridget were the alternates, ready to take a turn when someone wanted a break. There was much laughter and chatter as we all began threading our needles, excited to get started with this enjoyable task.

"When is the big day?" Mrs. Bruce asked.

"Hopefully in October," I said. "Ethan is already working on the house, although it may not be more than four walls and a roof when we move in."

"You are a very lucky young lady," she said. "When I married Mr. Bruce, we lived with his parents for a time. Not the most comfortable circumstances for a young couple in love, I can tell you."

"How old are you, Eliza?" Mrs. Fitzpatrick said.

"Nineteen last March," I said.

"That's how old I was when I got married," she said.

"I was a little younger," Mrs. Bruce said, "although we'd known each other most of our lives." She chuckled. "I hear you had a bit of an adventure recently."

"I'm not sure if I'd call it an adventure, but I did travel to New York to take care of my grandparents."

"And she got to go by train," Roseanne said.

"Yes. And I stayed until Grandma passed away."

"Your mother?" Mrs. Kilpatrick asked Mumma.

"No, my mother-in-law, God rest her soul," she said. "She hadn't been feeling well even before we left New York."

"I'm still worried about Grandpa," I said.

"I forgot to tell you, Eliza, we've had a letter. He's going up to Ontario with Letitia and her family."

"Oh good," I said breathing a sigh of relief. "I couldn't see him banging around that house all on his own."

"I want to hear more about how you met Ethan," Mrs. Bruce said.

"He rescued her on the side of the road," Roseanne told her, smiling wickedly and making it sound like he'd found a stray dog.

I laughed ruefully. "It was a strange way to meet someone," I agreed. "I was walking back from Port Hope on my own and not looking very carefully where I was placing my feet. I stepped in a hole, fell flat on my face, and twisted my ankle something fierce. It was all very embarrassing."

"That road can be treacherous," Mrs. Bruce agreed. "A young girl shouldn't be walking unaccompanied. It's unsafe."

I laughed aloud. "You can say that again. So there I was, sitting like a lump in the hot sun on the side of the road, with no way to walk and no way to get word to Papa to come and get me. Along came Ethan in the wagon, my gallant rescuer. Fortunately, he spotted me and pulled over. I can tell you, I was so grateful he happened along when he did."

"Or you would have been stuck there," Roseanne added.

"I'm sure there would have been others on the road that day," Mumma said.

"It was just meant to be," Mrs. Kilpatrick said. "Sometimes life takes you by surprise. You just have to be willing to go along for the ride and see where it takes you."

All of the ladies agreed. We covered many topics that morning. Annie had just been to see Mrs. Pottinger and told us things were looking up on that front.

"That's good news," Mrs. Kilpatrick said. "Maybe she'll remarry."

"She'll remarry out of necessity," Mumma nodded.

"What about you younger girls?" Mrs. Kilpatrick asked Annie and Roseanne. "Any special young man yet?"

Roseanne abruptly excused herself and left our circle.

"Did I say something wrong?" Mrs. Kilpatrick looked at her retreating form.

"I think we may have touched on a sensitive subject," Mumma said, then added, "My oldest son is courting." She winked at Annie.

Annie's cheeks turned pink, and she knotted her thread and pulled it through. "I'd better go find Roseanne," she said, excusing herself.

"I have three other sons who are single," Mumma said. "What about you, Katy?"

Katy was a sweet girl with brown hair that fell to her waist in waves. She was close to Roseanne in age but quieter and more reserved.

"I'm interested but not in any hurry," she said quietly.

Mumma wisely let the subject drop.

I paused to rethread my needle and noticed Emma and Bridget coming from the house, ready to replace Annie and Roseanne. We continued working until lunch. Having such a fine group of women who were experts with a needle, the stitching progressed rapidly.

At noon Mumma sent the children out to the field to deliver some food and replenish the water pail for the men. Moving our chairs and benches into a little group, but still under the shade of the oaks, we enjoyed a lunch of sweet tea, bread with butter and cheese, and some fresh berries. I ate quickly, eager to get back to work. While everyone was finishing, I pulled the quilt from the frame and moved it to a new section. When I looked up, all of the others had disappeared. I had just started to go look for them when I saw them returning from the house with parcels in their hands and beaming at me.

Taking their places again in our little lunch group, they made me sit in the middle. The younger children, who had come with them, each found a place on the ground near my feet. I could have squirmed from discomfort at being the center of attention. I felt absurdly like a queen holding court.

They must have been planning this for some time. Each person had made me something for my trousseau. With each package I opened, there were gasps of admiration. I was stunned by their generosity and in awe of the beautiful stitching. There were sheets and pillowcases edged with delicate embroidered flowers; hand towels and bath towels; a white linen tablecloth and matching napkins, each hemmed and perfectly square. By far the nicest gifts were those given by Mumma and my new mother-in-law: a fine-looking white blouse with lace on the collar, long cuffed sleeves, and small white buttons that looked like they were crafted from shells, and a beautiful, flowy, sheer white muslin nightgown. I gasped, picking up the nightgown, and then I felt the sudden heat of embarrassment rising from my neck to my face, knowing this was meant for my wedding night.

"This is the final present," Mumma said, handing me a small parcel.

I looked at the writing. It said, "To: Eliza Jane, From: Grandma." I looked up at Mumma, blinking back my tears.

"Open it," my sisters said.

Inside the package was a lovely ivory-white crocheted shawl. Grandma's wedding shawl.

"She sent it to me knowing you girls would be married in time. She wanted to make sure you had your 'something old,'" Mumma explained.

"It's so lovely," I whispered and handed it to Roseanne and Emma.

I wiped my tears and expressed my thankfulness to each person. "I don't deserve to be treated so royally," I said. "I'm so very grateful and truly appreciative of your fine work."

I was such a lucky girl, so richly blessed to have these women in my life. With so many items completed for my trousseau, I would have time to sew some new undergarments. I had been dreaming of a special wedding dress, but the cost of such an extravagance went against my frugal nature.

Nellie and Maggie took the gifts back to the house to place on Mumma's bed until later. For the remainder of the day we committed ourselves to completing the quilting. Roseanne rejoined the group, buoyed by the joy of the small party. Everyone knew better than to bring up the topic of beaux. Instead the older women shifted their interest to childbirth, seemingly to take it upon themselves to give me the benefit of their wisdom, all having raised numerous children.

"When Mr. Bruce and I were starting out, there was so much to be done, and the babies just kept coming every couple of years," Mrs. Bruce confided. "When we moved here to Michigan, and Robert was born, I just tied him across my chest with a shawl, and he slept and nursed as I kept working," she said with a laugh.

"It's wise to space your children a couple of years apart so you can get one out of diapers before the next is born," Mumma said.

Pregnancy and childbirth made me nervous. I knew I wanted children, but after Mumma's miscarriage, I was a little frightened. I wasn't about to admit that to anyone, as I knew full well that I'd probably be pregnant within the year. I'd just have to see what came to pass.

The women went on discussing their experiences. I wasn't the only one who wished they'd stop. I saw Roseanne and Annie look at each other and roll their eyes.

Annie piped up, "Do you think it will rain any time soon?" The older women looked up as though surprised the younger ones were still there.

Mumma shook her head doubtfully. "My husband says the farmers are talking drought."

"We had rain just before the last time we walked home," Roseanne said, "but I guess that was quite a while ago."

"It's not only the lack of rain but also the temperature. This is the hottest summer I can recall," Mrs. Bruce said.

"Eliza and I have to sleep up in the attic at Stafford House," Roseanne told everyone. "In a tiny bedroom with a window that doesn't open," she added dramatically.

"Oh, my goodness," Mrs. Fitzpatrick said, "that doesn't sound healthy."

"The window probably could open at one time, but someone painted it shut," I said.

"I think you should ask to be moved somewhere else or have the window repaired," Mumma said. "I'm sure there's another room in that big house where you could sleep."

"We're going to have to do something if these temperatures keep up," Roseanne agreed. "If we could open the window, at least we could get the benefit of the breeze off the lake."

"Maybe," I said, "but the room is on the opposite side from the lake, and it also gets the heat with the afternoon sun."

"My husband is concerned about his crops. And every August we worry about losing the well," Mrs. Bruce said.

"Couldn't we just dig deeper?" Annie asked.

"It's easier said than done," her mother replied.

Just as we finished the last rows of stitches, the men and boys came in from the field to get cleaned up. Ethan, his dad, John, and Will arrived soon after. Tommy, who had to come all the way from Grindstone, was the last to arrive.

Annie and Katy helped me remove the quilt from the frame and fold it up.

"It turned out so pretty. Now all you have to do is the binding," Annie said. "I'll bet you're getting excited about the wedding, aren't you?"

I smiled at her. "Yes, and I just love all the beautiful gifts everyone gave me today. It makes me feel like it's really going to happen instead of just a dream."

"Soon we'll be sisters," Katy said.

"I know," I smiled at her. "I can hardly wait until the waiting is over."

Mumma had the boys bring the chairs and benches back up to the house and carry the table out to the yard for supper. Nothing needed to be cooked since everyone brought food to share, and it was served cold. With every family bringing their favorite dishes, there was so much food. For dessert we had raspberries and cream. It was all so delicious and an absolutely lovely day all around.

It was the first time Ethan's family and mine had come together, and it was extra special having our best friends the Bruces with us too. Ethan and I sat together on the ground. I told him about the quilting and about the wonderful gifts everyone had given me for our home.

Billy was working hard at ignoring Roseanne. He sat with my brothers and laughed loudly at whatever they were talking about. Roseanne sat near Mumma and didn't even look his way. So different from the many gatherings over the past year and a half. I nudged Ethan with my elbow and nodded toward my sister. His eyes traveled across to where the boys were becoming more raucous.

"Billy makes me so angry," I said. "I can't stand to see Roseanne so sad. Why does he have to act so indifferent?"

"I don't think he's doing so intentionally," Ethan said. "He probably just doesn't know what to do about the situation. She'll be all right when she gets over him."

"I suppose. But she may never get over him. She was really in love with him."

Ethan shrugged, unconcerned. Finished eating, he stood and gave me a hand up, then gave me a quick peck on the cheek and went over to join the boys' conversation. I picked up our plates. On my way to take the dishes into the house, I motioned to my sister to join me.

"Stop pining over him," I told her when we were out of earshot.

"I can't help the way I feel," she said, leaning against the sideboard.

"What would you tell me if I were in your shoes?" I asked, knowing full well she would never let me get away with acting so glum.

She looked at me then. "I know you're right," she said with a shrug. She went back outdoors to gather the rest of the dishes. By this point the younger children had started a game of tag nearby and were shrieking and laughing, and soon the older girls dragged Roseanne by the hand and joined in the fun.

Near sunset the children, tired from playing, gathered back to where the adults were still sitting around the table talking. Mrs. Bruce called to my sister, who had flopped down on the grass with Ben in her lap. "Sing us a song, would you, Roseanne?" The children clamored in agreement and shouted out some of their favorite songs.

"When the shades of evening fall, zip, zip." She began to sing "The Mosquito," and the children joined in making the buzzing noises. "We can hear this insect call, z-i-i-ip!"

My sister had the sweetest, most pleasant-sounding voice. It was the envy of every young woman who heard her. And when she sang she had a way of lifting everyone's spirits, regardless of how she might be feeling herself. After a few fun songs for the children, she went on to the lead us in "The Star-Spangled Banner" and "The Battle Hymn of the Republic" in honor of the holiday just past. Everyone joined in on the chorus. Then she sang "Greensleeves" and, although she never looked at him, I knew she sang it for Billy.

I laid my head on Ethan's shoulder, and he put his arm around me. I glanced across to where Billy sat with my brothers. The look on his face was almost comical, so entranced was he while he watched her sing. I smiled and thought to myself, *Billy, my boy, you may think you're not in love with her, but I think you protesteth too much.*

By the time the first stars began to twinkle and the fireflies could be seen across the field, everyone had gone home. We carried Ben and Nellie to their beds, already asleep.

CHAPTER 28

With two and a half months to go until my wedding day, I returned to Port Hope. There were more people at Stafford House that summer, with relatives coming and going from back east and the Stafford girls home from school. With the added laundry and cleaning, there was time for little else. I was looking forward to the day I could walk away from this job and into my future as a wife and homemaker.

The hot summer continued without a drop of rain in sight. Roseanne courageously asked Mrs. Stafford to have a worker fix the window in our room so it could open and provide some ventilation. We also propped the doors open throughout the house to keep the air circulating. However, it didn't matter what measures we took; we still felt like we were being slow-roasted every night.

A couple of Stafford House guests had taken to their beds from dizziness and heat exhaustion. Dr. Dickinson paid a house call and came to find me after he had tended to them.

"Miss Ludlow, I know I can trust that you will make sure my patients drink plenty of fluids. Tea with honey or clear water will suffice," he instructed. "And I would prefer that everyone concerned would unlace those torture contraptions, or stop wearing them completely, and reduce the number of petticoats they deem necessary."

I squirmed in embarrassment and had to stifle a nervous giggle. It occurred to me that it would be a blessing to work for a man who wouldn't allow his household help to wear a corset.

"Yes sir," I said. "Could you suggest that to Mrs. Stafford? It would probably be better coming from you."

"Yes, I will," he agreed. "How are you and your sister getting along? I understand you are soon to be married?"

"Yes," I said, "in early October, to Ethan Kilpatrick."

He patted my hand in his grandfatherly way. "Congratulations, young lady. I'm sure you will make a fine wife and mother."

Mrs. Stafford passed on the doctor's orders to us that evening, that it would be permissible for us to leave the corset off and wear only one petticoat. What a relief that news was.

Roseanne tended to the guests' needs so I was able to get through more of my regular chores. The ladies were in the habit of having their tea in the shade of the large porch in the afternoons, and I was envious at how much fresh air they were able to get. I wondered how our family—all the farm families, for that matter—were doing in this heat wave. I knew Mumma, who had more common sense than most, would make sure everyone drank plenty of water.

Counting the days until the end of the summer, I had gone to Leuty's again and bought some plain white cotton for drawers, a petticoat, and a camisole. I dedicated every spare minute to sewing the remainder of my trousseau.

*　*　*

As I walked home from Stafford House for the last time before my wedding, I was grieved to see how the usually colorful countryside had turned to drab shades of brown, all of the vibrant vegetation bleached out from the intense sun. Some of the fields had already been harvested, and those that hadn't were clearly suffering from lack of rain. There was a smokiness in the air that left the sky hazy and dull.

The trees were shedding their leaves early too. My shoes crunched through piles of them, already dry and curled and fallen by the roadside.

I doubted I'd even be able to find any wildflowers for my bouquet. Maybe Mumma would have some flowers in her garden.

When I arrived home, Mumma was in the process of dabbing witch hazel on a heat rash that both Nellie and Ben had. She looked flushed and harried, the perspiration gathered along her forehead, and tendrils of hair were plastered to her skin. But when she looked up and saw me, her face burst into a welcoming smile.

"Oh, my goodness, Eliza, is it the end of August already?" she exclaimed.

"Yes, I'm at the final countdown, and I have a little more work to do on my trousseau," I said, giving her a hug. The little ones, tired and wilted, lay down for a rest, too old now for naps.

"I'll be able to help you in the evenings. We still have plenty of daylight," she said.

"How are Papa's crops?" I asked.

Mumma's face clouded with concern. "Dry as a bone," she said. "He thinks he'll be able to salvage the wheat, although it looks a bit stunted. Dick and Georgie are out harvesting with him now."

"How about the garden?"

"I was able to keep it watered until a couple of weeks ago, but the well level has dropped so low I didn't want to waste any drinking water. We still have the potatoes, onions, turnips, and beets that are probably going to be fine. Emma's out there now picking what's ripe. We've had fresh food daily, and I've been canning and drying everything extra."

I remembered it was almost two years ago, when I'd first met Ethan, that I'd had blisters on my hands from paring apples. I smiled at the memory of that first outing.

"This has sure been a dry summer," I said, "and hot. I don't re-member it ever being like this in New York. Everything is parched."

"We've had quite a dry spell, that's for sure, but it's almost autumn. It should rain soon."

"Not soon enough," Dick said, tramping through the doorway. He walked over to Mumma and showed her a nasty cut on his hand.

"Go wash your hands so I can see what I'm doing," she told him. "I may need to stitch that up."

"Aw, Mum, can't you just wrap it up?" he complained.

"Just do as you're told, Richard," she snapped.

My brother, who had reached his full adult height this year, stomped off to the pump to wash.

"My goodness, he's grown," I said.

"He's taller than Papa now." Mumma smiled.

Dick came back in with a look of panic on his face. "Well's dry, Mum," he said.

"It's not dry," she said impatiently, "you just didn't pump it enough."

"Yes, I did," he argued.

Mumma rushed past him out the door and to the pump. I stood by watching helplessly while she frantically grabbed the pump handle and lifted and pushed, lifted and pushed, over and over, to no avail. With fist to mouth, I bit down on my knuckles wishing and hoping the water would suddenly burst from the spout. Mumma finally gave up. She stood back, wiped her brow, and put her hands on her hips. Papa had always known he would have to dig the well deeper, but with so much to do, he'd just kept putting it off.

"Let me fix up that hand, and you can go out and tell Papa," she said softly with a defeated tone in her voice I had rarely heard.

She was near tears, I realized. Being out of water was a disaster of epic proportions. We used water for everything from cooking, cleaning, and laundry to bathing and drinking. In this heat, we had to keep drinking, especially the men and boys working in the field. A feeling of panic rose in my chest. I wanted to ask, what now? But I held my tongue. Papa would know what to do.

My parents were no strangers to the complications of life. They had both emigrated from Ireland as very young children whose parents had struggled to make a living in a new world. And here they were, a generation later, still struggling to put food on the table. They had to succeed because there were no other options. *Papa will know what to do,* I repeated to myself.

Papa strode in from the field with long, urgent strides, clearly dismayed but not surprised that the well was dry.

"Susan," he said to Mumma, "send the children to the lake with some buckets." Then he removed the bolts from the base of the iron pump and pulled it back. He knelt down and took a long, hopeful look into the hole.

"It's dry," he confirmed.

"Now what?" I asked.

"Nothing to do but dig it deeper. Dick, see if one of your brothers can come to help, then run over to John Carson's and borrow his auger."

Anxious to help, I said, "I'll go fetch the water." I pulled Georgie by the arm. We grabbed a couple of buckets, and he and I and the dog trotted down the path to the lighthouse by the lake. We walked out to the end of the long dock and filled the buckets. As we lugged them homeward, the water sloshed over the brim of mine and onto my skirt. Georgie carried his with two hands. His lips were drawn in a thin line. He had to stop every ten steps, pushing the dog away to keep him from drinking.

When we got back to the house, Mumma said, "Put them on the porch. We'll have to let it settle for a while."

We were on tenterhooks. I kept wondering what we would do in the long run if they couldn't reach water. Georgie, Finn, and I made more treks to the lake over the next few days.

On the weekend Roseanne came home to find the well dismantled and the men hard at work. "I needed a break," she said, and flopped into a chair. She was perspiring heavily from the strain of walking from town in the hot sun. "It's so hot and hazy that Mrs. Stafford's been having trouble breathing. The family left for the city for a few days. She's been running me ragged since you left, Eliza."

I frowned. "It hasn't been much of a picnic here either." I rubbed my forearms. "Georgie and I have been hauling water from the lake to help us get by while they work on the well."

"Why didn't you just go down to the creek?" she said, then hit her forehead with the heel of her hand. "Silly question." Her brows knit. "How long do you think this is going to last?"

"Papa says not to worry. Now it's so close to fall, it will rain any day."

"Sooner than later, I hope," she said.

By Sunday evening, after days of working the hand-operated drill, the well finally brought forth water. They had dug deep enough that it wasn't likely to go dry again this year. We all rejoiced in relief. Papa and the boys cleaned up with fresh water from the pump, and we all had a good, long, refreshing drink.

We ate a cold supper late that evening outside in the yard. Then my brothers headed home, and the little ones were sent to bed. The sky darkened with the onset of night, and I began looking toward the sky for stars but was unable to see anything for the smoky haze. I pulled my chair over next to Papa's, facing west.

"Beautiful colors tonight," I said, pointing toward where the sun had set and the sky had taken on a reddish glow.

Papa grunted and lit his pipe. "Farmers are burning the fields. Something I was going to do myself before I had to dig a new well."

I didn't respond for a time. Then I said, "I'm going to walk over to see Ethan tomorrow. I want to see how the house is coming along."

"I don't want you walking that far alone, Eliza," Papa said.

"I've done it a dozen times," I argued.

"It's not safe. Air's so hot and dry, we might as well be sitting in a tinderbox," he said, his brow furrowed with creases.

"Are you worried?" I asked.

"Burning's got to be done," he said with a shrug.

"Well, I'm going to turn in," I told him. "Goodnight, Papa." I leaned down to kiss him on the cheek.

"Sleep well, daughter."

Disappointed not to be able to visit Ethan, I sat in Mumma's rocker to write him a quick letter. Then I went to bed, lying down on top of the covers and praying for a cool breeze. I thought about what Papa had said: *We might as well be sitting in a tinderbox.* What I took to be Papa relaxing at the end of a long day of sweltering under the sun maybe wasn't relaxing at all. He'd been tense and vigilant. Usually he'd be sound asleep when the sun went down. Did he think something awful was going to happen? A feeling of unease ran from my brain to my gut.

Too hot and tossing and turning thinking about Ethan, I didn't sleep well that night. I felt like I'd just finally dozed off when the rooster began to crow.

Chapter 29

For all intents and purposes, that Monday should have been like any other Monday in the dog days of summer, except it was a hundred degrees. In the shade. At seven o'clock in the morning. There was an odd sky. It had looked strange for days, but today it was eerily peculiar. The cerulean blue was masked by the yellowish-gray of smoke and dust-filled air. And the sun appeared, unbelievably, like a small, orange orb glowing through a shroud. It looked so bizarre that prickles ran up my arms and the back of my neck. I had already broken out in a head-to-toe sweat, and I hadn't even begun my chores. I washed my face and hands in a basin of cold water and then poured it over my head. It felt absolutely heavenly as it trickled through the tightly bound strands of my hair, down my neck, and through the layers of my clothing.

"What in the world?" Roseanne remarked as she and Emma came outside.

"What's wrong with the sun?" Emma asked, frightened.

"I think it's all the smoke in the air," I said. "Papa says the farmers are burning off their fields, and a lot of them are burning leftover piles of slash."

"They used to do that in New York too," Roseanne said, "but I don't ever remember the sky looking like that."

I shrugged my shoulders, not knowing what to think, and went back into the house for something to eat.

We had a cold breakfast of bread and butter and cheese, some boiled eggs left over from the day before, and coffee. Papa and Dick had gone out to one of the fields at daybreak to turn the soil with the plow before the heat of the day. Emma, along with the younger children, was given the job of moving the bound sheaves from the grain harvest to the hay-mow, at which she screwed up her face in dislike. I sympathized with her, although not enough to trade places. It was sheer misery in this heat to be covered in dried pieces of grass, dust, and mites. Mumma took on the suffocating job of canning inside the hot house so as not to lose any of the produce from the garden. Roseanne and I tended the laundry. Everyone was so busy, we hadn't even noticed the wind pick up in the early afternoon.

About the time I heard Mumma's heirloom clock dong once through the open door of the house, my stomach started to growl for lunch. It was getting more difficult to see, and without looking up I smiled, hoping it was rainclouds moving in. *We could sure use a downpour of rain,* I thought. But within a few minutes, the daylight had become so dim it looked like dusk. I glanced up from where I was running clothing through the wringer to find a darkened sky. The previously orange ball of the sun was now red, but it wasn't from rainclouds.

The horse and cows, who'd been put into one of the fields to chew on the stubble, were making a lot of racket, neighing and mooing. The horse was excitedly circling the field at a gallop. Roseanne and Nellie, who had been laughing as they pinned sheets to the clothes line, suddenly began screaming. Mumma came to the open door.

From the west I could see smoke billowing our way. Lots of smoke. *Oh my God,* I thought, stomach churning in fear and bile rising into my throat.

"Fire!" I screamed.

Papa and the boys came running in from the field. I went to fetch the children from the barn, and Mumma quickly brought out a stack of napkins that had been worn as dust masks during the harvest and soaked them at the pump. The little ones ran to her side, and she deftly tied a wet napkin around each of their faces, covering nose and mouth. She ordered them not to remove it. I followed suit, placing one around my own face and then helping my brothers and sisters with theirs.

"Get all the food moved into the cellar," Papa shouted. "Dick, we've got to try to soak down the house."

I went into the house to find Mumma trying to strong-arm the old clock from its position on the wall.

"What are you doing?" I yelled to her.

"Get Papa. We've got to save the clock," she yelled back to me.

Papa and Dick stopped what they were doing to help Mumma. They tipped the clock onto its side and carried it out to the field. "Grab that shovel, Eliza," Papa ordered.

I followed him bringing it along and wondering what good it was going to do.

Papa frantically dug a trench the length of the clock, and they buried it under a hill of dirt. I ran back to find Roseanne and Emma rushing back and forth from the house and garden moving every food item they could carry down the stone steps into the cellar under the house. Not bothering to pick the vegetables from the vines and bushes, Mumma was pulling up whole plants from the garden, leaving only the root vegetables in the ground. I pulled the still-damp sheets off the line and threw them over the food, hoping against hope that they would provide some kind of protection.

The sky was ominous. Daylight was obliterated, plunging us from a dark day into nighttime. Particles of ash rained down as we worked, and the heat was so intense I felt like I was breathing fire. No one said a word but carried out their assigned tasks. My heart was in my throat as I ran about trying to salvage pots and pans, dishes, utensils, clothing, whatever I could get my hands on, putting everything in the cellar.

Papa was throwing buckets of water onto the house. Roseanne, Emma, Mumma, and I joined the effort, and I worked the pump until I had blisters. Dick had made his way onto the roof with a rope, and he and Georgie worked out a system of hauling the buckets up to soak the shingles.

John, Tommy, and Will came at a run from their place and grabbed the buckets out of our hands. "You're out of time," my oldest brother yelled. "The fire already burned through Huron City to the Bruces'. We've got to take cover!"

Papa stopped in his tracks. We all froze in place and looked at each other. Dick climbed—almost jumped —down from the roof.

Where? Where was there shelter from fire? I looked around me. Everyplace, everything, everywhere was flammable.

"The field," Papa yelled.

Nobody questioned or even considered doubting this solution. We ran for our lives. I grabbed up Ben in one arm and Nellie by the hand and ran as fast as I could.

Papa and the boys dug shallow holes and ordered us to lay on the ground with our faces in the dirt. I quickly showed the little ones what they were to do. The soil, which had been hard-packed, had just that morning been turned with the plow and was loose and supple. I dug deep, my fingernails breaking off with the effort, taking handfuls of soil and packing it around Ben and Nellie, covering them as completely as I could. I turned to look for the other children. Emma and Roseanne were lying face down, but Georgie was nowhere to be found.

I began to yell, "Georgie!" my heart throbbing in my chest and my throat quickly closing up as panic overtook me. This was no time for him to be pulling one of his disappearing acts. I continued to scream his name. Mumma and Papa turned around, confused.

"The dog!" I yelled, guessing where he was. "He went to find the dog!"

At that moment, Georgie appeared like a wraith through the smoke, stumbling over the clumps of dirt, his thin young arms wrapped desperately under the dog's forelegs, clumsily dragging him along. Boy and dog were nearly the same size in this vertical position, but Georgie persisted, determined to save his beloved pet. He stumbled forward next to me, a racking cough jarring his whole body. He stubbornly held onto Finn with one arm around his neck lest he decide to give in to instinct and run from the smoke.

No time to scold. I was having trouble breathing myself, and my eyelids felt like sandpaper rubbing against my eyes. In an eerie, unnerving howl, the wind changed directions, sending the fire right at us and bringing with it a torrent of ash and cinder. We were on death's doorstep with no place left to flee. Quickly I buried Georgie and Finn as best I could.

All of us lay there in the dirt and hoped against hope that the perimeter of the plowed field would provide some kind of shelter. With my head in the hole, sound became muffled except for the thumping of my own heart as it pounded its way out of my chest. My breathing was labored, and I sucked air in from the ground through the napkin around my face. I couldn't bear the sound of the children's crying next to me. In spite of the thin, protective layer of earth, they were completely and totally exposed to the elements. We were far and away from anything resembling safety.

There was no stopping the nightmare. The roof of my mouth prickled like needles, and I felt a weight settle in my chest as I was filled with dread. *God help us!* my mind pleaded. *We are going to die here, burned alive in the middle of Papa's field!* Every part of my being screamed at me to get up and run.

The wind that had blown so powerfully from the south and west suddenly changed direction again and blew with a gale force from the north, like the roar of a monstrous mythological beast. Burning embers found us, easy victims, unprotected and unable to defend ourselves. I jumped with a start as the cinders found their way through the layers of my clothing and burned my skin and hair. My sisters began to scream, and I heard Papa order them to stay down.

What about the animals? The chickens were surely roasted alive. The horse probably jumped the fence and headed for the lake, leaving behind the poor cows and pigs.

Ethan's handsome face flitted across my mind. *Oh my God, I'll never see him again.* I choked back a sob. I could not, would not, think of him as dead. I conjured up an image of him in my mind's eye, laughing with that cocky smile and those teasing blue eyes. That was the only way I would think of him. I couldn't bear to imagine him any other way. And what about our best friends, the Bruces, and all of our other neighbors?

And poor Mrs. Pottinger, widowed with all those children to care for on her own? *Dear God,* I thought, desperately trying to pray, but I couldn't put words together to form a prayer.

Suddenly there was an earsplitting eruption from the direction of the barn. *Maybe the hay,* I thought. We were in the center of it now. An inferno was ingesting the barn, the house, and all the dry vegetation that surrounded us. I was sure it was the end of the world and fought to keep the panic from overwhelming me. Any minute it would be over. We would be dead, wiped from the face of the earth.

The mythological beast surrounded us, trying to find a way to reach the succulent humans trapped in the middle of a dirt field. It snapped and roared in ferocious rage, spitting fire as it devoured our farm. *Please make it stop. Please make it go away,* the child within me begged. Desperate screaming and crying of my brothers and sisters filled my ears. I longed to soothe them, to wake them from the nightmare that engulfed us. Then I realized it wasn't the little ones after all—it was the sound of my own screams I was listening to.

I choked back my cries and listened for the sounds of the rest of my family, but all I could hear was the roar of wind and fire as the conflagration burned on. One by one the sugar maples along the fence line exploded into fire. I was lying on my face in the middle of a battlefield. An eternity seemed to pass. The minutes crept by. The monster, consuming all in its path, was still looking for sustenance. Snapping and sizzling, it burned on. I couldn't imagine there was anything left for it to devour except our poor selves. I couldn't breathe. *Oh, sweet Jesus, let me live,* I prayed.

Eventually the monster, having tired of the game, moved on to a better place. The roaring became distant, and around me I could hear the small sounds of fire that had burned down to coals. I chanced lifting my head up to look around. The sky glowed an evil red-orange, and the air hung thick with smoke. It looked like another place, another time, another existence, one I had no frame of reference to identify. Nearby a single blue flame danced eerily a few feet from the ground, mesmerizing me. I began to choke as my mouth filled with ash and smoke.

Papa heard my coughing and yelled, "Stay down. We aren't out of this yet."

Immediately, I lowered my face back into my shallow grave. The minutes and hours ticked painfully by. Our purgatory continued throughout the night, bringing cinders from the air, torturing us with burns over our heads, backs, and limbs. Every so often, I heard one of my brothers or sisters yell out in pain. I prayed none of us would ignite.

CHAPTER 30

Exhausted from my vigilance and starved for oxygen, I must have finally lost consciousness because the next thing I knew it was morning. Except for areas still smoldering around us, it was quiet—deathly quiet. No bird song, no animals lowing for feed, no leaves blowing in a gentle breeze. No sound of life anywhere around me until I heard Mumma's voice, raspy and soft, tell Papa to check the younger children.

I'm still alive, I thought. That in itself was a miracle. I rolled over. The rising sun barely lit the earth, nothing but a red ball glowing through the clouds of smoke and ash that hung over us and blotted the sky to the horizon.

I sat up, retied my napkin over my nose, and turned to uncover the little ones, scooping the blackened soil off their little bodies, hoping against hope they would be breathing. Papa and I rolled them gently over. They had fallen asleep or had perhaps fainted. Dry riverbeds of tears cut through the soot covering their little faces. When they awakened, their eyes, circled in red and bruised from rubbing, were wide with fear. Neither spoke nor cried. They made not a sound, but they were alive, and for that I was grateful.

I reached over and touched Georgie, who still had the dog in a strangle hold. Quickly I crawled over to him and rolled him over. Finn rose and shook himself violently, but didn't leave his boy's side. Several spots on Georgie's face where he had been burned oozed blood through the ash and dirt, and he was not moving. I tried to speak to get Papa's attention, but all that came from my voice was a croak. I leaned down, placing my ear against his chest. His young heart still beat. He had just passed out.

Papa, noticing my distress, crawled over to where Georgie lay and made a quick examination. He was breathing, but his lips were slightly blue.

"I don't think he's getting enough air," Papa said.

Mumma was checking the girls. Emma was writhing in agony, her cry bursting forth as a hoarse screech. She held up one of her long braids, burned almost through and hanging by just a few hairs. Her hands went to her head, patting to check the damage, and what she found there made her weep the more. Glancing over I was relieved it was only her hair that caused her distress. Roseanne was in similar straits as Georgie but was aware. She had a racking cough and was wheezing to bring air into her lungs. Her clothing was burned through in small sections.

I looked over my own clothing. It was a miracle it had not caught fire. My dress was dotted with holes the size of quarters. I looked at a spot on my shoulder where bare skin showed through and a scab had already formed mixed with blood and soot. Sores on my legs and arms were angry and oozing, and other skin was covered in little blisters, but there was nothing life-threatening. I could barely recollect when they had happened. Mumma made her way to me to look at the sore on my shoulder, but I pushed her away.

Papa led the way as we dared to move from our haven in the middle of the field to the pump. John carried Georgie, who still hadn't woken up, and Tommy carried Roseanne, whose breathing was so labored and weak she was unable to walk. We had to be especially careful where we stepped, as parts of the ground were hot as coals where the fire had followed the roots and burned down into the ground. As cautious as I was, my feet felt as though they were cooking, and I was sure the soles of my shoes were melting.

Mumma and Papa, holding the youngest children in their singed arms, glanced around at the desolation. Their faces, completely blackened except for the whites of their eyes staring raccoon-like at our surroundings, told the story. All was lost. The fire had consumed everything their little farm had had to offer. Everything they had owned in the world had been stolen from them. The stone fireplace and chimney standing stubbornly amid the smoldering ruins marked where the log house had once stood. The only sign that this had once been a home. The barn was gone, as was the chicken coop; no clucks, neighs, or moos greeted us. The animals had disappeared, having either run away or been roasted alive.

After checking for heat, Papa pulled off his shirt and used it to grasp the pump handle, pushing and pulling until the water that came forth was clear, the ash having infiltrated absolutely everywhere. We untied the napkins from over our faces. Fresh, cold, heavenly water we drank, cupping a hand under the pump, each taking a turn, until we were sated.

Then we ran the napkins under the water and dabbed at sores on backs, heads, and necks. We cleaned up the best we could, although the ash, soot, and dried blood stubbornly clung to the skin with our sweat. Papa thought it best to retie the napkins as the air was still too foul to breathe.

We all huddled together there in what used to be our yard, afraid to move, afraid to speak. My feeling of terror had passed, and in its place was numbness. I stared through the smoke-filled haze. I couldn't cry, my tears having dried up. I was bereft. All of our hard work, Papa's hours toiling day in and day out—it was all gone.

Mumma and Papa knelt next to Georgie and tried to wake him up. Mumma had washed his face and poured cool water over the back of his head. Minutes passed. We held our breath waiting for some sign that he was going to be all right. Finally, his eyelids fluttered open, and we breathed a collective sigh of relief. He didn't speak, just closed his eyes again and rolled onto his side, curling himself into a ball.

"We can't stay here," Papa said. "We need to go find help."

"What about the cellar?" Dick asked. "Do you think any of the food is left?" He started toward the ruins of the house.

"Get back from there, Dick," Papa said. "It's still burning. We'll wait until we're sure the embers have burned themselves out."

It was at that moment I remembered my trousseau. The clothing, linens, and the beautiful wedding quilt had been carefully folded and stacked in a corner awaiting my move to my new home as a married woman. I looked longingly toward where they had been and hung my head, grief-stricken. All gone, nothing left. All of my months and months of work. I buried my face in my knees. Emma, who had been watching me, moved over and put her arm around my shoulders.

"I'm so sorry, Eliza," she whispered. I put my arms around her, grateful for her comfort.

"I'd like to go up to our place and check on the damage," Tommy said.

"No point," John answered. "I'm sure it's in the same state."

"We all need to stay together," Papa said. "Let's walk to Port Hope. The fire may have burned out once it reached the lake. The village might have been spared."

"Is it safe to walk?" Mumma asked. "The ground is so hot it might burn through our shoes."

"It's a chance we'll have to take," Papa replied, resolute. He gathered Georgie's coltish body up in his arms with Finn following at his heels.

Dick picked up Ben, Nellie was hoisted onto Will's back, and John and Tommy supported Roseanne. It would be a very long and treacherous hike in these conditions.

When we reached the shore road, we heard a yell and turned to look. A group of people, including the Bruces and Mrs. Pottinger, her children, and her farm worker were walking toward us. The looks on their faces mirrored ours. Shock and terror still held us all in their grasp.

John left Roseanne and hurried to Annie's side where they embraced. I watched as he tenderly kissed her forehead and then her lips. Billy rushed to Roseanne's side to replace John, and put an arm under her to help her walk.

A ragged group of refugees, we slogged slowly southward, trusting that Port Hope would live up to its name and provide food, shelter, and medical attention. Although nobody came through unscathed, some burns were worse than others and would need careful tending.

It was the longest walk I'd ever taken to town. With every intake of air, I felt as though I was breathing fire, so raw were my lungs. When I looked over to Roseanne, I knew I was much better off. And Georgie, I couldn't even consider his condition, so frightened I was every time I looked at the blue tinge of his lips. The sores on my legs and back stung relentlessly, but I reminded myself that as long as I could feel pain, I was alive.

Some of the sights we passed were sure to give me nightmares for years to come. Animals of all kinds, having been overtaken by the firestorm as they raced to the safety of the lake, had had their coats and skin burned off, leaving charred remains of muscle and skeleton by the roadside and in former pastures. Luckily, we only saw animals and no human corpses, although there was not one single farm left standing as far as I could see in any direction. I wondered what was going to happen to us, left with only the clothing on our backs, no food or shelter to sustain us.

As we walked, my mind kept straying back to Ethan and his family. What had happened to them? *Ethan,* I cried out in my mind, choking down my fear. *Please, dear heavenly Father, let him live.* I could not bear it if anything had happened to him.

The village had not escaped the fire. Everything near the lake, the salt factory, the saw mill—including all the logs and lumber in the yard—and some of the shops had been burned to the ground. Even Stafford's dock, stretching out into the lake, was burned to the point of uselessness. The tall stone chimney, a part of the mill, remained. The singular remnant of a thriving business, it stood stark and alone. There was a swath of black soot on one side of the structure, evidence of the disaster it had survived. A couple of men, faces hidden by scarves drawn across their faces, were surveying the damage, kicking bits of debris with booted feet and shaking their heads in dismay. Out in the lake, a ship stood at anchor. Dozens of people were standing on its decks along the rails.

"Look, Pa," Dick said, pointing.

Papa nodded. "Only way back to port now is to row ashore."

On we trudged, silently hoping to find help, all of us in our party exhausted, hungry, filthy, and in shock. To our great relief, it looked like the lakefront was the only part of the town that was destroyed. We walked up State Street to find that most buildings remained almost unscathed. It was as if a line had been drawn and the fire had not been allowed to pass.

Two men were loading up a wagon with supplies at Angus McDonald's store. Papa, still carrying the limp body of Georgie, approached them and asked for help.

"The Masonic Hall," one of the men said, gesturing up the street. "That's where the others are. The docs have set up a hospital there."

Papa nodded his thanks, and we continued up the road.

We weren't the first to arrive. I gazed around at the crowd of people already there. I hadn't realized before then how far and wide the destruction was. Only the most seriously injured were allowed to enter. The rest were camped outside on the large porch that wrapped around the outside of the building and on the lawns. It was an eerie scene. Nobody was crying. Nobody was even speaking. All had the same wide-eyed look of shock and horror. I gazed at one group after another, all of them in the same condition as us. My eyes lingered on a boy about Georgie's age pulling on the leather sole of his shoe where it had burned through to his foot. It made me suddenly conscious of the sore spots on the bottoms of my own feet.

As soon as we entered the building, I saw Dr. Dickinson. I touched Papa on the arm to get his attention and pointed.

"That's Dr. Dickinson, Papa," I said. I went ahead and approached him. I was grateful that he recognized me.

"Eliza, my girl," he said, then turned to find the rest of my family, followed by the Bruces and the Pottingers.

"Could you have a look at my brother and sister and some of the rest of us?" I asked.

"Bring them over here," the doctor said. He tended to Georgie first, taking his thin body and laying him down gently on a bench. He did a quick examination and called for one of the women who was assisting him. She bustled over, wiping her hands on her stained apron. He listed what he needed, and she rushed off. He moved on to Roseanne and had her sit down at the end of the bench. The woman returned with another in tow, handing some supplies and bottles of medicaments to the doctor.

He quickly tended to Georgie then said to the second woman, "Take these people and treat their burns, then they can go outside to wait." We were led away, leaving Georgie and Roseanne behind.

"I'll stay here with the children," Mumma insisted, not wanting to leave Georgie in such a state.

I put my arm around her shoulders and pulled her along. "Don't worry, the doctor knows what to do to take care of them. We'll be right back after we've tended our hurts." She reached up and grasped my hand at her shoulder then followed me reluctantly.

My raw wounds stung and were covered with a sticky concoction of lard and honey, but somehow I felt better. We were sent back outside with the others who were deemed fit. As organized as the makeshift hospital seemed, there were no other creature comforts. Donated blankets were used for the more desperate fire victims. The rest made do with gunny sacks. I didn't mind, though I was longing for some soap to scrub away the irritating soot.

The peculiar silence remained. I sat down on the ground, and Ben and Nellie climbed into my lap and clung to me for dear life. Mumma was agitated. She sat, fiddled with the burned hem of her skirt, then stood and began to pace.

"I need to go back inside and check on the children," she said. Papa put his arm around her shoulders and tried to soothe her, but she pulled away from him. "I can't just sit out here," she said, her voice trailing off.

While they lie inside on the brink of death, I thought.

CHAPTER 31

I PEELED THE LITTLE ONES' FINGERS FROM MY DRESS, PASSED THEM OFF TO Emma, stood up, and took Mumma's arm. We found Roseanne and Georgie sleeping peacefully, both breathing a little easier. We sat down on the floor beside them. They were lying next to each other and covered with a large quilt. Neither stirred. Mumma took hold of Georgie's hand and held it tightly in her own. She bowed her head as if in prayer. I sat opposite her, near my sister, willing them well.

I gazed down at Roseanne's ravaged face, and tears sprang to my eyes. I'd spent so much time being jealous of her beauty, talent, and exuberant personality, none of which I shared. I was always so irritated with her. What would I do if I lost her? What would I do if there were no Roseanne in my life pushing me forward? I shivered at the thought and vowed that if she recovered, I would try to be a better sister.

The minutes and hours ticked slowly onward. I gazed around the large room, which was now full of people of all ages clinging to life. Hoarse coughing could be heard throughout the room as breathing had become a more desperate task than dealing with the burns that covered so much of their bodies. I knew not all would survive but prayed anyway, asking for God's mercy.

They say miracles often come in threes. That evening near dusk, Mumma and I took a short break and went outside to the rest of our family and friends. I sat down next to Annie. A horse and wagon had pulled up in front carrying several large pots of steaming soup and loaves of freshly baked bread.

"It's a miracle," I heard Mrs. Bruce say under her breath.

"A loaves and fishes miracle," Annie said to me. I nodded my head in agreement.

Cups, bowls, and spoons were brought out from the kitchen inside the hall, and we formed an eager queue to receive our portions. Several aproned women from the town began to tear chunks of bread and pass them down the line while soup was being ladled into the first few bowls.

A meal had never tasted as good to me as this simple chicken soup made with creamy milk. It was so filling and so satisfying that I couldn't help but sigh aloud as my fears of starvation receded. The stark, ashy faces with their wide-eyed stares were miraculously transformed. I saw many express their appreciation through smiles, murmured thanks, and a few tears of relief.

The second miracle was delivered from heaven that evening in the form of a downpour of rain. The skies that for months had refused to give up their life-giving water now opened their floodgates and poured down upon us. I heard some bitter expletives and a few rueful chuckles from adults around me. Some of the children began to spin and dance, their young faces tilted heavenward. It was a joy to watch. Their dance itself was an expression of thankful prayer.

Many who were now drenched to the bone crowded up onto the large covered porch. Women with young children and the elderly were allowed into the main hall to stay dry. I longed to join the ones dancing in the rain, so eager was I for a shower. Had they been able, Georgie and Roseanne would have been part of the dancing. Thinking of them, my moment of joy evaporated as I became aware of the uncomfortable coldness of the rain splattering against my clothing and the sores on my skin.

Mumma and I went back inside to continue our vigil. Roseanne awakened periodically for sips of water, but then she would lay back down in exhaustion. Georgie barely moved enough to indicate he was alive. The hospital room was abuzz with the murmurings of the additional people sheltering from the rain.

From my place beside Roseanne, I gazed around the dim room. I watched the elderly doctor shuffling from patient to patient and the village women who helped change dressings and give comfort and consolation. My eyes fell upon a young, yellow-haired woman sleeping across the room from me. The burns on her sweet, angelic face were covered in ointment and bandages. Vaguely, I wondered what her story was. My thoughts returned to Ethan, and waves of worry came crashing against me. It had been two days, and I had received no word. I wasn't going to be able to just sit here doing nothing. I had to move. To help. To find purpose while I waited.

I went to the kitchen where the bowls and cups were stacked in precarious piles. One of the women had filled a dishpan with warm water and soap.

"Here, let me do that," I said, grabbing a dishrag.

"No, no, dear. I'm fine. Go take your rest."

I shook my head. "I really need something to do," I said insistently.

"What is your name, dear?" she asked.

"Eliza Jane Ludlow," I replied. "My whole family is here."

"Aren't you one of the girls who work for the Staffords?" she asked.

"Yes," I said, nodding, "but I had just left my job to get married. But now…" my voice choked, not able to speak my worries aloud.

She patted my hand and pointed to an apron hanging from a peg on the wall. I quickly tied it around my waist and got right to work.

I worked through the night. Having finished the dishes, I moved through the rows of patients, helping wherever I could, even if just to give them a drink of water or walk them to the outhouse. Time passed quickly. Just as I finished with one patient, another was in need. In the wee hours of that morning, a third miracle occurred. Georgie woke up.

"Eliza Jane," Mumma called to me, "come quickly."

I rushed to her side, and lo and behold, Georgie's eyes were open. The first words from his mouth were, of course, about Finn.

"Where's my dog?" he rasped.

We laughed aloud. A waterfall of tears poured down Mumma's face. "Outside with Papa," she told him.

"What's the matter?" Georgie asked.

"Nothing, now," I said and smiled at him through my own tears of relief. "You had us pretty scared for a while there."

A young doctor who had just arrived on the scene to assist with the injured noticed our commotion and came over.

"So our young patient is recovering," he said, smiling.

"It seems so." I smiled back at him.

He extended his hand to Mumma. "I'm Dr. Herrington," he said, shaking her hand.

"I'm Mrs. Thomas Ludlow," she replied, "and this is my eldest daughter, Eliza Jane, my son George, and this young lady," she motioned to my sister, "is my second daughter, Roseanne."

Roseanne had awakened and was looking up at us from where she lay, her eyes shining clearly for the first time since the fire. I knelt down next to her and asked, "How are you feeling?"

"Better, I think," she said, her voice still hoarse.

"It's very nice to make your acquaintance," Dr. Herrington said. "I'll be back shortly on my rounds. Miss Ludlow, perhaps you could see if there is anything left of that soup for your brother and sister."

The rain had certainly doused the remaining fires, and later that day it let up. The men of the village divided themselves into groups with horses and wagons and set out to make the rounds of the area, searching for survivors, and to bury the dead. I prayed Ethan and his family would be found alive and well. The more time that passed, the sicker I felt with dread. They could have gone to Port Austin looking for help, but until I saw him, I would continue to worry.

By Thursday of that ill-fated week, most anyone who needed help had found their way to the village. The men who'd gone out to search had returned with grisly tales of the devastation throughout the county. I approached one of the men and inquired about Ethan's family. But the man shook his head.

"They live just off the shore road, a mile or so past Huron City. It's a big place," my voice trailed off as the man continued to shake his head.

Emma put her arm around my shoulders and pulled me away. "Maybe they didn't get that far," she said. "There's still a chance, Eliza. Maybe the fire missed them completely. You know how many times we've heard how it destroyed one building and missed the next."

I shook my head woefully. I didn't want to give up hoping. Until I went there and saw for myself, I would keep thinking of him as alive. But as the days passed, I had become more and more fearful of the worst. I returned to my duties tending the injured. I joined Dr. Herrington on his rounds that evening. I threw myself into my work, listening intently as he examined the people who had arrived on the wagons. Their injuries were gruesome, as they had gone without medical attention for so many days.

"Are any of these going to make it?" I asked him.

"Some, God willing," the young doctor replied. "They're very emaciated."

"What does that mean?" I asked.

"They've been without food and clean water and are wasting away," he replied.

The following morning, the town leaders met and voted to send Mr. Stafford to Detroit to solicit aid for the victims in our area. Meanwhile, the community continued to pool their resources. Mr. McDonald and the other shopkeepers emptied their shelves to help provide food for us, but the Masonic Hall and other nearby churches were full to the brim with survivors in need of everything required to sustain life. I had no doubt citizens from all over would respond when news of our need was brought to them, but I also knew it would be days, maybe even weeks, before more help arrived.

I was in the kitchen washing dishes again and thinking about our dire situation. The town wouldn't be able to keep this up forever. With nothing left but the ragged clothes on our backs—no money, no home, no food, and nobody to take us in—what was to become of us? Our only relatives were in New York and Ontario. Grandma was gone. Grandpa had moved to Aunt Letitia's. My head was constantly spinning but with no answer forthcoming.

I kept hearing people say, "God will provide." But I wondered where God had been when the fire had burned away all the farms and animals, killing some people and leaving others destitute. A feeling of bitterness was beginning to set in.

CHAPTER 32

"Eliza! Eliza Jane," Emma called out breathlessly, coming into the kitchen at a run. "He's here! Ethan and his father just walked into town."

I dropped the dishcloth into the soapy water and followed Emma at a run.

When I spotted Ethan, I stopped, feeling a little light-headed. He was blackened and dirty, and his clothes were hanging on him like rags, but he was the finest thing I had seen in days. I felt like a cool, clean wind had just swept through my soul, blowing all the worry and sorrow from my mind and replacing it with love and hope. I ran to him, put my arms around him, hugged him fiercely, and then gave him a quick once-over to check for injuries. So relieved I was at this first sight of him that I failed to see the look in his eyes. Finally satisfied that he was alive and well and not simply a wraith or vision, I looked up into his face. The lively, laughing eyes were dull and empty. The cold, unrelenting dread returned a hundredfold. He would not look at me. The light in his eyes was no more.

"You're safe," I said, my voice wobbly with emotion.

He nodded his head.

"You must be starving," I said. "I'll get you some soup."

"No," he said, voice low and expressionless. "We have to talk."

"You'll feel better after you've eaten," I insisted, taking him by the hand.

"No," he said, loudly, pulling his hand back from mine. "I have to talk to you. Now."

I looked around for someplace to go. "There isn't much privacy here," I said.

"It doesn't matter," he said.

I braced myself. "All right then, talk to me. Where are your parents and the children?"

"Dad's here with me." He looked away again. "The rest—" he choked, "the rest are gone."

"What?" A rushing sound filled my ears. I couldn't hear properly. "What did you say?" I asked stupidly.

"Mum, the girls, baby Johnny. They're dead, Eliza. All of them."

My mouth dropped open, and my hands came up to push against him in denial as I shook my head from side to side, stunned.

"They were in the well. Dad thought it would be the best place to keep everyone safe while we fought the fire. They all climbed in, all the way down to the bottom."

"But," I started to interrupt.

"There wasn't but a foot or two of water," he rushed on, trying to get the whole dreadful tale told. "Then the wind came up," his voice became so soft only his lips were moving.

"Ethan?" I asked.

He looked back at me and into my eyes. "They suffocated," he whispered the words.

I put my fist in my mouth to stifle the scream that was trying to escape. My stomach, which had been near empty for days, churned sickeningly. I placed my arms around him to comfort him, but he pushed me away.

"Stop, Eliza. Let me say what I'm here to say," he said, looking away from me. "I'm leaving."

My heart stopped. Then it started again with a pounding like it was trying to leap from my body. I put my hand up to my throat and tried to breathe. Had I heard him correctly? Before I could form a question, he continued, "Dad wants to go back east to his family. I'm going with him."

"But why, Ethan? Why do you have to go?"

"There's nothing left here for me, Eliza."

His words stung. I felt immediately hot then cold all over.

"It's all gone. All of it. I can't stay in that place anymore." His voice trailed off, and he looked toward the water.

But what about me? I wanted to say. *Don't you love me anymore?* But I couldn't bring myself to say it.

"Wh-when are you leaving?" I choked, my voice small.

"Right now. I'm only here long enough to say good-bye. There's a ship that's offered free passage to the city. Then we'll probably go on by train."

"Will you send for me? After you get settled, I mean?" I almost begged, leaning into him.

He shook his head. "Let it go, Eliza. It's over. It's all over. The house is gone, burned to ashes. Everything is gone. I'll not be marrying you with nothing to offer. I just don't have it in me to do it all again."

I swallowed hard. "Will you write to me?"

He didn't answer. He didn't hug me, or kiss me, or even look at me. He turned on his heel and walked out of my life.

I didn't call or run after him. I just let him go. I stood there, frozen in place. A deep, heavy weight dropped from my heart and settled in my stomach. I slumped to the ground, buried my face in my hands, and cried out in grief. I wanted to scream, to rage at the unfairness of it all. I wasn't sure for which I felt more grief—the loss of his whole family or the loss of my love, my future with him.

Annie found me there in a crumpled ball of tears. She put her arms around me, trying to comfort me. But I was inconsolable. Surrounded by grief on all sides, my one and only hope was gone. I pulled away from her and stumbled, blinded by my tears, into the crowded hall. People called to me, but I ignored them and stumbled on. In the back, in a corner, I dropped down onto the cold, hard floor. With no blanket, not even a gunny sack for comfort, I turned toward the wall and closed my eyes, shutting out the awful, desolate world.

This isn't happening, I thought. *He loves me. He didn't mean what he said. He doesn't know what he's saying. He's just in shock. He'll come back to me. Please come back to me,* I begged silently. I knew in my heart of hearts he must still love me.

In my mind's eye, I conjured an image of us, Ethan and me, standing before his preacher. I wore a beautiful dress with grandma's shawl draped over my shoulders. My hair was swept up, curled and shiny, and I was holding a little nosegay of wildflowers. I saw myself gazing up to him adoringly, and I saw his eyes shining down on me, loving me back. He was my present, my future. I wasn't "Plain Eliza Jane" anymore. Inside my mind, I screamed. Someone had chosen me. Me! And I had chosen him. I wouldn't give him up. I would hold that image close to my heart where nobody could take it away.

Precious sleep overtook me. Unaware of time passing, I slumbered dreamlessly through the rest of that day and night. Nobody bothered me. Nobody came to check on me. In the early morning, my little sisters tried to wake me, but I rolled over and went back to sleep, unwilling to face the day. I wanted to be left alone to sleep, to forget, to hide my face from the world. I had had all the grief a body could take. I didn't want to go on. I couldn't go on, not without Ethan.

Eventually, Mumma came to wake me. I woke with a start and sat up. I hurt all over from laying so long on the cold, hard floor.

"Eliza, you must eat something," Mumma said, squatting on the floor next to me.

I looked at her dumbly, trying to recall where I was. Memory came crashing in on me, and I leaned into her, laying my head in her lap, and wept. Mumma tried to soothe me. Her hand, cool and comforting, smoothed my filthy hair back from my brow. Not usually one to give in to self-indulgence, she must have had some idea of my pain, for she allowed me my tears and self-pity.

"He's gone, Mumma. He doesn't love me anymore." I hiccupped and pulled back to wipe my nose with my tattered sleeve.

She did not answer me right away.

"I never should have given him my heart," I said.

"That's just the bitterness talking, daughter. Life has its ups and downs. It's times like these when we realize how very lucky we have been."

"Lucky?" I looked at her incredulous. Surely she had never had her heart broken like this. "I feel like the unluckiest person in the world," I said angrily as resentment poured in on top of my self-pity.

"Eliza Jane Ludlow," Mumma said sharply, "you should be ashamed of yourself. Your betrothed has lost his whole family. It's not his lack of love that drove him away. It's the unfathomable grief of knowing they're dead. They're not coming back. Just look around you. Yes, you've suffered a great disappointment, but you'll get over it. These people," she motioned around the room at the dozens who were gravely injured and still clinging to life, "have lost a lot more than you, and they are able to hold on. You, my girl, need to think more about others than yourself."

I hiccupped again. Stung, I didn't know what to say. *This is so unfair,* I thought. *I've just lost my whole life, everything I had to live for.* But I said nothing and just ducked my head.

"Get yourself up, and let's find you something to eat and perhaps a cup of tea." She stood up and strode off, expecting me to follow.

Reluctantly I dragged myself up off the floor. I felt like an old woman with rheumatism. I went to the kitchen and found a piece of bread and a cup of water, then wandered outside. People were beginning to recover from the effects of the fire. There was more talking, children were playing, and I even heard a chuckle or two. Annie saw me and rushed up, putting a comforting arm around my shoulders and leading me to where our families were sitting together with other refugees. I found a spot on the outskirts of the group and sat down on the grass, gnawing on the dry bread. Annie smiled at me encouragingly as she returned to her place next to John. Even Roseanne was there with Billy's arm protectively around her shoulders.

I felt strange and light-headed from sleeping so long and not eating. The group was talking in low tones of what they had heard tell from the men who had returned from their search for survivors across the county. These stories would be told over and over for years to come every time the subject of the great fire came up.

"Parisville lost a good many," an older fellow with a singed and grizzled beard said to Papa and Mr. Bruce. "I went there with the search party. Most awful thing I ever saw. A mother and her children on their knees in a circle, burned beyond recognition." Everyone shuddered and their heads hung a little lower. "And young Jensen," the man went on, "his little ones as well as his folks, all dead. Nicest family you'd ever want to meet."

"It's a crying shame," his wife said. She was about Mumma's age and so thin her clothes hung loosely on her body. "Only one to survive was the pretty young wife. She walked all the way here on her own. Her face was burned, and her beautiful blonde hair was burned almost off her head."

"The worst I heard was the man who came into town late Tuesday night." My brother Will related another gruesome tale. "He was carrying the remains of his wife and kids in a ten-gallon bucket." Everyone winced.

Now that people had begun to talk, there was no stopping them. It was as if by talking about it, they could come to accept it. They continued to talk of families taking cover, like we had, in newly plowed fields or ditches, soaking their heads, clothing, and the surrounding ground in water and hoping for survival. Then there were stories about others less fortunate, like the man who had sent his family to take cover in a cornfield thinking the green corn would protect them, only to find their remains the next day. All listened with ghastly interest. I should have been horrified but couldn't seem to get myself to get up and leave.

"There was a hunter I heard of out near Ubly," Will went on. "He'd just shot a moose and was dressing it out when the fire overtook him. He climbed into the carcass and lived to tell the story."

I watched Roseanne put a hand over her mouth in revulsion. I brushed some stray hairs out of my face and took another bite of my bread. My eyes fell on a man who shuffled up to eavesdrop on our group. He stood behind Papa and scratched at the scraggly hair on his cheek. I had a strange sense of foreboding. I felt like I was outside my body watching myself watch him.

"Did you hear about the family who hid down in their well?" the man said. Almost as soon as he spoke, I had the impulse to run away, but remained rooted to the spot.

"A lot of people took shelter in wells," somebody else said.

"But this was a mother and five children," the man went on. "The man and his son were fighting the fire."

I was paralyzed. I could hear my heart pounding in my ears, and for a moment I thought I would pass out.

"Wind came up," the man pressed on. "Must've been gale-force, because it picked the young man up and blew him into the next field. Then it picked the roof up off the house and dropped it right over the well."

My family started to put the details together. One by one, they looked my way with startled glances. I knew this was Ethan's family he was talking about. I gulped, swallowing the bile coming up from my stomach.

The man continued, "The boy rushed back to find his dad trying to lift the roof off the well, but the fire overcame them. They had to abandon it. Lost all of them, the mother and all five children."

I started to choke. The crust of bread slipped from my fingers. I stood up and my water cup tumbled out of my hand into the dirt on the ground. With a hand clapped over my mouth to hold in my scream, I stumbled away.

Chapter 33

I ran headlong away from the horror stories, blinded by tears, down the road toward the lake. I was going to throw up. I crumpled to the ground, crawled on hands and knees to the water's edge, and vomited the bit of bread and water that had been my only food in the last two days.

Wind came up. Must've been gale-force, because it picked the young man up and blew him into the next field. Then it picked the roof up off the house and dropped it right over the well, the story resounded in my ears. I pictured my brave, strong Ethan being thrown aloft by a great wind and landing in the blackened dirt of a nearby field. I saw him racing, running, breathing great gulps of rancid air, trying to get back to where he knew his family desperately needed saving. I could hear their cries and their screams and put my hands over my ears to block out the sound.

I slumped down onto the wet sand where tiny waves lapped against the shore, wrapped my arms around myself, and rocked back and forth in time with the gentle swaying of the reeds. I wept, my heart shattering into pieces inside my chest. I could picture the scene so vividly. My poor, poor Ethan, struggling to lift the roof in all that smoke and fire. And Kathleen, Bridget, Mary, and little Maggie, my sweet sisters, all trapped beneath it, stuffed in an old dried-up well with their mum and baby Johnny.

I heaved again, though there was nothing left to come up. "I'm so sorry, so very sorry," I sobbed to no one.

Suddenly there were arms around me, rocking with me back and forth, back and forth. It was a young woman, the blonde girl I had noticed earlier in the week. She cried along with me. Together we poured out our grief, and when there were no more tears to shed, we sat back and held each other's hands.

She was the one. I knew she must be. The young woman they had been talking about from Parisville who had lost her little children and husband. The remnants of her blonde hair were pulled back into a tail, and the burns across her forehead and cheeks had dried and scabbed.

I hid my face in my hands, ashamed. "I'm so sorry," I murmured. "I know who you are. I know you lost your family."

She nodded morosely. "I keep coming down here and contemplating walking into the water and not coming out." She shrugged. "But I haven't been able to go through with it."

"Oh, my goodness," I pleaded with her, squeezing her hands for dear life. "Please, please don't."

"Did you lose someone as well?" she asked.

Knowing what had happened to this beautiful woman, I felt as if my story paled by comparison. "My fiancé and his father left yesterday to go back east. For all these days, I didn't know what had happened to him. His mother," I paused, hardly able to say the words, "his sisters, and his little brother perished." *But that's not all,* I wanted to say. *He doesn't want me anymore. He doesn't love me.*

"I'm so very sorry for your loss," she said gravely.

I shook my head. "I know I have so much to be grateful for." I wiped my tears with the backs of my hands. "I'm so ashamed of myself, so selfish...," I trailed off.

"Loss is loss," she replied. "My loss is no greater than yours, except I've had a few more days to get used to it."

I considered that for a moment. How could she ever get used to it? "What will you do?" I asked.

She shrugged her shoulders. "I haven't figured that out yet. Today is about all I can handle right now. Tomorrow will take care of itself."

"That's good advice," I said.

We sat in silence for a time, gazing out toward the water where the small waves lapped rhythmically onto the shore. When we finally stood up, we made our way slowly up the street arm in arm. "If ever there is anything I can do for you, will you please let me know?" I said.

"You haven't told me your name," she said.

"Eliza Jane. Eliza Jane Ludlow."

* * *

I returned to the Masonic Hall, helping the doctors tend to the sick and working with the village women in the kitchen. Remaining busy was the best diversion from my grief and sadness over losing my betrothed. I worked until I dropped then slept a dreamless sleep, awoke, and began again.

A few days after Ethan had departed, Emma came through the door of the kitchen, where I was elbows-deep in dishwater.

She announced breathlessly, "Dr. Herrington is looking for you. He said to meet him at the Lutheran church."

The German Lutheran Church was full of people in similar straits as those at the Masonic Hall. I asked one of the ladies who was tending the sick where I might find the doctor. She pointed to a small room in the back corner of the church. I rapped softly on the door, and Dr. Herrington opened it. Inside the dim room was a young woman, face aglow with perspiration and lying on top of a table. She was covered with a blanket and in the throes of labor. She grimaced and whimpered in pain.

"Miss Ludlow! You got my message," he said, "Have you ever assisted at a birth?"

I shook my head. "I was fifteen when my mum had my youngest brother. I didn't help the midwife, but I was able to watch. And I helped my mum through a miscarriage last year."

He nodded his head. "That will do. She's been in labor since yesterday. I'm afraid the baby's turned," he said in a very soft voice. When he noticed my confusion, he added, "Not breech—he's just facing the wrong way. I'm going to try to turn him so her labor can progress."

"What do you need me to do?" I whispered.

"Keep her still. This is going to make her uncomfortable, but it will help," he said.

I positioned myself at the end of the table near her head. "Hello," I said, smiling kindly down upon the woman, "I'm Miss Eliza Jane Ludlow," I introduced myself. "I see you're going to have a baby today."

"Better today than a week ago, thank the Lord," she said back to me. "I'm Mrs. Margaret Huxtable." She stopped speaking abruptly, racked with another pain. I held her hand and waited for it to pass.

The doctor moved to his patient's side and said, "Your baby is facing the wrong way. I'm going to see if I can turn him. That should help move things along." Then he glanced at me.

Her knees were covered by a blanket, so I was unable to see exactly what he did. But the young mother cried out in pain, pushing back with her feet against the tabletop and lifting her hips. I kept my hands on her shoulders to hold her as still as I could and keep her from rolling off.

"Sh-sh-sh-sh," I soothed, "it will be better now." I looked toward the doctor, who nodded at me. She relaxed, but within a few seconds she was racked by another labor pain.

Several contractions later the doctor said, "Push, Margaret."

She let out a long groan and bore down. The blanket slid back from her knees, and I could see the baby was out. The doctor skill-fully placed the palm of his hand under the baby's head with his fingers gently on either side of its neck. Margaret pushed again, and she was born, bloody and waxy and perfect. The baby girl let out a healthy squall.

"You have a daughter," Dr. Herrington announced. Then he laid the babe tummy-down on her mother's chest. I covered her with a towel to keep her warm. The doctor deftly tied off and cut the cord then continued his ministrations.

I gazed down at the mother and child, the sweetest, most adorable sight I'd seen in a long, long time. Margaret crooned to the little thing while tears of joy leaked from the corners of her eyes.

"Florence," she said softly, "my little flower."

The first flower from the ashes, I thought, smiling through my own tears of happiness.

A while later I took the baby from her mother and used some of the warm water from the basin to clean her up, rubbing her vigorously but gently. She continued her healthy squalls as her skin turned a mottled pink.

"She's got a good set of lungs, it would seem," Margaret chuckled, smiling joyfully.

I swaddled little Florence in a fresh baby blanket, which one of the village women must have donated, and returned her to her mother.

Dr. Herrington was drying his hands and had a big smile on his face. "Just what we need to renew our faith in the future," he said. "Miss Ludlow, thank you for your help. There is a young man who is waiting for the news of his daughter's birth. Would you ask him to come in, please?"

I didn't have to go far to find him. He was with the reverend and an older man who might have been his father. I asked if he was Mr. Huxtable. He didn't wait to answer but rushed to the door to see his wife. My face, unused to smiling, grinned from ear to ear, and the reverend winked at me.

My work there finished, I left and slowly walked the short distance back to the hall. For the first time since Ethan had left, I felt better. The lump in the pit of my stomach had begun to relax, and I found I no longer felt like crying. I didn't feel like laughing either. I just felt calm. *Life goes on,* I thought. Just as plants shrivel up and die in the winter and spring forth into new life, the cycle continues. I was done weeping for what could have been, I resolved. I would just have to move forward, one step at a time, toward what would come next in my life.

Chapter 34

THE FOLLOWING WEEK, PAPA AND MY BROTHERS DECIDED TO GO TO THE farm to survey the damage. Finn and I went along. It was a warm fall day with a threat of rain. As we walked along, I realized I could see the air—actually see it with my eyes. It contained tiny bits of ash and soot picked up by the breeze as it swirled continuously around me. The dog wandered off to sniff for scents of life and then came bounding back to my side, whining.

I longed for the glorious fall landscape of the last two years, when it had been arrayed in vibrant colors. All lay stark and barren, stretching as far as I could see, in shades of mourning black. Once in a while there would be a single, lonely, leafless tree sticking up out of the ground. It would have seemed comical if it hadn't been so tragic.

I kept waiting for a surge of emotion, to begin crying out my sorrows anew. Surprisingly, I didn't feel any great regret or sadness as I walked; in fact, I felt almost nothing. I didn't feel despondent, but neither did I feel hopeful. But I did feel fearful. How were we ever going to survive winter in this lifeless land? I couldn't imagine remaining at the Masonic Hall until spring, living off handouts from the townsfolk, whose generosity was nearly exhausted. But I also couldn't see a solution. *And we'd better think of something soon,* I thought, *because the mild fall weather could turn at any time.* I shivered, thinking back to the frigid, windy snow storms of last winter. I caught up with Papa and my brothers to ask what they thought.

"Did you hear about the article in the *Detroit News*?" Will was saying. "They're already advertising land for sale on the thumb as 'rich and ready for planting.'"

The others chuckled. "It's going to be a lot easier to plow, now that all the stumps and trees are gone and the grass is burned off," John said.

"And underneath all that black, the soil is rich, just waiting for seed," Papa said.

I was surprised to hear how optimistic they were. When I turned to gaze at the stark landscape again, it was as if my eyes were newly opened. I could see potential instead of loss.

"What are we going to do when winter comes?" I asked.

Papa's face sobered. "Let's wait and see what happens when Stafford gets back from Detroit."

When we reached our property, we took a shortcut across the back from Stoddard Road. Even after two weeks' time, there were still places smoking. Papa said they were probably the stumps of downed trees. We went straight for the stone chimney, our only landmark. The boys left Papa and me there and continued on up the road to their place.

Papa said, "Before we start, Mumma wants me to check on the clock."

I followed him to the field just west of where the house and barn once stood, where we had taken cover on that awful day. I stopped and stared. I could still see the shallow holes that had saved our lives. The depressions, untouched by fire, made a cut-out shape of our family where we had lain side by side hoping not to get burned. I shuddered. It was a miracle, truly a miracle, that we had lived. I turned in a slow circle. The fire had devoured absolutely everything. There was nothing left alive. No grass, no trees, no animals of any kind, not even insects. I heard Papa whistle through his teeth. He had uncovered the remains of the clock: the hinges, hands, and pendulum were all that remained.

"Oh, Papa, Mumma is going to be so sad," I said.

He nodded his head but didn't reply. He just picked up the remnants of the only heirloom Mumma had owned and placed them in the deep pocket of his trousers. Then we went back to where the chimney stood blackened and alone amidst the ruins of the house.

The log walls of the stout cabin were nothing but piles of char. I felt pieces of glass from the windows splinter under my feet as I stepped gingerly through to where the kitchen used to be. The heavy iron stove had fallen through to the ground but was still in one piece. I moved ash and debris with the toe of my shoe and wished for a rake, but I stooped over to comb through the piles of charred remains with my fingers.

"Be careful there, Eliza. You could still get burned," Papa warned.

I looked up at him and nodded. Finn had been digging near the hearth, his claws turned out to be much more effective than my fingers. He had uncovered the Dutch oven.

"Good boy," I told Finn and patted him on the head. I retrieved the metal washtub, blackened but still usable, and dragged it over near the fireplace and put the recovered cookware inside.

"This is like digging for treasure," I said to the dog as I knelt down and continued to forage. Many of the items buried in the ashes were still warm to the touch. I placed each piece worth salvaging in the tub: cast-iron pots and pans, the kettle, silverware, utensils, and the poker from the fireplace. All were blackened but still usable.

"Eureka!" Papa yelled excitedly. He held a fist in the air.

"What is it?" I called, I picked my way carefully to where he stood. He held out a hand, and in it were several silver coins. We hugged joyfully, and I did a little dance.

"How much is it?" I asked hopefully.

"Not much, but more than we had a minute ago. Your mum had a stash of money under the mattress, God bless her."

"Good for Mumma," I laughed. Ever the practical homemaker, her coins could make the difference between whether or not we ate. We renewed our search, invigorated. When we finished with the house, we went to search where the beautiful barn used to stand. Now only the stone foundation remained. I recalled the explosions when the hay had caught fire and burned the massive building down to its pegs.

After a few hours, we took stock of what we had uncovered. Papa had found most of what he supposed Mumma had squirreled away for a rainy day, and we had a washtub full of odds and ends that could be cleaned and reused. We had had some success in the barn as well. Except for their wooden handles, we salvaged most of Papa's tools: chains for stump pulling, horses' bits minus the leather harnesses, and the plow, rakes, and scythe. It made me feel better finding these things—proof that we had lived and thrived at one time in this now godforsaken place.

We tried futilely to scrub our blackened hands at the pump and then took a drink of water. We decided to return to Port Hope without waiting for the others. "They're big boys," Papa said. "They'll come back when they're ready."

* * *

We existed in a kind of limbo as we waited and hoped for help of any kind to reach us. I had my work for the doctors to keep me occupied. I changed a lot of dressings and applied the sticky salve to burns. Sometimes young Dr. Herrington would refer to me as his nurse, and I would smile every time he said this.

The seed of an idea began to take root inside of me. I found myself wondering, could I become a nurse someday? It made me feel good to be of some use to people who were hurting.

One day when I was with Dr. Herrington while he was doing his rounds, I got up the courage to ask him, "If I want to become a nurse, how would I go about doing it?"

"There are two ways," he told me as he removed the bandages from around Mr. Hennessey's left arm. "You can enroll in one of the hospital training schools for nurses, like the one at Buffalo General Hospital, which would take a year, or you could do an apprenticeship with a doctor."

My heart began to race. I knew what an apprenticeship was. "Could I train with you or Dr. Dickinson?" I asked.

He turned and smiled at me. "Dr. Dickinson is going to retire. With so many people recovering from this fire, I was hoping you'd consider working with me."

I returned his smile, a ray of sunny hope shining through my days of despair.

"Sleep on it, Miss Ludlow," he went on. "It's a big decision. I know you have a job here in town. You would have to be willing to give that up, and the income. The hours are long, and it's a very demanding job. It would be a big commitment."

"Would I be able to learn midwifery?" I pressed.

"Yes, delivering babies is part of what you would learn. If the doctor is unavailable, you would be the only other medical professional in the area."

I pondered the idea of becoming a nurse under his tutelage. Now that I had actually put words to my desire, it wasn't whether or not I was going to do it but how and when. I was stuck here for the foreseeable future. And afterward, Mumma and Papa would surely expect me to go back to work at Stafford house to earn money. Sadly, my own dreams would have to be put on hold.

When we were finished seeing all of his patients, Dr. Herrington gave me directions on who needed tending throughout the day. I went outside in hopes of having some time to think things over, but, alas, it wasn't to be. Annie Bruce was waiting for me.

"Your mum asked for us to take the younger children down to the lake to clean them up," she said. We gathered her little brothers plus Nellie, Georgie, and Ben and herded them down to the water's edge. Georgie was not happy. He had a strong aversion to water unless it was to drink.

"Oh, come on, Georgie," I said. "It'll be fun. And Andrew has to come too."

We stripped them all down to their drawers and let them splash and play in the shallows.

I turned to my friend. "What's the matter?"

"Eliza, how long can we keep this up?" she asked. "I mean, we're sleeping outside, our clothes are nothing but rags, and we've hardly anything to eat."

"I don't know," I replied, having voiced the same concerns before. "However long it takes for help to arrive, I suppose."

"There are rumors that there've been thousands of dollars collected for relief to fire victims. Your brother said there have been reports in the *Detroit News*. But we've seen none of it. Don't you think that's strange?" she said while holding Robert's arm with one hand and scrubbing at his face with the other.

I shrugged my shoulders. "Maybe the money's going to other places, just not to us," I said. "I do know the doctors have received supplies sent from the city by ship. If they hadn't, we would've run out of bandages and medicine days ago."

"I wish there was more food. Even after the soup each day, my stomach is gnawing with hunger. And whatever are we going to do when the weather turns?" she persisted. "Mumma and Papa are talking about giving up and heading back east."

"Do you have family you can move in with?" I asked.

"Yes, but with so many of us, it might not be any better an idea than staying put until help arrives. The older boys were talking about going to the city to find work. At least that would bring in some money. But I'm more worried about how cold it's going to get."

Winter was months away yet. So far we had been very fortunate with a warm, mild autumn. But time was passing with no help in sight.

"It's always darkest before the dawn, as my Grandma used to say," I told her. "I know my family isn't going anywhere. There's only Grandpa and the aunts, and Papa's a stubborn Irishman. He won't want to give up."

"My pa is pretty stubborn too," Annie said, "but he's worried about keeping us sheltered and fed. But I suppose we're all worried about that."

Chapter 35

It seemed every moment I was not occupied, I spent worrying. My conversation with Annie ruminated in my mind as the help we all hoped for seemed a long time coming.

I started making a habit of walking to the Lutheran church to visit baby Florence and her mother whenever I had the chance. After being present at her birth, I felt especially close to her. She was so precious and new and filled my heart with the hopefulness I longed for.

The minister in the church led a prayer group every day, and I began to plan my visits so I could take part. I began to pray in earnest for the first time in my life. I had always said quick little prayers, like, "God, please help," or, "Please make it better." Our family had had a Bible, and we said grace before eating, but since making the move to Michigan and becoming so busy with farming and working at Stafford House, I had usually been too tired to pray. Sadly, I must admit, I never had taken to reading scripture. Even the few times I had attended church with the Stafford family, and the one time with Ethan, I'd mostly just sat there trying to figure out what the preacher was talking about.

After surviving a dreadful fire, losing our home, and almost losing our lives, I started to feel like I had been away from God for too long. Spending week upon endless week homeless and not being certain if we would have food to eat or a roof over our heads this winter, I developed a serious feeling of anxiety that only blessings from God would put to an end. It was past time to ask Him for His help.

One afternoon I got up enough nerve to ask the reverend if he had an extra Bible I might borrow. He dashed off to his office and returned with one.

"You are welcome to borrow this until you are able to get your own, miss," he said as he handed it to me.

I held it gently, feeling the texture of the worn leather cover, as if I had been given the greatest gift of hope. I felt my heart swell, and tears came into my eyes. *Maybe now things will get better,* I thought. I murmured a thank you. He smiled back at me and patted me on the shoulder.

"Keep doing the work you do for others, miss, only now do it in His name," he said and walked away.

I returned to the hall with my precious book and began to read that day. Each morning as I spent a few minutes in prayer, I felt uplifted. All of this grief and the uncertainty would pass. And God willing, someday I would become a nurse.

* * *

Mr. Stafford returned from Detroit and called a meeting. Mumma and Papa went to hear what he had to say while I kept track of the children. They returned with smiles on their faces. The good people of Detroit and others from all across the country had donated money to help us get back on our feet, just like Annie had been saying. Mr. Stafford was given some of the money to purchase food and supplies for our immediate use, which were being sent by ship, with promises of more relief to come. As soon as a system for distributing aid to the community could be set up, we would be able to apply for help for our family. Papa was still hoping to be able to plant spring wheat while the weather was still mild.

A few days later, more help unexpectedly came from New York. On the outside of the hotel, a white banner was unfurled bearing a large scarlet cross. Papa, Mr. Bruce, Annie, and I walked over with many of the other refugees to learn what the flag meant.

The newly founded American Red Cross had arrived in Port Hope. Its founder, Miss Clara Barton, had recruited volunteers from her hometown of Dansville. She had sent her agents and teams of men and women to White Rock, south of Sand Beach. But knowing there were many victims who were unable to make their way south, they had decided to come right into the communities most affected by the fire. That meant Port Hope. With energy and spirit, the volunteers set up shop, using the hotel kitchen until their own camp kitchen could be established. They brought crates of clothing, shoes, and food. Before they were even open for business, a line had formed outside the hotel and down the street.

Every time I looked at that white flag with the bright cross of red, I felt a newfound hope. And I wasn't the only one. People seemed re-invigorated, like the worst was finally over. Everyone, no matter how tired, hungry, or injured, perked up a little. They had a brighter look in their eyes and a more optimistic sound in their voices. Some dropped to their knees to praise God that help had at last arrived.

Dr. Dickinson sent me along with Dr. Herrington to pick up the supplies and medications the Red Cross volunteers said they had for us. Dr. Herrington was very pleased with the variety of medicaments, and we each carried a large boxful back down the street to the hall.

Mumma and Mrs. Bruce were singing praises of thanksgiving for the hoped-for bars of soap, washrags, and towels. That very evening Annie and I, plus the rest of my sisters, headed down to the lake. It was the most heavenly bath and hair washing I'd ever had, cold though the water was. Each of us had something clean to put on, including fresh undergarments. The clothing wasn't new or the perfect size, but it was clean. The ladies of the Red Cross who worked in New York for Miss Barton must have burned the midnight oil washing and mending to provide for us. The thought of their hard work and generosity filled my heart to overflowing. There were even knitted sweaters and hats, and we gladly traded our thin feed-sack blankets for real woolen blankets and quilts. My new skirt, gathered full about the waist, hung loosely on my skinny frame and dragged on the ground as I walked, but I didn't mind. It had no holes and was clean. The hem could always be taken up if I could get ahold of a needle and some thread.

Within the week, Red Cross camps were set up throughout the thumb area. The crowd on the front lawn of the Masonic Hall began to break up and move to camps closest to their own villages. My family moved to one near Huron City. There we set up housekeeping in an old Civil War-era tent.

"It looks too small for all of us," Roseanne said, looking at our tent with a skeptical eye. "Are you sure we'll all fit?" She went inside and looked around.

"Don't say it," I said.

"What?" she said, feigning innocence. Her nose was already twitching, and I could see she had all she could do not to cover her nose and mouth.

It did smell musty, but it would keep the rain out. "Beggars can't be choosers," Mumma told her. "Besides, you and Eliza will be going back to Stafford House once Mrs. Stafford returns."

My sister and I had walked up to Stafford House earlier in the week. We were happy to see it had come through the fire unscathed. I had heard the stories of Mr. Stafford's efforts to organize firefighting crews to save as many buildings as they could. I remembered thinking it looked like someone had drawn a line that the fire had not crossed. I wondered if that was due his team's efforts. We inquired at the house to see if the family had returned with Mr. Stafford from Detroit. We were told they weren't home as yet but were expected any day. It would be good to get paid for working again. I didn't mind doing my part to help our family get back on our feet.

Meanwhile, the Red Cross had been so generous in their provisions. Each family received extra clothing, cots, and blankets to keep us warm. Mumma and I scoured the pots and pans and silverware I had collected from our place so they could be used again. Firewood brought from south of Sand Beach, along with provisions of coal, provided a warm campfire each evening. It wasn't home, but it was comfortable. Everyone became a little bit happier once they had a place to hang their hat, even if the walls were made of canvas.

The Bruces set up camp nearby, although, like Papa, Mr. Bruce and Annie's brothers spent most of their time at the farm. There was a sense of urgency with the oncoming winter months. Planting was of utmost importance, not only to provide a cash crop in the spring but to hold the soil as well. Seed and tools were shipped in so farmers could plant wheat and grass for pasture. Mumma was able to get a variety of seeds for a winter garden: carrots, parsnips, onions, radishes, turnips, spinach, and cabbage. If the weather cooperated, we would soon have fresh food again.

John, Tommy, and Will, who were not considered as needy since they were unmarried, were toward the bottom of the wait list for aid. They threw in with us, and the Bruces and the Ludlows worked together plowing and planting all three farms.

The Red Cross set up a community kitchen in our camp. Volunteers worked tirelessly to provide meals, including hot cereal for breakfast and bread and beans or soup for dinner. We also were given meat or fish at least once a week. With two hearty meals a day, the feeling of starvation that loomed over us began to diminish. All of the women and girls took turns helping with food preparation and serving. Annie, Roseanne, and I took dinner to the men and the boys, who continued to work until dark each evening.

Things were beginning to look up. Papa applied for building supplies for a new house and barn. Intending to build a better house than we had before, he kept saying he hoped the supplies would arrive sooner than later so he could start building before winter. Eventually he secured a cow, some chickens, and bales of hay and feed grain to see the animals through until the grass started growing. Papa and Dick built enclosures and lean-to shelters for the animals.

* * *

In late October the Staffords returned from the city, and Roseanne and I went back to work. Unsure when we would be home for a visit, we hugged each of the children and Mumma. I said good-bye to Annie and her mother, and Roseanne and I went south once again along the shore road to Port Hope.

As we tromped along the wet muck of the roadway, I had to hold my overlong skirt up to keep from tripping on it. My shoes were my same old ones with holes burned through the soles, so before we were halfway to Stafford House, my feet were wet and sore. Roseanne sighed loudly. It was the first sound she'd made since we'd left the camp.

"What's the matter?" I asked.

"What do you mean?" she said.

"I mean you're not usually this quiet. What are you thinking about?"

"Billy, of course. I'm already missing him," she said, sighing. "I'm really sorry things didn't work out between you and Ethan."

I shrugged my shoulders. I wasn't sure I was ready to talk about Ethan. "Whether or not he stayed, I don't think we would have gotten married anyway," I said.

"Do you think he was going to call it off before the fire?" she said.

"No, that's not what I mean, although who knows? Wouldn't we be in exactly the same position everybody else is in? No roof over our heads. No money. No food or clothing except what has been given to us through charity. Ethan would not have married me under these circumstances," I said morosely.

"That's probably right," she agreed. "Nobody is going to be getting married for a good long time."

"Do you still have your heart set on Billy?" I asked.

"Oh yes," she exclaimed with a little secret smile. "We're both young. We have plenty of time. I can't imagine his family leaving like Ethan and his pa did."

"I wouldn't be too sure about that," I said. "Annie was telling me that her parents were considering going back east. They have family there that they stayed with when they arrived from Ireland."

"Oh, I know about that," she said airily. "They all discussed it, and I can tell you I was really worried for a bit, but the boys said they'd rather go to Detroit to work for a while than give up on the farm completely."

"Thank goodness," I said, "because besides your being in love with Billy, I think John would miss Annie."

"I'm sure if she did leave, he'd eventually go after her. They are courting, you know," Roseanne said. Then she looked at me and her cheeks had flushed. "Maybe Ethan will come back for you."

I shook my head. "No, he won't. He's gone for good."

"How can you be so sure?"

"I'm sure," I replied.

She looked at me but didn't say anything. I was glad she let it go.

"Besides," I said, "I think God has another plan for my life."

"What do you mean?"

"I want to become a nurse," I told her. Once I said it aloud, I was surer than ever that it was the path I was to take.

"You'd make a good nurse, Eliza Jane," she said encouragingly. "When are you going to start?"

"I don't know. I haven't even talked to Mumma and Papa about it yet. They are going to need every cent we can earn right now. There's no hurry. I'm still young," I said echoing her words.

She hooked her arm through mine and said, "Yes, we are."

When we got to Stafford House, we were greeted by Mrs. Stafford as if we were long-lost relatives. She gave each of us a big hug.

"Oh, thank the Lord you are both safe," she said. "I've never been as beset with worry as I have been these past weeks, unable to know who survived or to be able to help in any way."

"We're very happy to be back," Roseanne replied.

"Eliza, I thought we were losing you to marriage this month," she went on.

I braced myself. "There isn't going to be a wedding," I said. I didn't want to elaborate.

"I'm so sorry, dear," she said sympathetically. "I'm very happy to have you back. Cook is waiting to see you. Go down and say hello before you get settled, would you?"

I fell back into my old routine of housework drudgery. I was feeling the rub of being back to working in someone else's house rather than my own, since my hopes and dreams had gone up in smoke, so to speak. I felt annoyed and then guilty, because I knew I was very fortunate. I knew I should be thanking God for all the blessings in my life, but I couldn't bring myself to do it. I was so confused. I threw myself into my work with renewed vigor borne of the anger I felt deep down at the change in my fate.

At sunset I was back in our little attic bedroom with my little cot and warm bedding. Roseanne, who was still recovering from the fire, was sound asleep. I tiptoed quietly around the room removing apron, dress, and petticoats and hung them up on hooks. Then I got out of the horrid and unnecessary corset and crawled into bed in my underclothes. I thought over the day and our greetings from Mrs. Stafford and Cook and felt more lost and forlorn than I had since Ethan had left. I missed him terribly, although I would never admit that to my sister. Going back and forth between hating him for leaving and wishing he would come back, I finally fell asleep from exhaustion.

CHAPTER 36

By the turn of the year, we were happy to bid good riddance to 1881. Most people who had suffered loss in the great fire had either returned to the east, moved in with relatives, or were still hanging on camp-style until their homes could be rebuilt. That winter, strangely enough, was not a cold one. It remained mild with temperatures rarely dipping below freezing. Snow was infrequent. I thought this was a gift from above and said prayers of thanksgiving that the families who were still homeless, including my own, were at least given this small reprieve.

By the end of February, I was feeling restless, having never been apart from my family for so long a time. Sadly, we had skipped Christmas that year. Even the Staffords had decided to go without the extravagant food and decorations they normally indulged in. It had been a very subdued holiday season. There would be no maple syrup this year, nor parties in the sugar bush. No secret, stolen kisses from a lover.

My sister and I decided to go home for a visit in the middle of March, just after my twentieth birthday. It had been half of a year since the fire. As we approached Stoddard Road, we were shocked to see a beautiful two-story clapboard house where the old cabin had formerly sat. Papa had built the new house around the original fireplace, extending the chimney above the second floor. A barn at least as magnificent as our other one was in the framing stages. We could see the men out in the field. The Bruce men and my older brothers were working with Papa, Dick, and Georgie. They had plowed several times more land than Papa had done before, and acres of wheat looked to be thriving.

When Roseanne realized Billy was there, she broke into a run. I continued toward the house. On the way through the yard, I heard Finn's excited bark and the sound of Nellie and Ben shouting my name. They came running toward me and almost knocked me over with their hugs.

"I've missed you so much," I exclaimed, kissing them on top of their heads. "How are you?" Finn was happy to see me as well. His tail wagged and thwapped against my skirt. I stooped to scratch his ears.

"We're good," Nellie answered, and they ran off again with the yellow dog following on their heels.

I opened the door to find Mumma sweeping the floor. "That's quite a crowd out in the field," I said.

"They are splitting their time between the three farms, like they did right after the fire," Mumma told me. "The work seems to move along a lot faster with three plows working. Did Roseanne come home with you?"

"Yes, but she went out to see Billy," I said. "We were surprised to see the house. I can't believe how fast Papa got it built."

"Papa always said he intended to replace the old house with a better one," she replied. "And all the Bruce men and our men worked together to get our house and the Bruces' framed and roofed. They still have to build a house at the boys' place, but for now the boys are staying here. I can't tell you how wonderful it is to have a roof over our heads again."

I looked around. The walls had been plastered smooth, and the whole place had a much warmer feel than the old cabin. I admired the kitchen. A small pump stood next to the sink where a window looked out on the yard between the house and barn. No more hauling water from the well. That alone was a remarkable improvement. The iron stove had been cleaned up, and there was a large pantry next to the back door and stairs going down into the cellar. A great room stretched the length of the house with the old fireplace hearth in middle of the wall. There was plenty of space for our whole family to visit and share a meal. There were windows on both outside walls, and a staircase led up to four large bedrooms. The only thing missing was a water closet, and the furniture was sparse.

"It's really beautiful," I said, "and warm too."

Mumma put the kettle on the stove and said, "Let's sit down and have a cup of tea, shall we? How are you doing, daughter?"

"I'm all right," I said, shrugging. "Some days are harder than others when I think about what could have been."

She handed me an envelope. "I wasn't sure if I should save this for you or cast it into the fireplace," she said. "It arrived two days ago."

My heart pounded in my chest as I looked at the handwriting. Ethan's. I looked up at Mumma.

I didn't want to open it. As long as it remained closed, I could pretend there was still hope. Slowly and carefully I lifted the corner and tore it open. I unfolded the sheaf of paper. Desolation filled my heart as I read:

Dear Eliza Jane,

I hope this letter finds you and your family well and recovered from the tragic events of last fall. Dad and I are settled near his brother in Concord, and I have been working at a meat packing company for the past few months. We recently sold both pieces of land in Michigan to a family from Illinois, as neither one of us has any desire to return to that place.

I have met someone and fallen in love. Her name is Miss Eleanor Bingham of Concord, daughter of the resident minister at our church. We were married before Christmas and are expecting a child at summer's end. I wish you well and hope that you, too, will find happiness in the future.

Sincerely,
Ethan Kilpatrick

I dropped the letter onto the table. Mumma picked it up and skimmed the contents. I covered my face with my hands. I didn't cry. I couldn't cry. I was shocked and dismayed at having harbored a secret hope that he would return to me. I wasn't surprised that they probably would not be returning to the farm, but married and expecting a baby?

It was more than I could take in. How could he have forgotten he was in love with me so quickly? How could he leave me here desolate and alone? Had he ever really loved me? How could I have been so stupid to fall in love with someone who could hurt me so?

"It isn't healthy to dwell on it," Mumma said as she refolded the letter and put it back in the envelope. "Someone else will come along."

I shrugged my shoulders. "I'm not interested in anyone else coming along. I don't ever want to feel this way again as long as I live. Not ever," I said with finality.

Wisely, Mumma didn't argue. She stood up and put her arms around me. It was then that I cried. Bitter tears of disappointment rolled down my cheeks as I wept onto her shoulder. Once again my anger reared its ugly head, and I pulled away, wiping impatiently at my tears. I wasn't going to shed one more single tear over him. I wouldn't give him the satisfaction. In my mind I could hear Roseanne saying, "Hurray, Eliza Jane. You might be getting a backbone yet."

"I'm going for a walk to clear my head," I said. "Maybe I'll stop in to see Annie."

I started walking up the shore road but passed the Bruce farm and walked on to where Ethan and I would have made our home. Of course, nothing was the same. The beautiful view that would have been mine out the kitchen window of the new house was no longer there. It was all gone. Turned to ash and swept away on the wind, just as our love had been. The love, the dream, the hope, the future. All gone. All that remained was the stone foundation of our house, blackened with soot and outlining what could have been. I sat down in one corner and propped my chin on my hands.

I sat there for a long time. It was eerily quiet. This was where Ethan had told me he loved me for the first time. The place we had become engaged and planned our life together. Had he meant any of it? If the fire hadn't killed his family, would he have rebuilt like my family, and the Bruces, and all the other farm families who had chosen to stay?

The fact that he hadn't returned to me, or even come back to take me to New England with him, spoke volumes about his character. How could he forget me that quickly, fall in love with another woman, and marry her? That was the horrible truth of it. Would I have ever wanted to be married to a man who didn't love me as much as I loved him? That was a hard fact that I had to face. The doubts I had had about him, the night I'd found him drinking and flirting with another girl, had been correct all along. I should have trusted my instincts then and ended our relationship.

I walked across the dry creek bed to the Fitzpatrick farm. The house, like so many others, had been burned to the ground. I knew the gruesome story of what had happened here, but there was something about standing on the very place where the family I had grown to love had been murdered by a violent firestorm that brought the truth home to me. I searched for where they had buried them. I found five unmarked mounds of earth. They must have buried baby Johnny with Mrs. Kilpatrick. I sat down on the barren, blackened earth and cried for the loss of such a wonderful family.

I finally understood. I could never have remained and rebuilt here, had I been Ethan's father. It finally made sense. Was it the voices of their spirits that helped me to comprehend the unfathomable grief that had driven my lover away from me? I took a deep, cleansing breath and blew it out, letting the anger go with it. I would have done the same if it had been my family. It was never meant to be. I would need to find a new dream, a new future.

When I came in the door, Mumma stopped what she was doing at the stove and turned toward me. "What is it?"

"I want to become a nurse," I blurted out.

Mumma didn't say anything for a moment but filled our cups with tea and brought them to the table.

"That must have been some walk you took," she laughed.

"You're not taking me seriously," I said. "I really want this. I've been thinking about it for months, ever since I helped Dr. Dickinson and Dr. Herrington with the injured last fall."

Mumma did not reply. She sat perfectly still and observed me.

"I need to find a new dream and start my life over," I went on. "I'm twenty years old. I don't want to be a maid for the Staffords the rest of my life. I want to make my own future."

She looked at me for a long moment, then asked, "What do you need to do to become a nurse?"

"Dr. Herrington told me I can either go to a school like the Buffalo General Hospital Nursing School for a year, or I could do an apprenticeship with him."

"Going back to school would probably cost a lot of money," she said.

"Or do an apprenticeship with him," I repeated, "and I will be able to become a midwife, which is something I've been interested in since Ben was born."

Mumma took a long sip of her tea. "Eliza, he's an unmarried man. I don't think it would be proper for a young woman to be working so closely with a bachelor doctor."

I laughed out loud. Truth be told, I hadn't given any thought to his being married or single.

"This is about what I want to do for my life's work. I want to become a nurse. I know I can't afford to go to the school in Buffalo, but if Dr. Herrington is willing to take me on as an apprentice, then that's what I intend to do."

She sighed. Ever the practical woman, she smiled and said, "Well, all right, then. Where will you live?"

"I don't know that part yet. He was planning to set up his practice in Grindstone City. Maybe I could find a place to board near there. Or," I said hopefully, "I could live here and work for my room and board with you during my off hours and walk to Grindstone City."

"That's quite a distance to walk," she said. She stood and picked up our empty cups. "I'll talk to Papa about it," she finally said.

I threw my arms around her, saying, "Thank you, thank you, thank you!" Tears of joy and relief leaked out the corners of my eyes.

Roseanne came through the door and said, "We'd better be going back, Eliza." She looked between Mumma and me, sensing she had missed something. "What's going on?"

"I'm going to be a nurse," I announced.

"Oh, I'm so happy for you. You'll make a wonderful nurse," she said.

I hugged Mumma again and skipped out of the house. I shouted a farewell to the little ones, the dog, and the men in the field.

* * *

That week I wrote a letter to Dr. Herrington stating my desire to begin my apprenticeship. I only had to wait a couple of days for his answer. In the return letter was his business card:

W. J. HERRINGTON

PHYSICIAN AND SURGEON

CALLS ANSWERED PROMPTLY AT ALL HOURS
DAY OR NIGHT, RAIN OR SHINE

GRINDSTONE CITY, MICHIGAN

I broke the news to Mrs. Stafford. Surprisingly, she didn't complain about losing a maid but shook my hand and wished me well. On my last day, when I was packed and ready to leave, she gave me my pay with a bonus of two dollars to start me off on my new career.

"A very admirable pursuit, Miss Ludlow," she said, "Mr. Stafford and I wish you all the best in your endeavors."

The following Monday, as I walked the miles to Grindstone City, my feet barely touched the ground. All around me I saw newness. New houses and barns, new plants in the fields, plus sunshine and a light breeze off the lake. Everything seemed full of life. A Bible verse that I had read in Ecclesiastes popped into my head:

For everything there is a season, and a time for every matter under heaven: a time to be born, and a time to die; a time to plant, and a time to pluck up what is planted; a time to kill, and a time to heal; a time to break down, and a time to build up; a time to weep, and a time to laugh; a time to mourn, and a time to dance…

I had been reborn. The grief from the past year was finally behind me. I wanted to laugh, and sing, and dance all at the same time.

When I arrived at Grindstone City, I had no trouble finding Dr. Herrington's office. He had hung a sign over the door that read: W. J. Herrington, Physician and Surgeon. There was a wagon and horse tied up out front. *There must be someone else here,* I thought.

I checked to make sure my blouse was tucked in and dusted off my skirt. Taking a deep breath, I placed my hand on the doorknob and pushed it open. A small bell jangled as the door closed behind me. Nobody was there. A desk and chair sat vacant and covered in books and paper, and I could hear murmuring coming from a room toward the back. Suddenly Dr. Herrington's face appeared in the hallway.

"Miss Ludlow!" he greeted me. "Welcome. I'm with a patient. Come on back."

Tentatively, I approached the room and looked through the door, unsure of who and what I would see. Inside was a tall young man sitting on the examination table with his shirt off. The first thing I noticed was the lean muscular build of a working man. I smiled at him. His face turned an embarrassed pink, but his warm dark brown eyes shone brightly as he smiled back at me. I felt a momentary flip of my heart.

"Young Mr. Herrington here has done himself an injury," Dr. Herrington said.

Herrington? I looked quickly back to the doctor.

"My younger brother," he said. Just then the doorbell jangled again. "Business is picking up," the doctor said and he winked at me. "Irvin, this is my nurse, Miss Eliza Jane Ludlow. I'm leaving you in her very capable hands," he said and handed me a rolled bandage. "His ribs are bruised, not broken. Wrap him tightly, but leave him room to breathe." And with that he left the room.

"You're my very first official patient," I said to him as I wrapped the bandage around his ribcage.

"I'm honored," he said with a deep, husky voice.

"Your brother has offered me an apprenticeship to hone my nursing skills," I told him. "What do you do for a living, if you don't mind my asking?"

"Nothing as sophisticated as doctoring," he laughed and then winced at the pain in his ribcage. "I'm a simple farmer. Or rather, I'm trying to be a farmer."

"How long have you been here?" I asked.

"I got here as soon as the boats were able to break through the ice on the Erie Canal," he said.

Gooseflesh rose on my arms, and a prickling went up the nape of my neck. Grandma would have said someone had just walked over my grave, and some people would attribute those feelings to clairvoyance.

I chuckled. "Just about the same time my pa and brothers came this way three years ago."

"So your family must have lived through the fire?"

"Yes, we survived and rebuilt," I said proudly.

"I'm glad that you survived, Miss Ludlow," he said, watching me intently as I tied off his bandages.

He took a breath and patted my wrapping job with satisfaction.

"Maybe I should come to the doctor more often if I want to see you again," he said, smiling a warm, friendly smile.

A year ago I would have turned beet red and not looked at him, but instead I met those warm brown eyes and returned his smile. "Oh, please don't hurt yourself again," I retorted. "Maybe you could just stop by and take me for a walk."

About the Author

Lila Osborn Mechling is a retired teacher and writer. She lives on five acres in rural Multnomah County with her husband, Mike. She loves to delve into genealogy and the history surrounding people of the past.

Find out more at lilamechling.com.
Ordinary People, Extraordinary Lives.

www.ingramcontent.com/pod-product-compliance
Lightning Source LLC
Chambersburg PA
CBHW061601100726
47898CB00002B/471